NO LONGER PROPERTY
OF ANYTHINK
RANGEVIEW LIBRARY
DISTRICT

The Perfect Love Storm

D0057461

The Perfect Love Storm

Anna Black

www.urbanbooks.net

Urban Books, LLC
300 Farmingdale Road, NY-Route 109
Farmingdale, NY 11735

The Perfect Love Storm Copyright © 2019 Anna Black

All rights reserved. No part of this book may be reproduced in any form or by any means without prior consent of the Publisher, except brief quotes used in reviews.

ISBN 13: 978-1-60162-102-3
ISBN 10: 1-60162-102-7

First Trade Paperback Printing Janaury 2019
Printed in the United States of America

10 9 8 7 6 5 4 3 2 1

This is a work of fiction. Any references or similarities to actual events, real people, living or dead, or to real locales are intended to give the novel a sense of reality. Any similarity in other names, characters, places, and incidents is entirely coincidental.

Distributed by Kensington Publishing Corp.
Submit Orders to:
Customer Service
400 Hahn Road
Westminster, MD 21157-4627
Phone: 1-800-733-3000
Fax: 1-800-659-2436

Prologue

The Storm men were all gathered out back near the grill, and the women were posted up in the house at the round kitchen table with glasses of red and white wine, champagne, and apple martinis. It was the eldest son, Lance's, birthday, and his wife had decided to have a party at their house instead of the civic center that the family normally used to celebrate birthdays, anniversaries, baby showers, or whatever occasion the Storms thought called for a party.

As with all the parties the Storms threw, there was a huge turnout. Everything they did was big and done with style. They were well known in East Texas for their construction company, Storm and Sons Construction. Their family was responsible for most of the homes that had been built in the last thirty years. Every six months or so, they were breaking ground to start a new project or rehabbing a worn-down community.

Starting with rehabbing and moving to selling, their grandfather had opened the business in the early eighties. Now, the business had flourished into a Fortune 500 company. They had expanded into different regions of Texas and hoped to someday be even larger.

"Enough talk about these crazy kids of ours," Gina, Lance's wife, said, getting the ladies' attention. "Let's talk about this wedding."

All eyes landed on Madison, the newly engaged bachelorette. She had somehow won over the well-known playboy of East Texas, Chase Storm.

Tasha chimed in. "Yes, Madison, how nervous are you? I mean, you *are* marrying the infamous Chase, the East Texas Ladies' Man," she taunted. The other ladies exchanged high fives and chortles.

Madison slowly took a sip of her drink, paused, and then smiled. "I'm fine. I'm not nervous at all. And for the record, Chase has changed. He loves me." She blushed.

"True," Deena said, agreeing with a nod.

"Well, if I would not have witnessed this with my own eyes, I'd tell you to run as fast as you could," Gina added.

Gina was married to Lance and had been in the Storm family the longest. Tasha was married to Damon, Storm number two, and Deena was married to Travis, Storm number three. Chase was the baby, the fourth and last Storm, known for being a heartbreaker. He was now 34 and was finally settling down with one woman—Madison.

She was a woman no one would have ever thought in a million years he'd choose, let alone marry. Chase was now a reformed ladies' man, womanizer, or as some would say, playboy.

Before Madison, the only women they'd ever seen him with looked like runway models out of some fashion magazine. Drop-dead gorgeous, fit, and sexy to the max. But not Madison. She was not a thin supermodel. Far from it, and was definitely not the norm for Chase. She was pretty as can be, but she was at least fifty or sixty pounds overweight. What society called a BBW, or plus-sized.

Even though full-figured women were making a mark in the new-aged world, Chase selecting her still had half the folks in town scratching their heads. Madison was kind and supersweet, but no one believed for a moment that Chase had fallen for her. Especially not Hope Gardener, the town's beauty queen. She and all the locals thought Chase would settle down with her when he was ready to stop running around. But he hadn't.

Instead, he fell for Madison, a plus-sized, caramel-com-
plexioned princess. She was soft spoken, truly humble,
and the only daughter to William and Martha Atkins. She
had honey-colored eyes—not hazel, but golden—and a
smile that would brighten a sad man's day. Not rotund
and sloppy, but shapely with curves, she was attractive . . .
beautiful, some would say, because she had the face of an
angel. She had a headful of naturally curly hair that hung
past her shoulders at one time, but the day of her first
date with Chase, she had cut it all off. Her new do was
just as gorgeous and complimented her heart-shaped
face.

"Well, that was my initial reaction when he first asked
me out, but after I accepted, he was serious, and I discovered he's actually a great guy," Madison smiled.

"I guess . . . In all honesty, I think you changed him,"
Deena said. "The more he hung around you, I noticed a
change in him."

"Well, as you all know, I didn't know of his past, nor did
I have the 411 on Chase and his whorish ways. I just went
out with the man I met, who seemed to be sweet and
genuine." Madison hunched her shoulders. "This Chase
you guys constantly speak of, I've never met him."

"Well, good luck," Tasha said and rolled her eyes. She
loved her brother-in-law, but he was absolutely not her
favorite person. "Because I'm still not convinced."

Madison ignored their comments about Chase and got
up to refill her glass. They didn't know him like she knew
him. She believed their union was real. After all she had
gone through and then meeting Chase, she felt blessed.
He was not only wealthy, and from a line of great men,
but he was also, without a doubt, fine as hell. He stood at
six feet, with a set of abs and arms that made a woman
weak. His back looked sculpted like an artist had molded
it, and Madison enjoyed giving him massages. He had

dark eyes, brows thick to faultlessness, and long eye-lashes. His strong jawline, sexy-ass lips, and mustache and beard lined to perfection turned heads everywhere he went. His body was right and tight, and he dressed like a million bucks, even on a casual day.

Confident was an understatement if used to describe him because when Chase walked into a room, he owned it. He had been with every gorgeous gal in East Texas, one would say, and Madison could imagine how the majority of them felt when he settled with her. Even Deena, her best friend, thought it had to be a joke when she told her he had asked her out. Now, after only a little over six months, Madison's left hand housed an enormous engagement ring that was a conversation piece. And they had set a date for only three months away. The city of Tyler was still gossiping about the two of them, but the nonbelievers were finally starting to believe.

"So, this is really it?" Lance asked his little brother. The crowd had gone, and the only ones left at the party were the brothers and their mates. The women were now out-side on the deck off the kitchen, while the men claimed the deck off the family room. Lance and Gina had a huge custom-built home, with a wraparound porch and three decks. One off their master bedroom, one off the kitchen, and the third one off their family room.

"Yes, this is really it, man. I mean, Madison is the one."

Head tilted and a brow vaulted, Damon asked, "Chase, seriously, you're not going to pull a crazy stunt or dump her the night before the wedding or leave her at the altar, are you?"

"No! Damn, man, why can't y'all believe me when I say I'm in love with her? I mean, do you guys think I'd go to this extreme if I *didn't* love her?"

His three brothers looked at each other and burst into roars of laughter. "Yes, you would." Travis continued to laugh as he spoke.

"I mean, li'l bro, you won the bet," said Damon.

"You don't have anything else to prove," Lance added. "Yes, we all know that Madison is not your type, so you can drop the act."

Getting serious and trying to lower the roars of laughter, Travis said, "Yeah, Chase. You're going to hurt that woman. She loves you, and you took this bet thing way too far. We expected you to flee after the first date, but here we are, wondering why you took it there. Why did you ask that woman to marry you?"

"Yes," Lance said, "the three million is yours, plus whatever Dad has promised. I'll write you a check tonight before you leave. I know it was an extreme measure for us to offer you a mil apiece, but you were out there, brother. And, besides, we never counted on you winning."

Damon shook his head. "We didn't, God knows we didn't when we came up with it, but you won, little bro. I'll have a check ready for you tomorrow, first thing."

Travis took a swig of his beer. "Yes! Unfortunately, you did what we challenged you to do. Going out with Madison is something we all thought you'd never agree to, so you won the bet, bro. I'll drop my check off tomorrow before I go home."

"Listen, keep your money, okay?" Chase shrugged. "The bet means nothing to me anymore. I know that was the initial agreement, and I didn't think I'd win either. I mean, I was an ass. For you three to bet me to date Madison for six months was a bit much, but—"

"So, it *was* a joke?" Madison shouted.

The men turned in her direction. None of them had seen her approach.

Madison stood with four cold beers locked between her fingers. Her hands trembled so much that the glasses clanked. The women had been taking turns checking on the guys and replenishing their drinks, and it was her turn to serve them a round of cold beers. She had headed around the porch smiling, but paused when she overheard them talking. She shouldn't have eavesdropped, but when she heard Travis say, *"Yes! Unfortunately, you did what we challenged you to do. Going out with Madison was something we all thought you'd never agree to, so you won the bet, bro. I'll drop my check off tomorrow before I go home,"* she couldn't help but listen in on their conversation.

Chase stood up quickly. "Madison!" he cried. She heard the nervousness in his voice. "Baby, hold on; it's not what you think."

"Really?" she said and walked up to him. She put the beers on the table and slid the ring from her finger. "You won the bet, so you might as well collect your cash. Stay the fuck away from me, Chase!" She dropped the ring in a glass of dark liquor in front of where he had been sitting and rushed off.

"Fuck!" Chase roared and ran after her.

Chapter One

"You're leaving?" she asked her lover when she opened her eyes and saw a fully dressed man standing over her king-sized bed.

"Yes. I have some things to take care of before Simone and the kids get here this evening."

"Like what?" Madison inquired. "You said you'd spend the day with me," she reminded him.

"I know, sweetheart," Tony huffed.

"So that's what I expected you to do," she droned.

He continued to button his shirt. "Look, Madison, I'm sorry. I got a text from Simone saying they will be here later on this evening instead of tomorrow, so I have to cut our time short."

She sat up and blew out a breath.

"Come on, baby, don't start making me feel bad about it. You know I would spend the day with you if I could."

"I'm not trying to make you feel bad. It's just I'm tired of this situation with us, Tony. I mean, Simone doesn't even live here with you, but it seems like she sees you more than I do sometimes."

"Well, Simone is my *wife*, Madison."

"Damn, Tony," she spat, "I know that. I don't need you to remind me of that every time I bring her up, Tony. I know what and who she is!" she shot at him.

"Look, baby, I'll see you in a couple of weeks. If I can get away sooner, you know I will see you before then."

"Now it's a couple of weeks? She was only going to be in town for a week. When did it become two?"

"Well, they'll be here in Tyler this week for Spring Break, then next week, I'll be in Austin with them."

"Whatever," Madison mumbled under her breath.

"I'll try to come by when I can, babe." He kissed the side of her head.

"No, don't bother. I can't be your sidepiece anymore. It's not enough for me."

"Are you serious right now, Madison?"

"Dead serious. Enjoy your time with your family, and when you're done pretending to be a good husband, don't bother ringing my bell."

"Madi—"

Cutting him off, she threw up a hand. "No!" she barked. "I should have never gotten involved with you in the first place, Tony. That night at the ranch, when we reconnected, I should have done the right thing, but I got caught up. This, this," she said shaking her head. "This is *not* who or what I am. I know better than this." Now tears fell from her eyes. "Please, stay away from me, Anthony Reed. I don't want to do this with you anymore." She lowered her head. "This was wrong, and I don't know why I even got involved with you," she cried.

"Are you serious?" he asked. "We have history, Madison. We should have been married. You and I were always meant to be," he defended.

"No, we weren't, and the only reason I can say that I ended up messing with you, Tony, is because you were familiar. It was just safe, but the two of us are dead wrong, Tony, and I'm more than ashamed of myself for this. Now, please, go."

"Just like that?" he asked. His voice was shaky, but she didn't look up at him. "You don't have any feelings for me?"

"I did once, Tony, but that was long ago. This right here was just physical. I knew that because I never thought you'd leave Simone for me. This brief moment of insanity is over. I'm ready to get my life back on track, and maybe even fall in love again, and being your mistress isn't what I want for myself."

"Wow," he said standing there, and she wondered why he was so shocked. They had only had sex four times during their brief affair, and those times were because she simply could no longer ignore the aching between her thighs. She had told him she only wanted to be friends, but she had weak moments when she had given in to him and let him put out her fire. She knew she was wrong and would feel terrible afterward, but not terrible enough to not see him again, but that day was different. That isn't what Madison dreamed her life would ever be like, and she was now mad at herself for allowing such foolishness to happen.

"I'll just go, if that's what you truly want, Madison." She nodded yes and was happy he didn't argue. He kissed the top of her head and slowly walked toward the door as if he wanted her to change her mind, but she silently watched him leave.

She leaned back against her headboard. *Why did I allow myself to become his mistress?* she questioned herself again.

Maybe because they did have history, and she felt safe with Tony, she thought. That had to be the only logical reason for her to go out like that.

Tony was gorgeous, and he was her type—tall, chocolate, and with a hard body. He was a cowboy, and he had come back to Tyler to tend to their family ranch when his dad fell ill. Since his kids were settled in school in Austin, and his wife, Simone, owned a business there, they'd decided to live apart, until Tony either found someone to take over the ranch full-time or he sold it.

A couple of days after he had arrived, Madison and her mom had run into him at the store. She was shocked to see him and wanted to run in the other direction. They had dated awhile back in high school, and he was her first love and sexual partner. She'd gone off to Huntsville to attend Sam Houston, and he went off to Texas A&M. They had grown apart quickly. By winter break, they had both moved on. Later, they both married and had kids. Tony had settled in Austin, while Madison and her family settled in Houston. A few years later, Madison moved back to live with her parents after losing her husband and 3-year-old twin boys to a car accident. When it happened, she fell into a deep depression and cut herself off from the world. She stopped working and gained eighty pounds over the years of her isolation, going from a size six to an eighteen. She had just been forced to rejoin the world when she ran into Tony.

She was out shopping with her mother, and Tony called out to her mom. Since Madison had put on so much weight, she knew he probably didn't recognize her.

"Mrs. Atkins?" Tony said.

"Yes?" Her mom looked up. "Oh my goodness, Tony, how are you?"

He hugged her. "I'm fine. How are you?"

Madison wanted to die when she realized who her mom was talking to. Her first love stood before her eyes, and she looked like a damn beached whale.

"Wonderful, son. How is your father? I heard about the cancer," Martha said, placing a hand over her heart.

"He's not doing too well. The cancer is aggressive, but he's strong and hanging in there."

"I'm sorry," she said and then turned to Madison. "Madison, come over here and say hello." Madison looked on, scared to move in his direction.

"Madison?" Tony said. His eyes bulged, but he then smiled.

She knew what he was thinking, but she smiled and pretended she was her old self. "Hey, Tony," she muttered and tried to avoid eye contact.

"Come here, Madison." He pulled her into his arms and gave her a tight hug. "It's good to see you. I didn't recognize you."

"I'm sure you didn't. I'm like two of me now," she said with sarcasm.

"Madison," Martha said and swatted her arm.

"But you're still gorgeous," Tony said. Madison gave him a look.

"I heard you were married now," her mom said.

"Yes, ma'am. And I have two boys, twelve and ten. They're home in Austin. I'm here working for my dad until I sell the ranch or get someone I can trust to take over when I go back."

"Well, I'm sorry to hear your dad isn't getting better. Why don't you have dinner with us? You know every Sunday I whip up a feast."

"I'm there," he smiled.

His smile was even more gorgeous than Madison had remembered. Anthony Reed had been a good-looking guy back in high school, but now, he was a grown-ass man who was even more delicious. She looked at Tony lustfully, wondering if he looked as good as she imagined under those clothes of his.

She jumped when she felt her mother touch her. "Yes? I'm sorry, Mother, what did you say?"

"I said it would be nice to catch up over dinner."

"Yes, yes, ma'am. It would be."

Tony smile at them both. "Well, it was nice to see you two. Tell Mr. Atkins I said hello, and I'll be there on Sunday."

"Okay, son," her mother said.

Tony gave her and her mom a final hug, and Madison could have sworn he squeezed her even tighter that time. The two women watched him walk away.

"That Tony is even sexier at thirty-something than he was at seventeen," Martha said.

"Mom, please, you know nothing about sexy."

"Humph, your tongue tell lies, chile. Hell, your daddy was, and is still, sexy in my book. That man used to come over my house with them tight-fitted jeans and that hat. . . . Humph, girl, makes my temperature rise just thinking about it." Martha playfully fanned herself, smiling.

"Mom, please, Daddy is *not* sexy."

"Chile, please. Every woman in East Texas wanted your father back then, but I had that man on lock. I don't know about these New-Age men, but back then, voluptuous women like myself had to beat these Texas fellas off with a stick. But with your daddy, that wasn't the case. When I first laid eyes on him, I put these hips in motion and got that man." She strutted a little and did a little dip. Madison looked around in embarrassment, hoping no one was watching them.

Martha Atkins was the opposite of her now timid daughter. She was pleasantly plump, and she was sophisticated. No one ever caught her on a bad day, and even though there was barely a black strand of hair left on her silver-colored head, she rocked a nice, tapered haircut. In her 60s, she was in great health, and although retired from the hair salon she owned and ran for forty years, she still made an occasional appointment for her church sisters.

"Mom, please don't do that in public."

"Well, if you would loosen the hell up and put some makeup on your face and stop wearing that tired ponytail on the top of yo' head, you might find another husband."

"I don't want another husband, Momma. Dre was the only man for me."

"Baby . . ." Martha moved in close to her daughter and then lowered her voice. "It's been over four years now. It's time to get your life back, Madi. I'm sorry you lost them, baby, but you're only thirty-three years old. You have a full life ahead. There is someone else out there for you, but you have to get back into the swing of life."

"Mother, please drop it, okay?"

"I won't. I'd be a horrible mother if I let you wither away. You have a great education, and it's time you got back to work. Your father and I love having you, but you are grown, Madi. Now, your father has told me to leave you alone. He's okay with taking care of you, but you're not a child, and I want my house back. Your father and I want our lives back, Madison. I brought you out today to tell you the things your daddy just won't say because you're his baby girl, and he coddles you like you're a child, but I'm here to tell you that it's time to rejoin the world. It's time to get back to living and get some love and happiness back into your life."

Madison sighed at her mother's words. She was living with her parents, but not living *off* them. She had received a substantial amount of money from the policies that were on her husband, and the company that hit them paid out a huge settlement, so all she had to do was go. She didn't burden her parents financially, because, although her mother usually tried to refuse it, she paid them rent. She'd pay a utility or two when she caught the mail before her mom did, and she bought groceries because she loved to cook.

She hesitated and then said, "Fine, Mother. I'll find another place and get out of your and Daddy's hair." She tossed the blouse that she had taken off the rack before seeing Tony onto a nearby table and then headed out of the store. She went straight to her mother's Mercedes.

Martha followed behind trying to talk to her, but she kept moving. "I didn't mean it like that, Madi. I just meant you have to start living again. Your father and I adore you, but if we continue to allow you to stay, we'll be enabling you. The person you have now become is not the person we raised."

They got into the car, and Martha started the engine and turned the AC on blast. Madison didn't say a word; she just stared out the window.

"You are stronger than what you think," Martha added. "It's tragic what happened to Dre and my grandbabies, Madi, but you have to find a new life."

Tears rolled down Madison's face.

"I'm sorry if I hurt your feelings, baby." Martha grabbed Madison's hand and squeezed it.

"It's okay, Mom. You're right, and I know you mean well."

"Yes, I do. I want what's best for you, sweetheart," Martha said.

They rode home in silence after that.

The next day, Madison met with her friend, Deena Storm. She was a real estate agent, and her husband and his family were builders.

"As you can see, this community is going to be gorgeous when all the houses are completed." Deena was showing her a house in one of her family's newer developments.

"I like this one, but I really liked the one with the back of the house facing the lake. Can we look at that one again?" Madison asked.

"Of course." Deena walked across the room and turned off the light switch. "Now, that one is twenty grand more than this one. The view, the upgrades, the fifth bedroom, and fourth bathroom are why the price tag is a lot more. This one has four bedrooms, three baths, and only one fireplace. There, you'll have the two-sided fireplace on the main floor and the one in the master," she explained as they walked toward the door.

"I understand. That is exactly why I want to see that one again. I know it's a lot of house just for me alone, but who knows."

"I know losing Dre and the boys was hard on you. I mean, you stayed off the scene so long, I was worried about you."

"I'm better now, Deena, and I'm sorry for shutting you out like I did. I didn't mean to treat you that way when you were trying to help me."

"It's okay, Madi. At the time, I had recently married Travis, and we were in honeymoon mode, so I know it was an undesirable situation for you to be around us back then."

"Yeah, it was, but I'm better now."

"Good," Deena smiled, and the two women walked to her Jag.

They drove a short distance to the house that Madison loved. It didn't take much convincing for her to put in an offer.

"Okay, of course, we are the sellers, so I'm going to get you that family-best-friend rate. I know this one is twenty more than that other one, but after I work my magic, your price will be the same or as close to the other home as I can get it," she winked.

Madison hugged Deena. "Thanks so much."

"Thank me after I run the numbers by my brother-in-law, Lance. He drives a hard bargain."

"Well, I'll be waiting for your call," Madison said.

Chapter Two

Chase tapped the steering wheel of his Audi, bobbed his head to the music, and sang along with Blake Shelton while he drove, on hold to speak to his big brother, Lance. He was going to suggest that he get another station for the hold music. Even though he liked country music, it didn't seem to be the best hold music.

"This is Lance Storm," Lance answered.

"Hey, L, what's going on? I called your cell phone a few times. Too busy for your baby bro?" he kidded.

"Some of us do actually work," Lance said, and Chase could hear papers shuffling. His brother was always in work mode, and he wished he'd relax and kick back but work always trumped everything.

"I work, but I'm out of my office by three. I don't have to work ten hours a day to do what I do."

"What is it you do again?" Lance joked.

"Ha, ha, ha, big bro, you're so funny. You know what I do. I make sure those numbers look right on those supply orders, baby. You know I'm the one that keeps us on budget for each job and underbudget if I stay late," Chase laughed.

He was the head accountant. He oversaw a staff of twelve, and their numbers were always on point to the penny. And whenever they finished under, his department got a bonus, and Chase was all about making bonuses, so he did a stellar job. He wasn't just good at what he did, he was superb, and he knew his brothers knew it.

"Yeah, yeah, you handle your end like a pro, so, to what do I owe this call? I have mortgage applications to comb through."

The continued sounds of paper shuffles were a hint to let Chase know he had to get to the point of his phone call before he'd be greeted by a dial tone. Lance worked just as hard as he did. It was why their business was so lucrative.

"Okay, I'll hurry so you can get back to work. I don't need the 'Time is money' speech today, big bro."

"Then out with it, Chase. You've already wasted two valuable minutes of my time that I can't get back," Lance said.

Chase laughed lightly. "I need a model home for the weekend. I tried to hit up Deena, but you know she never answers my calls close to the weekend."

"Why can't you take your dates to your real home, Chase?"

"Dude, are you crazy? I would never reveal the location of my home. That is play rule number one. These chicks are crazy as hell. The one and only woman who may get lucky enough to be called Mrs. Storm won't know my true location until *after* the honeymoon."

Lance laughed. "You are truly a piece of work, little brother. But, unfortunately, if you want to know what's still empty and staged, you will have to get with Deena. I don't keep track of that anymore."

"Damn, Deena hates my guts, and she said that last time would be the last time."

"And she said that before that time and the time before. Go by her office, dude. Ask her for the list."

"Damn damn damn. I don't want to do that."

"If you want a place to lay up with one of your fans, you have no choice, because I can't help you, and I gotta go. I have work to do, Chase."

"I guess I'll have to," Chase sighed. He pulled off the highway to head back in the other direction.

"You know you are going to have to settle down one day, Chase, and stop chasing skirts. Momma and Pop must have known what you'd grow up to be when they named you that."

"Listen, marriage and settling are *not* on my to-do list. Maybe when I'm fifty, I'll consider it."

"Whatever, Chase. Don't break another headboard, and make sure you have the service clean up this time. Deena said if she ever walks into another model home that you left a mess, she was going to roast you like a pig."

They laughed.

"Okay, man," Chase said. "I'll have it cleaned. The last time, it just slipped my mind."

"Well, your dates are not too bright if they can't figure out these are staged properties. I mean, not one personal picture and only a couple of items in the fridge and closet."

"Well, we spend time in the bedroom, bro, not in the kitchen and closets."

"Okay, on that note, I'm hanging up. Get yo' life right." Then he hung up.

Chase chuckled at his brother's last comment.

He headed to Deena's, mentally preparing himself for the tongue-lashing she was going to unleash on him. She was a cool sister-in-law at times . . . until the subject of his love life was up for discussion. She frowned on him and acted as if he didn't have a right to mingle. Hell, he was still single.

Chase arrived and parked in the closest empty spot near the door he could find. He put on his designer sunglasses and got out. He spoke to the women that passed him by on his way to the entrance. One sister deserved a second look, so over the rim of his shades, Chase eyed the sway of her hips and ass. "Damn, baby, fine," he said and continued to the door. He walked in and was greeted by other staff as he made it to Deena's door. It was open, so he tapped the frame to get her attention. "Deena, Deena, Deena, my favorite sister-in-law, you're looking lovely today," he sang when he walked into her office.

"Get out, Chase. Lance called me already, and I told you no more hookups in our model homes. You bring too much drama to this company. Got chicks showing up in trench coats looking for you and ready to fight me when I say that you don't live there. I'm not for it."

"Deena, Deena, Deena. Come on, sis. I won't forget to clean it this time, and I'll make it clear that it's a rental while some construction is being done on my house. That usually keeps them from coming back."

"Chase, why are you so damn foolish?" She shook her head at him but went for the list.

All of his sisters-in-law were plus-sized. Beautiful, but too big for his taste. His brothers had a thing for hips, butt, and gut, he guessed. He thought back to when Travis married her. Deena used to be thick, but a decent size. But after three kids, she was no longer thick. She was fat, in his opinion. Even though he didn't care for her physical appearance, he loved her for being the right woman for his brother.

"Here." She slapped the list into his chest. "Make your decision now so that I can take it off my show list. Lord knows I don't want to come in on you and God-knows-who, doing God-knows-what."

"Thanks, sis." He gave her a wet kiss on the cheek. On purpose, because he knew that always irritated her.

She gave him a playful shove. "Boy, go on now. Your lips done been in too many places."

"Well, Travis wasn't a saint before you."

"Maybe not, but I know he wasn't as bad as you."

"True," he agreed and scanned the list. "Damn, the lake view one sold?"

"Yep, two days ago. To my girl Madison."

"Madison . . . Madison . . . Madison . . ." It sounded familiar.

"Quit playing. You know Madison."

"I heard of her, but I don't think we've ever met."

"Well, you have, I'm sure. She's my friend from high school that lost her family a few years back, and she was in a deep funk, so she didn't move around much. She's Martha Atkins's daughter. I'm sure you remember her."

Still looking over the list and only half-listening, he nodded. "No, I don't, but okay. I'll get this one on Lancaster. I'll only need it one night—tomorrow night."

"Who is this chick, Chase? Do I know her?"

"Nope. She lives in Dallas. Coming to visit some family here, so she and I are hooking up tomorrow night."

"Dallas, huh?"

"Yes, Dallas, why?"

"I see you're expanding your horizons."

"Well, I've had all of the beauties in Tyler, so why not?"

Deena frowned. "Eeeewwww, Chase. Get your ass out of my office."

"As you wish," he said and made his exit, stopping to grab the house key from the keyboard.

He bumped into a plump sister on his way out.

"Oh, I'm sorry," she said.

"Don't mention it." He didn't look back. She was pretty but didn't hit the double take list.

He got in his car, planning to head to the grocery store for wine, fruit, and finger foods. He'd order takeout for his Dallas Delight, take her to breakfast after he serviced her right, and drop her back off where he scooped her up.

"Damn, I love being single." He slid his sunglasses on and pulled off.

Chapter Three

"So, when can I close?" Madison asked Deena, anxious and excited.

"In less than two weeks. Lance didn't remember meeting you at the wedding, but when I reminded him of what you have gone through, he quickly agreed on this price."

Madison smiled.

"You chose to pay everything outright, which is saving you a ton of interest. Even though you have excellent credit, no interest sounds a helluva lot better to me," Deena giggled. "Damon is going to break out in a happy dance when he hears this."

"Well, thanks to the huge settlement from the accident and my husband's insurance policy, I'm pretty much set for life. I don't have to, but I am going back to work so I can get back to what some would call a normal life. Something I never imagined I'd have again since that day, but it's time to live again. I've decided to manage my mother's salon. It's outdated and old and in need of quite a few upgrades. I'm going to turn it into a more upscale, modern salon. I want to talk to someone at Storms about remodeling or even building from the ground up. I want Martha's to step into this modern world and cater to more than just church folks," Madison laughed.

"That sounds great, Madi. I'm so happy to see you getting back to living. A new man may be your next new beginning," Deena added.

"I don't know about that, Ms. Deena. Honestly, love is the last thing on my mind. I just want to get back into the swing of life. If love happens, however, I'll let it." She smiled. She was just about ready for anything, but love had never entered her mind until Deena's mention of a man. Tony was good for sex and a good time, but since he was married, he was safe. She'd never fall in love with a married man. If she ever fell in love again, he'd have to be single and, hopefully, childfree.

"Well, you never know what's in store for you, Madison," Deena winked.

"You're right," Madison agreed. "So, what's next?" she said, getting back to the house business.

"I'm going to get everything over to Lance, and he'll give you a call with your exact closing date."

"That's it?"

"Yes, ma'am, that is it. I have everything I need from you, and since there is no financing, this will be a quick and easy process."

"Well, I guess I'll hit up a few furniture stores this week because I'm sure when I open the storage unit that houses all my old things, the memories are going to come flooding in. I don't know if I wanna keep those things or sell them and start fresh."

"Well, I'll go with you if you need me to when you go, so don't worry. And if you decide to sell it all, let me know, because we do staging, and I'm sure you'll have some items we can use."

"Thanks, Deena."

"No thanks needed, Madi. We've been friends since forever. I hate what you went through."

"Me too. I miss them every single day, but now I can go without crying every other day. When I think of them, I smile more now. I'm finally starting to feel alive again."

"That's wonderful."

"Well, I'll get out of your hair. I have to go by the salon and do a walkthrough, meet the stylists, and survey all of the immediate damage."

"Oh yeah, let me give you a card. Give Marcus Storm a call. He is Travis's cousin and our head architect. Just tell him I referred you, and he'll take care of you."

"Wow, thanks. I do hope he can renovate it because I don't want to change the location. It's been in that spot for over forty years and to move it would be terrible."

"Well, one thing about our company is we work around the clock. Usually, they can move things around to give work access while they work. Like, you may be down to two bowls for a couple of weeks, and things will be tight and noisy. But we've done salons before that turned out fabulous. Check out Lucy's Locks and Styles by Jackie when you get a chance. We got them remodeled without a hiccup in their businesses."

"I will." Madison stood.

"Oh, and since you're back in the land of the living, mark your calendar for the Storms' thirty-third anniversary party. It will be at the convention center, as always, and it's taking place a little over a month from now, so get you a sexy ballroom gown."

"Sexy? Ha," Madison laughed.

"We are not all meant to be skinny. And you know big Texas men love big Texas women."

"I didn't know until my mother schooled me on that. I would love to attend, so I'll make sure I hit up Mrs. Henderson. She can make a dress in five minutes."

"Well, you better get on it, because she's making my and my sisters-in-law and our mothers' and my mother's-in-law dress too. She has almost finished ours. And so you will look like family and not just my best friend, our dresses are red," Deena smiled.

"I do look good in red." Madison smiled back and made her exit.

When she left, she headed to her mom's salon. After a walkthrough, she wanted to tear the building completely down. "Oh Lord, what have I've gotten myself into," she said. There was old everything, even though it had been renovated a few times since the seventies.

She dialed Marcus, and he agreed to meet her the next morning. Not like Madison, he was impressed by some of the architectural details. He told her the arches and hardwoods were in great shape and said he'd definitely try to keep those. He promised to have her plans with a new layout in two weeks. She smiled as he shook her hand to leave. He was attractive.

She hadn't been out in so long, and being in the presence of Marcus for that short time made her realize just how much she missed the scent of a man. His cologne smelled so damn good on him, and when he spoke, she couldn't help staring at his lips, and when he pointed out certain things, she stared at his muscular arms and wanted to reach out and touch him. "Am I really ready to date?" she asked herself aloud when he made his exit. Rejoining the world was one thing, but finding love again was something else entirely. She wondered if she was ready to give her heart to another man.

She locked the shop's door and was about to head home but decided to stop by the furniture store to look.

Seeing new and updated styles, she agreed her stuff in storage had to be sold. Even though she hadn't closed on the house yet, she dropped seventeen grand on a new bedroom set, living room set, kitchen table and chairs, and office furniture. She'd keep her cookware, dishes, art, accessories, and other valuables, and put her old bedroom set in one of the spare bedrooms. She couldn't imagine sharing that bed with anyone else anyway.

When she got home, her parents had jazz coming from their room, and she could smell the scent of Jasmine, her mom's favorite fragrance. Her mom and dad were older, but still madly in love, and although she hated it, she still had to wear her headphones to bed . . . in case they decided to be intimate. She had known to be home and across the hall from their room would be horrible, but when she lost Dre and the boys, she couldn't bear to be alone. She had fought with her in-laws about burying her husband in Tyler because they wanted him in Houston. But as his wife, she had the power to bury her husband wherever she wanted to.

She lay in her bed and decided to listen to an audio book. She had become a bookworm in her secluded days and was able to listen to a book while she enjoyed her other hobbies—quilting, crocheting, and knitting. She also played the piano and could sing, but that had never been her passion. Her momma wanted it to be, so Madison had piano lessons and a vocal coach when she was younger. Martha had put her in every talent show under the stars, but by junior year, she told her mother she didn't want to participate anymore.

"Mom!" Madison said when she looked up to see her mother at her door. She had been listening to an audio-book with her headphones on and did not hear her come in.

"I knocked," Martha said, coming in carrying the phone. She had on a black lace teddy with matching robe. She extended the hand holding the phone and held her nightie closed with the other.

Madison was unfazed by her mother's usual nighttime attire. "Who is it?"

"Anthony. He wanted your cell, but I figured if you wanted him to have it, you'd be the one to give it to him." Madison took the phone. "Don't forget, darling, he's a married man. Don't fall for *no* bullshit," Martha said and left.

"Hello," Madison said.

"Madison, hey. You're a hard woman to track down."

"Hey, Tony. I was out all day."

"I know. I called several times. It's crazy your folks still have the same number."

"Yes, this number is older than me."

"My pop does too."

"So, what's up, Tony? Why are you calling me?"

"I wanted to see you and catch up. I heard about your husband and your twins. I'm so sorry, Madi."

"Thanks, Tony. I'm healing now, finally. It was super-hard, but I'm so much better now."

"That's good to hear, Madison. I can imagine you went through a tough time."

"I did, but time is the healer of all things."

"Indeed, it is," he said. The line went silent.

"So, Tony, what do you need?"

"I wanted to meet for a drink. It's been some time since we've seen each other, and I'd like to see you, Madison. If you're not busy, maybe you can come by and have a drink with me. This thing with my dad is tough to deal with, you know."

"I can imagine. Sure, I can come by. I'm not busy."

"Great, that will be just great."

"So, I could be there in an hour. I need to change."

"That's perfect."

They hung up, and Madison sat on the side of the bed. *Okay, all I have is sweats and housedresses,* she thought, looking down at her attire. She only had two cute outfits, and she had worn one to house hunt and the other earlier that day.

Martha stepped in. "What did Anthony want with you, chile?"

"Nothing too much, Momma. He just wanna talk. He's having a hard time dealing with Mr. Reed being ill. Asked me to come by for a drink."

"Madison Grace Atkins-Morgan, don't you go to that man's house for a drink. He is *not* available. He is married with sons, and that's not a good look for you."

"Mother, I'm aware of that. I'm not interested in Tony, so please don't turn this into something it isn't."

"Okay, but I know how men are, and it's been more than four years since you've had your cat stroked."

Madison's eyes bulged. "Momma!" She couldn't believe her mother had just said that to her.

"Oh, Madi, don't play coy with me. I'm your mother, and I've never sugarcoated anything, and I'm not going to start now. I tell it like it is. Don't get caught up with another woman's man, because in the end, if the mistress wins, she later becomes victim to the same thing." Martha turned and left.

Madison showered and pulled her long curls up into a high ponytail. She grabbed a new pair of yoga pants that she had never worn and a V-neck tee shirt. After looking in the mirror, she went for her makeup bag, only to find most of her cosmetics were dried up. "Okay, I must get new makeup too," she told herself. She slowly approached her parents' door and tapped.

"Come in," her mother said.

Madison stepped in to find her daddy under the covers, and her mom leaning in close. She thanked God that the aroma of sex she had smelled when she was a teenager wasn't in the air.

"Mom, I need makeup, please. Mine is dried up."

"In my bathroom in the left drawer," her mom said.

"Thanks, Ma." After getting the makeup bag, Madison started to leave.

"Madi," Martha called out.

Madison paused. "Yes, ma'am?"

"Remember what I said."

"I will."

Madison hurried to the hall bathroom and spruced up her face before grabbing the keys to her Suburban.

She pulled up to the gate of the Reeds' ranch and got out to open it. She figured Tony wouldn't shoot because he was expecting her. After clearing the gate, she got out and closed it. Just then, Tony approached on a horse.

"Oh my God, Tony, this cannot be Bandit."

"No, Bandit died about seven or so years ago, but this is one of his offspring." Madison approached, and Tony tugged the reins so that the horse wouldn't react.

"He's gorgeous. What's his name?"

"Booker. I came to open the gate, but I see you remember the trick for the latch."

"Yep, I do. Did it plenty of times when we were younger."

"Well, come on in. Daddy is already sleeping."

"Okay."

She got in her truck, and Tony and Booker headed toward the stables, while she headed toward the main house.

Chapter Four

Her mother was right.

Madison walked into a familiar floor plan that had been renovated. The house's décor had been updated, but it still had the feel of the house she used to visit when she was a teen.

"What would you like?" Tony asked.

"Wine would be nice if you have it; I'm not into heavy liquor."

"Wine it is," he said, going toward the kitchen.

The house now had an open concept floor plan. The wall that had once divided the kitchen from the living area no longer existed.

"The place looks nice. I see that, like my parents, your dad renovated."

"Yes, thanks to me. He thought things were fine the way they were, but things were falling apart. Half of the drawers in the kitchen wouldn't open or close all the way. The ranch was doing well, so why not? I got with the Storms, as everyone in this town does, and they came in and did an overhaul. No new added space—there is still no master bathroom in my dad's room—but every room got a face-lift." He gestured for her to have a seat on the sofa and then handed her a glass of white wine.

"Well, when you come over Sunday, you'll see the same thing went down at my parents' place. House is still pretty much the same layout, like here, but it's now open as well. And that fourth bedroom no longer exists. My parents expanded their room and added a master bath and an enormous walk-in closet."

"I imagine it's nice," Tony said.

"It is, and it's always where I'll call home no matter where I live."

"I know, right? My home out in Austin is nice. We have five bedrooms, a loft, my own man cave, and a pool, but somehow, I feel more at home here." He excused himself to get his drink and moments later, joined her on the sofa. "It's very nice to see you again, Madison. I can't believe how the time has zoomed by."

"I know. It seems like just yesterday we were teens running around this ranch."

"You were like my heart back then." He smiled.

"You were mine too, but we grew up, and that puppy love quickly faded. Mother told me that it wouldn't last, and I didn't believe her. But like most things, she was right."

"Well, yes, unfortunately, she was, but I still think about you now and then. I miss a lot of things about you."

"Really? I thought that wife of yours would be the only one on your mind."

"My wife? Oh boy, my wife. I love her, don't get me wrong, but, honestly, I don't miss her. I mean, she's a pistol. Always got something smart to say, always wants the last word. She's from New York, and they are a different breed than us Texans."

"Like my momma always used to say when I'd complain about Dre, 'You knew who you were marrying.' I'm sure you knew who you were taking the plunge with."

"I did, but she has gotten worse," he laughed.

They continued talking and catching up. By glass number three, she was good and tipsy and starting to remember all the reasons why she liked Tony back then. He was easy on the eyes, and she remembered him being a great kisser.

At that thought, she stood. "I'd better be going."

"Don't go," he said. He stood up and moved directly in front of her.

"I have to, Tony. I mean, it was great catching up, but if I stay . . . I-I-I—You're married now, so I definitely need to go." She headed for the door, but he beat her to it and blocked her exit.

"Just tonight, baby, and I promise I'll never bother you again."

"Tony, I just, I can't, I—" Tony pushed his tongue in between her lips, cutting her words off.

A man hadn't kissed Madison since Dre. Her nipples sprouted against her satin bra. They became so hard that they ached to be sucked, touched, and pulled. He moved down to her neck as his hands palmed her ass.

"Tony, wait. Wait-wait," she pleaded trying to pull away from his strong embrace. He was so deliciously aggressive, she had to free herself before things went too far, but he held her. She knew that he wouldn't deviate from his plan of seducing her, so she gave up the battle. She secretly wanted him, but also knew she was dead wrong for even allowing him to kiss and fondle her body. He felt so good, after so long of not having a man's touch, she wanted him, but wished he was the single Tony she dated back in high school.

"Don't fight it, baby, I want you," he breathed against her neck. He pushed her back, toward his old bedroom, and she allowed it. Once inside, she wasn't surprised to see that it had also changed. It was now a grown-up room with adult furnishings instead of posters, trophies, and smelly clothing covering the floor. And a huge king bed replaced the full-sized one that she and Tony used to fool around on.

She knew she should have run away from that situation, but once they were naked, she surrendered and let Tony remind her body of what it felt like to be with a man. He caressed her skin and licked her all over. He had turned into a skillful lover. He treated her to two body-numbing orgasms induced by his magic tongue licking her clit and sucking on her lips.

It had been over four years, and when he penetrated her, it hurt like hell, like their first time. When they noticed blood on the condom after the first round, she became embarrassed, but they both agreed it was just like the first time when the same thing happened. She wanted it to be good, but it was painful. She moaned in agony more than pleasure.

"Slow, Tony, slow. It hurts." He was not much bigger than she remembered, but her tight walls hadn't had a workout in a while.

"I'm sorry. I don't want to hurt you." He slowed his strokes. "Is that better?" Although it wasn't as bad as it was, it was far from better.

She buried her face in his neck and let him enjoy himself. Tight and painful for her, but tight and pleasurable for him, she thought, giving him all of her. When his body jerked, she knew he had accomplished his goal.

"Aaaaw, baby. Aaaaw, baby, you feel so damn good," he groaned. He rested on top of her for a few moments and then got up to dispose of the condom.

Then it's like reality hit her like a ton of brinks. She'd just fucked a married man, and the feeling of culpability overcame her.

"We can't ever, *ever* do this again, Anthony Reed. You have a wife and kids, and I'm horrible! What we just did was horrible," Madison said in a panic.

Tony rushed to her side to comfort her. "Hey hey hey, calm down, Madi. Relax, baby."

She jumped up and started searching the dimly lit room for her panties. "Tony, this is not who I am. My mother told me to be careful, but did I listen? No! I do not mess with other women's husbands or men, as a matter of fact, and what we did—" she cried gathering her belongings.

"Okay, you're right. We went too far. It's just after seeing you, Madi, I started thinking about you nonstop. I'm sorry. We won't do this again."

"You're damn right things went too far and, we will *never* do this shit again," she spat. She dressed as quickly as she could and hurried out.

She got into her Suburban and headed home, feeling like shit. She slept on the sofa in the den. It was one in the morning. No way was she going to chance her mother coming in to talk to her if she went upstairs to her bedroom. She couldn't lie to her mother's face and say she and Tony had just "talked."

She felt awful. Even though she was no longer close to God, she prayed and asked him to forgive her. She had stopped talking to him after he took her men away, but that night, she needed his mercy, because she knew she was wrong.

Tony came over a couple of days later for Sunday dinner, and as soon as he left, her mother said, "I don told you about that damn Tony, Madison. You play with fire, and you *will* get burned."

"Momma, I'm not sleeping with Tony," Madison defended.

"Madison Grace, stand in my face and tell me another lie and I will slap you to the floor."

"Okay, Momma, I'm sorry. I did the other night. And it will never happen again."

"Somehow, I don't believe that. I saw the way you two carried on at the dinner table. I saw the lust in both of your eyes. In my day, many'ah women fought over men, but I've never respected one that opened wide for one that had a wife. Now, I'd give them gals a run for their money for a single stud, but I've never wanted to share anything in my life, especially no man. Don't let Tony reel you in, Madison," Martha said and brushed Madison's hair behind her ear. "As your friend, I don't want to see you hurt, and as your mother, I don't want to see you hurt."

"I know, Mother, and I have this thing with Tony under control."

Or so she thought.

The night she moved into her house, he was inside of her again. He and a few of his friends helped her move into her new place, and after everyone else left, he stayed behind. She tried to resist but gave in again and not proud of it, she knew she had become Tony's mistress.

Chapter Five

"Oh my God!" Deena gasped.

"What?" Gina asked.

Deena nodded toward her brother-in-law Chase and his companion. "This boy is a piece of work. Where is the rest of his date's dress?"

Tasha's eyes widened. "Oh, hell naw. Let me find Damon right now. They have to do something about him. This is an elegant affair, and Chase will not embarrass this family." With Gina and Deena in tow, she stormed off to find her husband. "Go and get your brother," she said when they found him. "That ho he has on his damn arm just strolled up in here looking like she belongs on a corner. We worked too hard to put this tasteful night together, Damon."

Damon turned to see what his wife was talking about. "Aaaaw, Tash, it's not all that bad."

She scowled. "Damon."

"Okay, okay. I'll go and talk to him." He hurried over to Chase and tapped his shoulder. Chase turned and smiled when he saw his brother. "Hey, bro, you know Sarah, right? Sarah, you remember my brother, Damon."

"Hey, Damon," she said. Her shrill voice drawled the words. Damon smiled at her; then he pulled at Chase's arm. "Hi. Would you excuse us for a sec?"

"Go 'head, I'm ready to get my *drank* on," she cheered and then bopped over to a server holding a tray of champagne.

"Chase, seriously? You bring *that* up in here?"

"I know. I told her something sexy but elegant."

"And when you saw that dress two inches below her pussy, you should have left that trick on her corner."

"Chill on that, Damon. I asked her to come, and I couldn't just tell her she was suddenly uninvited."

"Chase, do you *really* want Mother to see her in that dress?"

Chase took another look at Sarah and the bottom of her ass cheeks peeking from under her dress. He had to admit that his big brother was right. It was more than trashy. She looked like a working girl for real. "Okay, I got you. I'll take her home."

"Now," Damon demanded.

"Okay, bro. Damn, I'll take her now."

Lance and Travis hurried over, both with identical scowls on their faces. "Oh hell," Lance said.

"Oh hell is right," Damon said. "I just told him to get her ass out of here."

"What in the hell was he thinking?" Travis asked as they watched their baby brother practically drag his date out of the ballroom.

"We have to do something about him," Lance said. "He's going to end up being killed by one of these crazy women or contracting something a shot can't cure. Not to mention tarnishing our family's name. The Storms get married; we don't keep company with whores. Chase is almost thirty-four. It's time for him to grow the hell up and start acting like the valor men of this family. I mean, we've all played the field, but Chase has outplayed us all, and we need to do something about him before he gets any worse."

"Yes, indeed, and tonight we talk to him," Damon added.

"And say what?" Travis inquired. "It's going to have to be a sweet deal for him to listen to us. We've been preaching the same damn sermon for years, and he hasn't changed, and if there's something worse, I'd hate to see it."

"How much are you willing to gamble to tame this young beast?" Lance asked.

Damon raised an eyebrow. "What do you mean?"

"What if we challenge him to a little wager? Like, let's say if he stays with one woman and gets to know her for at least six months, we'll each give him a mil?"

Travis agreed first. "One million for six months? I'm in. No way he'd last that long," he said shaking his head.

"Hell, I'd offer two million just to see him settle down and act like Storm blood is running through his veins," Damon said. "Do you know he showed up at my house with three women the other night? Asking if he could use my hot tub."

"What?" Travis frowned. "I know Tasha was heated."

"Heated is an understatement, bro. She was on fire. Cussed his ass out and told him to get the hell away from our front door with that bullshit."

Lance shook his head. "Why, when he has a hot tub of his own?"

"I know, but Chase don't be wanting these crazy women to know where he lives. All this using our model homes for his sexcapades has to stop, Lance. I'm serious. I told Deena the other day not to give him that list or another key ever again."

"You're right," Lance said. "I'm in for a mil. He has to calm down and settle down. He's running through his money like water, and it's time he grew the hell up. The right woman will make that happen. And we're going to find her for him." He pointed at a curvaceous, plump woman in a red dress. "Her."

Travis and Damon looked in her direction.

"Her, right there?" Damon asked in disbelief. "Chase is not going to be interested in someone like her."

"Yes, her," Lance confirmed.

"Man, are you crazy? Do you know who that is? Deena would have a heart attack, and Chase would laugh his ass off," Travis said.

"Deena?" Lance tilted his head.

"That's Madison, her friend from high school who lost her husband and kids a few years ago."

"Yes. That's Madison Atkins-Morgan, Martha Atkins's daughter," Lance said. "She bought a house not too long ago from us, and regardless of what Deena or Chase may say, I say she's the one."

"I say good luck with that. My wife is going to freak out, and Chase is not going to go for her."

"If he wants the money, he will. Chase is not going to turn down $3 million—money that he doesn't have to work for handed to him on a platter. Oh, he'll bite. I promise he'll do it for the money."

Travis looked nervous. "And my wife?"

"Listen, brothers," Lance said, "I understand your concerns, but I'm *sure* she's the one. She'd whip Chase into a real man. He needs a real, mature, grown-ass woman, and she's it. This is between us. We don't have to tell anyone about the offer. And if Madison can tame him, it will be a win-win. Deena wants him to settle down just as much as we all do," said Lance.

Damon shrugged but then agreed. "Count me in."

They continued to discuss their plan of approach while they waited for Chase to return. As soon as he walked back into the ballroom, they rushed over to him and escorted him to a smaller, empty room.

"What is this, some type of intervention?" Chase grinned devilishly.

Lance spoke first. "You can say that."

"Well, save your breath, because I love my life, and I'm not about to change how I live because you three don't agree."

"What if there was a reward involved?" Travis rubbed his hands together, nodding.

"A reward?" Chase cocked an eyebrow. "I'm listening."

Damon's baritone voice boomed in the empty room. "We've discussed it, and we all agree that it's time for you to settle down and find a wife. You can't find a good girl if you keep bed hopping, so each of us is willing to give you a million dollars apiece to date one woman for six months. That will give you time to get to know, and possibly even get close to, her."

"Man, you guys are kidding me, right?" Chase laughed out loud and looked at his brothers like he was waiting for someone to laugh with him.

Travis took the floor. "No, li'l bro, we are dead serious. One million each, for six months."

Realizing that they were dead serious, Chase quickly agreed. "That's a bet," Chase said. He shook their hands one at a time. When he got to Lance, the eldest Storm didn't let go right way.

"Not so fast there, little brother, there are two tiny details," Lance added.

A frown immediately took over Chase's face. "Oh shit, here we go. I knew this deal was too sweet to be true."

"No, the offer is real. But we have to pick her, and no smashing on the side."

"Oh, hell no!" Chase shouted. "Absolutely not. Hell no. No deal!" he disputed.

"That's the deal, Chase," Damon said. "We have your best interest at heart, so you know we are not going to toss you just anybody. And if you are still fucking around with other women, what would be the point of this? We want you to settle down, so we're going to choose someone that we think will be good for you."

Chase settled down after hearing Damon out. "I don't know. I mean, I know I'm capable of getting to know the right woman, but I want her to be gorgeous. And no side-piece? What if she's holding out for marriage or some shit like that? My dick can't bear the thought of no pussy for six months, man; come on now. That's being unrealistic."

"She'll be gorgeous, and I believe she'll be good enough to make you wait if you have to. Or, she just might be willing. Those are tiny details. Besides, Chase, according to your reputation and track record, you're charming enough," Travis winked. "I'm sure you'd be hard for her to resist."

"Chase, you have to turn over a new leaf and try something new for a change if you want a wife and kids," Lance said. "All of this whoring around you're doing is not a good look. We settled down long before we were your age. And the way you're running through women, you're going to miss the opportunity to find a good one while you're young enough to enjoy her, have kids, and pass on your legacy."

"Okay okay okay. You don't have to lay it on so thick. It's a deal, but she'd better not be a troll, I swear."

"Man, we'd never do that," Travis said. "She'd be the mother of our nieces and nephews."

"So, do we have a solid deal?" Damon asked. "You can't back out, and you have to be a man of your word, Chase Storm."

"It's solid." Chase shook all three of his brothers' hands again, and they headed back to the party.

Satisfied that they had convinced Chase to agree to their terms, the Storm men worked out the plan for Chase to be introduced to Madison. Since Travis knew her, and Lance had met her at closing, Damon, who was the smoothest, was elected to be the wingman.

"Madison, right?" he said, approaching her.

"Yes," Madison turned.

"I'm Damon, Damon Storm. I heard you were the one to get that gorgeous house by the lake in our newest development."

"Yes, that was me."

"Well, congratulations. I know you'll love it."

She smiled, and Damon noted how beautiful she was.

"Yes, I do love it. Every morning before I head out to work, I sit out back and enjoy my morning coffee."

"I bet. You're Deena's friend, right?"

"Yes, I am."

"Nice to meet you. I've heard a lot about you. I'm sorry about the loss of your family. I can imagine that was tough to go through."

"Yes, my husband and boys passed away a few years ago. It was tough at first, but I'm better now."

"That's good. And I'm glad you are doing better now."

"I am." Madison gave him another smile.

Damon smiled back at her. "Well, a woman as beautiful as you are won't stay single for long."

"So I've heard, but I'm starting not to believe it."

"You know, I have someone I'd like to introduce you to. Do you mind?"

"No, not at all."

"Come with me." He walked her over to where Chase stood. The youngest Storm's eyes widened when he laid eyes on her.

"This is my brother, Chase. Chase, this is Madison. She's the one who snatched up the lake property in our new development." Damon could see the lack of interest, but they had a solid deal. His baby brother had no choice.

Chase extended his hand politely. "Nice to meet you, Madison."

"Likewise," Madison smiled.

"Well, I'll leave you two to chat," Damon said and hurried off.

"Why in the hell is Chase grinning in Madison's face so damn hard?" Deena said between clenched teeth. She was about to march over and tell Chase to get the hell away from her friend, but Travis grabbed her arm.

"Now, baby, they're just talking. And they are grown, so don't march over like you're their mother."

"You're right." She let out a deep breath. "I don't know what that Chase is up to, but Madison is one of the good ones. She's been living under a rock for the past few years, and I'm sure she has no idea that he's a wolf in sheep's clothing."

"And you're not going to tell her, either."

"Hell if I'm not. Baby, I love your brother, but he's a dog, and I can't stand back and watch him play with her. You know she's not his type. I've never seen Chase with, let alone date, a girl who wears double digit-sized clothing."

"Well, this may be just what he needs, so let grown folks be grown. Madison is a smart woman, baby, so can you please promise me you won't meddle?"

She hesitated. "Baby, Chase is a do—" Travis kissed her, cutting off her words. "No meddling." He kissed her again, this time on the nose.

"Baby, she's my friend. She's been through enough as it is."

"Deena, Deena, darling. They're only chatting, baby. You have no reason to warn her."

"Okay okay okay, I'll stay out of it. But if your brother is up to no good or if he hurts her or-or-or—I'm going to gut him like a fish, is all I'm saying."

Travis laughed and pulled his wife close, thinking he'd beat her to it.

Chapter Six

The older Storm brothers stood outside and watched Chase walk Madison to her car. The men had kept their wives from interrupting the couple that night, and they were surprised that Chase hadn't headed for the hills. They watched him give Madison a friendly hug, and he even closed her door after she got in. He waved as she drove off, and the brothers were a little impressed.

Chase approached the group. "You guys are so full of shit. You know damn well I don't date big girls."

His brothers laughed.

"She is beautiful, and she carries her weight well. You have to admit that," Damon said.

"You can handle her, can't you?" Lance joked.

"She can't possibly be too much woman for a Storm man." Damon and Travis joined him in laughter.

"You know what? Fuck all of y'all. In six months, after I have romanced her and gotten to know her, I'm going to let her down easy with the 'It's not you, it's me' line; then I want my money. *All* of it."

Damon chuckled. "You'll get your money, but you'd better play by the rules. You have to date her, Chase. Meaning introduce her to Momma and Daddy, bring her to get-togethers. Actually *date* her, or else all bets are off."

"I bet you once you get a chance to be between them warm thighs of hers, your take on plus-sized women will change," Lance teased.

"You know it," Travis agreed. He, Lance, and Damon high-fived.

"Whatever," Chase barked. "I'm going home."

"Alone, right? If we catch you smashing and dipping, no deal," Damon reminded him.

"Yes, alone. I know the fucking rules," Chase yelled over his shoulder.

Chase headed home, cussing and fussing at himself. He hated that he had made a deal such as he did with his brothers because he couldn't go back on his word. It wasn't about the money so much, because he had plenty of money; he just wanted to be an honorable man about his decision to accept the bet. They already didn't have any respect for him or see him as a responsible man, so if he caved, they would never in a million years let him live it down. And the chance of them ever respecting him would be slim to none.

His phone vibrated, and he saw Tracy's name on the screen. She was one of his regulars and could suck a nut out of him within minutes. With a sigh, he reached over, and for the first time, hit ignore. He'd never ignored a call from Tracy, and he thought he was crazy for ignoring it now. Hell, how would his brothers know, he thought, but then he decided to stick to the agreement; at least he could try. To give in just that easy would prove them right, and he didn't want to go out that easy.

Shaking his head, he said, "Y'all got me this time for real, but I got something for y'all too. Y'all think I'm going to cave, but six months is a breeze. Especially if I hit it."

Hell, I've never been with a big girl, he thought. *Wait, take that back. Maybe my freshman year of college, and it was good. And Rhonda wasn't all that big. She wasn't thin, but was she even considered a big girl? Or maybe I was just drunk and thought it was good. Hell, what does that matter now?* he pondered.

He pulled into his three-car garage, went in through the kitchen entrance, and tossed his cell phone and keys onto the counter. He went for a beer but decided he needed a shot instead, so he reached for the Cîroc and a shot glass.

Just as he downed his second shot, his phone vibrated. This time, it was Jessica, another one of his late-night specials. He wanted to answer, but knowing the Storm men, they had probably wired his house for sound. He hit ignore and wondered how long he would last. He wanted his dick sucked or to be in some pussy, not sitting around nursing a bottle of vodka.

He had to romance this BBW quick, so at least he could have someone to keep up his regular favors. His phone buzzed again. It was Ashley, and his dick throbbed. Ashley could do tongue tricks and was the most flexible woman he's ever had the pleasure of pleasing. He was used to answering his phone for his regulars, and it felt odd not to have one or two of them at one of his family's model homes, on their knees, fighting to please his dick.

"Damn!" he said out loud. "Why did I shake hands on this bullshit?"

He snatched up his phone from the counter and scrolled to Lance's number. He would call him and tell him no deal. But he stared at his phone for a moment and then put it down. *I can do this,* he thought. *I just have to refocus my focus. Focus on the money. Yeah, just think, in six months, you'll have an additional three million to spoil the ladies with.*

He grabbed the glass and the Cîroc bottle, went into his family room, and flopped down on the soft leather sectional. After pouring another shot, he reached for the remote. He turned on his new curved flat screen TV and admired the perfect picture for a moment before changing to the auxiliary mode and hitting his Roku remote to go to Pandora. The sounds of "Bed" by J. Holiday came flooding through his wireless speakers. He threw back his shot and bobbed his head, thinking about how badly he wanted to put a couple of his fans to bed that night.

His dick ached with need, so he grabbed his stiffness, deciding he'd take off his tux, shower, and drink himself into a deep sleep. Cîroc would be his wet pussy for the night.

He thought about the bet again. For his brothers to come up with something like that, to give up a million bucks each, meant he had to be worse than he thought he was.

"Am I that bad?" he questioned himself out loud. "Nah, I can't be." He paused. "Well, I guess at least they think I am." He threw back another shot before heading to his bedroom. He showered and moisturized his skin, something he did after every shower, and then threw on a pair of long basketball shorts and a tank. He went back to the family room and heard "Chocolate Legs," by Eric Benét, playing. The words penetrated his ears and put his mind right back on what he was missing, a set of long, sexy legs around his waist. He grabbed the remote and changed to the Rick Ross station. He didn't need to hear another song referring to sex.

He bobbed his head, took back-to-back shots, and woke up the next morning on the sofa with a hangover from hell. "Damn!" he said when he focused on the nearly empty bottle of Cîroc. He'd never drunk that many shots alone in his life. This was going to be the longest six months of his life. He grimaced and rushed over to the kitchen trash can. He didn't think he would have made it to the bathroom without spewing the previous night's appetizers and dinner onto the floor.

"Tomorrow," he said and slid down to the floor. "I'll woo her tomorrow."

Chapter Seven

"Thank you, Marcus," Madison said. He had presented his new design plans a few weeks earlier, but she had suggestions and different ideas, so he had gone back to the drawing board to tweak them. Now, they were perfect, exactly what she wanted. "These look great. I'm ready to get started right away, so let's talk cost."

"I have the estimates right here." He pulled out a file. "Now, this could be more or less, depending on the materials you choose along the way. Since we're expanding, we're going to have to stain the entire salon so that the new wood floors will match the existing floors. Different finishes—like knobs for your stations and cabinets—the tile you choose for the bathrooms, the brand of the dryers, fixtures, all that will affect this cost. I did my estimate based on middle-grade materials, but you can pull back on cost where you are comfortable and go up on cost where you want to splurge. This is only standard."

She gave the numbers a quick once-over and agreed that it seemed pretty standard. She had been expecting it to be a little higher, so she was comfortable with Marcus's rate. She just had to run the numbers by her mom. "Thanks, Marcus, this looks good. I have to run this by my parents, but I'd like to know when we can get started."

"Well, you give me a date, we get our guys, and then we start. Normally, we do 30 percent down, but Deena said you're good for 10. So, you tell me when you want us here."

"I thank Deena, but I plan to put 50 percent down and pay the other 50 when the project is complete. I won't be financing this renovation. My mom has wanted to upgrade and expand for years, and now that I'm here, I can run the business. She has the money, so I'll have your check to start with and another check when everything is completed."

"Sounds good to me."

"Marcus, what are you doing here?" The voice came from behind them. They turned to find Chase standing near the door holding a bouquet of flowers.

"Working," Marcus answered him. "What's up, cuz? You shouldn't have," he joked.

Chase smiled. "You wish. These are *not* for you, man; they're for Madison."

Madison had been biting her bottom lip and wondering why Chase was standing in her salon looking so damn delicious and bringing flowers for her. "Me?" she asked. "And I deserve those why?"

He approached the desk where she and Marcus were standing and handed them over to her. She immediately put them under her nose and took a whiff. "Because you left an impression on me the other night, and I wanted to offer you these in exchange for dinner."

Madison felt her face getting hot. Chase Storm was one of the finest men in East Texas. How in the hell was he interested in her? It made no sense. Yes, they had met at his parents' anniversary party. They had chatted about hot topics. *No*, she thought, *it had been more of a debate*. Every point she had made, he'd argued it. He had gotten her a couple of drinks and was gentleman enough to walk her to her car. They hadn't even exchanged numbers, and he seemed friendly, not interested.

"Dinner?" she questioned as if she hadn't comprehended what he said.

Chase smiled and removed his sunglasses. "Yes, dinner. I mean, if you don't have any other plans for dinner tonight."

Marcus cleared his throat. "Listen, Madison, I'm going to make my exit. Please let your family see those figures and give me a call when you're ready to get started."

Intent on smelling the flowers, she barely looked in his direction. "I will," she mustered up.

"So, is that a yes?" Chase asked after his cousin was on the other side of the salon door. "I mean, you *are* sucking all the scent out of those flowers, so I think you owe me dinner."

She looked at him, trying to discern whether he was serious. "You want to take me to dinner? Who put you up to this? Deena? I told that girl that I didn't want to be set up."

"No, she didn't. If Deena had her way, I'd stay as far away from you as I could."

"Why? Are you trouble, Mr. Storm?"

"Some would say I am, but I'm on a mission to change. I have a history and a reputation with the ladies. But I'm not getting any younger, so now, I'm looking for quality, not quantity."

"So, why me, Chase Storm? There are tons of gorgeous women in this town that you could be buying flowers for, so it's baffling that you chose me."

"I wanted to buy flowers for the woman standing in front of me. I have dated almost every woman in this town and could very well get any one of them, but you, Madison, are different from the rest, so that is why I'm asking you. I have to head back to my office to wrap up some things." He moved closer and handed her a card.

She could smell the sexy scent of his cologne. He was picture-perfect in his tailored suit. When he slid his sunglasses back on his face, Madison's pussy gushed.

"My cell number is on there. Call me and give me an answer to my dinner request." Chase walked away and then turned back. "Oh, I almost forgot. I'll take these." He took the flowers back.

"*Excuse* me? Did you *really* just take the flowers back?" Madison looked astounded.

"I did. The flowers are yours *in exchange for dinner*. No dinner, no flowers." He hit her with his sexy smile and then turned and walked toward the door to leave.

"Yes!" Madison blurted, surprising herself.

Chase stopped in his tracks and turned back to her. "Did I get a yes? You'll have dinner with me?" he asked.

"Yes, I'll have dinner with you, Chase, I'd love to," she blushed.

He walked back and handed her the flowers. "Well, the flowers are yours, then. I'll be at your place at seven thirty."

"Do you need the address?"

"No, I know exactly where it is," he said and walked out.

Madison grabbed hold of the counter to keep from falling. "Oh shit, oh shit. I have nothing to wear."

She hurried to get her purse and keys. It was a Monday, and the salon was closed, so she'd have to beg her mother to come there and do something with her hair. But first, she had to find the perfect outfit.

"You're going to dinner with that playboy?" Martha asked after Madison announced who had miraculously asked her out. Nothing like Madison, she had a life, and she knew the 411 in her town.

"Why does everyone keep saying that? I don't know if he's a playboy or not, Mother. All I know is we met, he seemed nice, and then today, he shows up with flowers and asks me out. I need you to make me pretty, and, please, no sermons. Just fix my hair and my makeup."

"Again, my daughter is setting herself up for failure. But I'll let you learn the hard way—as I always have."

"Mother, what does that mean? I'm *only* having dinner with him."

"Tony. Does that name ring a bell? I know that little cheater has been creeping around your place. You are so into not caring and not socializing that you don't know what folks are saying. People see when his vehicle is in your drive, missy, and you better hope that mess don't get back to Austin, and she comes here and put an ass whoppin' on you both."

"Well, Mother, folks should learn to mind their own business. And you're right. I can't lie to you, no matter how badly I want to. I was involved with Tony, but I told him that I was tired of being his sidepiece. It's been over a week since I've seen him, Ma. I promise I'm done with that."

"I hope so, chile, because you know that I don't condone that cheating mess, and I'm shocked that you carried on like that with Anthony, knowing he has a wife and two boys."

"Momma, I was wrong, I've repented, and I'll never do that ever again; you have my word. That was foul, and I'm over it."

"You better be, and now this baby Storm. I won't lie, I'm concerned about this Storm. Chase has a reputation. And he has been with every young lady in town, and I'm sure Longview too."

"I know, but he approached me; I didn't approach him. And today, when he brought the flowers, I felt like he was genuinely interested, Ma. If he's such a ladies' man, why would he ask me, of all people, out?"

"For the life of me, chile, I can't answer that. But I'm going to make him glad he asked. I think you need to spice it up a bit. Chase is edgy and dapper, I must add.

He is always looking his best, even if I've come across him in sweatpants at the market. So, you're going to have to glam it up, gal, and all this hair is for girls. Let's turn you into a woman."

"Ma, please. I don't want to cut my hair."

"I know you don't, but I highly recommend it. The look you have is boring, baby. I'm a seasoned stylist, and I'm not sayin' nothing to ya that I wouldn't say to a paying client. It's time to glam it up."

Madison agreed with her mother, but her hair had been long all her life. The thought of going short made her tremble. But maybe it *was* time for a change.

After a long pause, she said, "Okay, Ma, do it!" Martha turned her away from the mirror and got to work. After the cut, facial, and makeup were applied, Madison didn't recognize herself. "Oh, Mother, I look . . . I look . . ."

"Damn good. Fabulous. Gorgeous, if you ask me."

Madison smiled at her reflection. "I do." She looked at her watch. "Thank you so much, Ma, but I have to go. I have just enough time to go home, take a bath, and dress."

Chapter Eight

Chase dressed slowly, wondering if he dared to even show up. Not that he was afraid for him. He was afraid for Madison because he knew his intentions were not sincere. He was only out to prove a point and earn some cold hard cash in the process, not fall in love like they wanted him to. He hoped he'd be able to maintain and not lose by dipping off in one of his sidepieces. Six months was a long time to go without sex. His johnson hadn't gone without it for six *days* since he was 19.

"Okay, showtime," he said to his reflection in the mirror. "She's just a woman. Plump, a little more to love, but pretty, so I will be okay," he told himself. He grabbed his wallet and keys and headed for the door.

Walking to his car, he thought about how she had smiled at him earlier that afternoon when he gave the flowers back to her and the way her eyes danced when he looked at her. He'd go for pretty and plump over fit and gruesome. He had seen some slim women that he wouldn't date or kiss, let alone touch, even if his brothers were offering ten million apiece.

He pulled up to Madison's house and admired the newly added touches she had given to the already-beautiful landscaping. She had added a swing to the left side of the massive porch and a couple of wicker chairs with matching footrests and a little round table in between on the opposite end of the swing. The ledges had been laced with beautiful flowers in colorful pots, and more hung from hooks at evenly spaced intervals.

He remembered the door being yellow before it sold, but now it was bright red that looked better. Flowers in hand, he rang her bell.

"Coming," he heard her yell.

The door swung open, and his eyes widened. Madison looked more mature, classy. . . . No, sassy was a better word, he thought. Stunning was his final answer.

"Madison . . . Hi," he said. She looked beautiful.

Her dress was solid black at the top with wide band straps. The bottom was satin zebra print.

A red leather belt sat high on her waist, right beneath her breasts giving her a waistline that he didn't know she owned. He recognized her red shoes with red soles as being expensive, and she carried a matching little red clutch. Her diamond jewelry sparkled almost as brightly as her smile. She looked striking.

"Hello. Come on in. I just have to turn off a couple of lights, and I'll be ready."

"Take your time," he said, mesmerized. Then he remembered the flowers. "Oh, these are for you."

Madison took them and smelled them. "More flowers. These are just as beautiful as the ones you gave me earlier."

"I heard that women love flowers."

"You heard right. Come on in. I'd like to put them in water before we leave if you don't mind."

"No, of course not."

"Can you get that for me?" she said, motioning toward the door.

"Sure," he said. He shut the door and followed her into the kitchen. Well-endowed she was, but she was curvaceous, and his brothers were right, she carried herself well. He checked out her sway as she walked and got a look at her calves. They were those big, sexy legs that his father always bragged that his mother had. Out of his grandfather, father, uncles, and brothers, he was the only one who had never thought about hooking up with a big woman. But he had finally laid eyes on one that he thought might make him reconsider.

"You can have a seat if you like. This won't take long," she offered.

"I'm good." He looked out of the huge bay window facing the lake. "You got the home of my dreams," he smiled.

"Did I?"

"Yes. I love my house. It's gorgeous. And when we bought this land to build on, I always said whoever would get this lot overlooking the lake would be one happy homeowner. I mean, two other properties share this view, but you're smack dead in the middle, so your view is nicer."

"I got a good deal too. Deena and I have been friends since the ninth grade. Your family gave me a remarkable price."

"That's good to hear. I've heard your name before, but never had the pleasure of meeting you."

"You have met me before, Chase."

He frowned. "No, I don't think so."

"You've met me on a couple of occasions. Deena has said, 'Chase, you remember Madison, don't you?' and you'd say 'Yes' with a fake smile and move around. The other night, when we were reintroduced for maybe the fourth time, I decided not to mention that we've met before."

"Wow, I'm a jerk." He felt horrible.

"No, I wouldn't say that. I just hadn't caught your eye back then."

"Hmm . . . Maybe you're right."

"Maybe so. Are you ready?"

"Yes, let's go."

They walked to Chase's car, and for the first time, he found himself opening the car door for a woman.

"Thank you," she said, smiling. Chase shut the door and walked around to the driver's side, wondering what the hell had gotten into him. "Get it together, Chase," he told himself.

Tyler wasn't a large city like Austin, Dallas, or Houston, so he took her to the best place he knew in their town, Dakotas Steak & Chop House.

After they were seated and their drink orders were in, Chase gazed at her, trying to figure out why he thought she was more attractive than he had thought earlier that day and even the night he met her. Then it hit him. Her hair. She was now sporting a sexy, tapered cut, not the updo from the party or the homemade ponytail she had earlier.

"You cut your hair," he said, his tone in a higher pitch than he meant to say. It had finally dawned on him what was different about her and made her superattractive to him.

"Yes, I did. Did you just figure that out?"

"To be honest, yes. I mean, I was asking myself, what is it about her that is different? Why does she so look stunning tonight? I mean, you are a very beautiful woman, Madison, but this is the perfect look for you. It really brings out your beautiful features. I hadn't even noticed how light your eyes were before, and with the makeup, you look radiant."

"Come on, Chase, you don't have to lay it on so thick."

"I'm not; I'm being genuine. You look gorgeous, girl. That haircut is *definitely* you."

She blushed. "Thank you. I wanted to compliment you as well. You look really handsome tonight. When I opened the door and laid eyes on you, I thought I had to be dreaming. I mean, don't get me wrong, you're not the first good-looking man I've ever been out with, but I pulled them eighty pounds ago." She looked away. "Let's just say I'm a little apprehensive about your intentions with me."

"Why so?"

"Because, as I said, we've met before, and it was like I was invisible to you."

"Well, as *I* said earlier, I'm in the process of making some changes in my life. I'm not getting any younger, and I'm sorta looking for mother material, someone who has a head on their shoulders and is interested in me beyond my reputation, family name, bank account, and clout. If we date, you know, if you like me enough to allow me to stick around for a while, you may hear some things that are not pleasant about me, Madison. I just ask that you trust me when I say that is *not* who I want to be anymore. I turned in my player card, as they say."

"So, you want to transition from your playa-playa days with me?"

"If that's an option."

"With that said, I don't know, you know. What if you relapse?"

"What if I don't?"

"What if I fall for you?"

"What if I fall for you?" he countered. He knew there was little chance of that, but she intrigued him, and her conversation alone was enough to keep him interested. The night of the anniversary party, they talked for what seemed like hours as they debated everything from music to black men dating white women to politics to celeb gossip.

She was a challenge, and he enjoyed talking to someone who had an education and valid arguments, someone who didn't just agree with everything he said. Women before her were educated, maybe, but he had never wanted to get to know them for their brains. Women before her never got a dinner invite; they always had to eat whatever takeout he ordered. He'd occasionally do breakfast, but that was the furthest he'd go.

Over a good meal and exquisite wine, Chase and Madison shared endless conversation. Then just before dessert, a familiar face caught Chase's eye, and he prayed she'd respect he was sitting with someone and not approach.

But that didn't happen.

"Good evening, Chase." She released the words as sultry as she could make them sound.

He knew her, and this was why he never took his dates out on the town because he didn't like or want any drama. "Good evening, Hope," he said. She was the last person he wanted to see. They had been a hot item in high school but had split up before going off to college. She and he had hooked back up years later, and they hooked up on a regular for a long while . . . until she started shouting marriage, commitment, and settling down with her in his ears. He had told her that now wasn't the time for him, and he was far from ready for all of that, but if and when he was ready to settle down, she'd be his choice. A big fat lie, and he knew that bullshit was when he said it. That blatant lie was bigger than the state of Texas because although she was one of the most beautiful women in Tyler, she never made his dick throb or ache. He never longed for her, nor did he miss her when they were apart. Sex with her was good but routine. She didn't excite Chase, so that was not the one he'd choose to spend the rest of his life with.

"I hope I'm not interrupting," she said in her East Texas drawl. "I know you're all business, baby."

His brow arched. *Baby?* What the hell was Hope doing? he wondered. He had to make things clear and get her the hell away from their table. "I am, but this is not a business dinner."

"Oh, I'm sorry. Is this a relative?" she said, turning to Madison. "Forgive me; I'm Hope Gardner. How long will you be visiting?"

That time, Madison raised her brow. "Hi, Hope, I'm Madison Atkins-Morgan. It's strange how you suddenly don't remember me. Our mothers were friends since we were little girls, and we were considered best friends once. I'd never forgotten who you are. Or your family. Everyone in Tyler knows who your father is. He's the Car King of Tyler, right? A *hands-on* type of man, I've heard." Hope shifted her weight and readjusted her designer bag in the crook of her arm. "Chase and I are not related, but I'm sure you already knew this." Madison smiled at her.

They both watched as Hope tried to save face. "Oh my goodness, Madison, I hardly recognized you. I mean, the last time I saw you, you were . . ." She paused and used her tiny hands to indicate the shape of a smaller frame.

"Thin?" Madison shot at her.

"Yes, darling, that is correct. I didn't recognize you, sugar. I mean, with all those extra pounds, you look like a totally different person," Hope replied smartly. "But I do apologize for my intrusion. I'll let you two get back to your dinner."

With a smile, Madison said. "Yeah, you do that."

"You two enjoy your night, and, Chase, I'll talk to you later." Hope winked at him and then finally moved on, and Chase and Madison both laughed.

"I'm Hope Gardner," Madison mimicked, turning her nose up in the air and pretending to swing her hair over her shoulder.

"How long will you be visiting?" Chase chimed in. The two of them had a good laugh.

After multiple jokes about the great Hope, Chase looked closer at Madison. She was amazingly striking and funny as hell, and her laugh was melodious to his

ears. He was having a great time, a really great time. He
didn't even think that he just may dig her. He had never
laughed so hard with a woman or enjoyed a woman's
company as he enjoyed hers, and he was wondering why
he'd never considered that he could like her. He'd never
taken the time to get to know someone, and what he was
learning about Madison made her appealing to him. He
was starting to feel more than a mental attraction for this
vivacious woman. He wanted to kiss her. *Shit!* he thought.

"So, is she one of your old flings?"

"Yes. And there are tons right here in this town, so
brace yourself. I'm not going to lie to you, Madison.
Before you, I've been in the company of a whole lot of
women. But I've never shared a moment like this with
any of them. I'm having so much fun with you, and I'd
like to see you again. I mean, if that's okay." He shocked
himself with that question. They hadn't had any physical contact, and yet, he wanted to see her again. Maybe
his brothers were right. Maybe if he had tried to get to
know some of the others, maybe he would have been
open to a real relationship, but he hadn't given any of
them a chance. He had hit every one of them with the
same line up front, "I'm only looking for a good time."
If he was with one that talked too much, he'd never give
her another opportunity to be with him. If she asked too
many questions, he'd delete her number from his phone.
He liked his women sexy, freaky, and mute, but now he
didn't want Madison to be quiet. He wanted to know
every detail about her.

Madison smiled. "I'd like that too."

"So, are you ready for dessert?"

"Can you ask them to package it to go? I'm really stuffed
from dinner."

"What? You barely finished your food."

"Yeah, thank God you brought your appetite and finished
it for me."

"Well, I just assumed you would devour your meal." Immediately after he said those words, he realized how it sounded when it came out. He didn't mean it that way. He was only saying how good the food was, not that he thought she was a pig. "Wait, I didn't—I . . . mean for it to sound like—"

She tilted her head to the left and narrowed her eyes at him. "Why? Because I don't look like Hope? Because I'm a big girl, you thought I'd *lick* my plate?" she said with much attitude.

He knew that things had just turned bad. "No no no, babe, wait. That came out wrong. I didn't mean it to be insulting. I just meant that the food here is so delicious that I thought you'd clean your plate. That is all I meant, Madison."

This time, her laugh was sarcastic. It was clear she didn't believe him. "I have to visit the ladies' room. No, I don't want dessert. I would like it very much if you would take me home now, Chase Storm."

Chase stood. "Madison, please. Wait a minute, let me explain, please." He watched as she strutted to the bathroom without looking back.

Chapter Nine

Wow, the nerve of him. She paced the bathroom floor. The evening had been so perfect until he said that bullshit. She had felt so beautiful before he had said those words. Hell, that's an understatement—she had felt sexy, something she hadn't felt in the last couple of years. But after the brief visit with Hope and his comment, she felt differently. Did he think big girls were a safe choice because no one else wanted them? Did he think he'd have a good woman in her because no one would take a second look at her? Her thoughts raced through her mind as she paced. She didn't want to go back out to face him, but she didn't want to call anyone to get her. She'd be too embarrassed to say what truly happened on her first date with Chase.

She got a glimpse of herself in the mirror and then paused. She smiled at her reflection. She looked better than she had in years, and she felt good, so why was she hiding in the bathroom worrying about what his ass thought of her? She wasn't going to let Chase make her feel insecure just when she was finding her way back to being confident. Not a hair was out of place. She needed to touch up her lips, but her makeup was still flawless. She reapplied her lipstick, straightened her belt, and went back to the table.

Chase saw her approaching and stood, looking like a sad puppy, but she didn't give a damn. He was rude, and he wasn't going to choose her because he thought she was easy.

"Madison, I'm really sorry. I promise you that I didn't mean anything by that. I wasn't trying to be insulting. That came out completely wrong."

"It's okay, Chase. I'm good. Are you ready?" She hoped her tone would cut him like a knife. She didn't allow him to answer before she turned and headed for the door. Chase was the one lucky to be out with her, *not* the other way around, she told herself.

He opened the car door for her, and she got in. When he got in, it felt strange. The mood had changed. On their way to dinner, they had talked nonstop, but now they rode in awkward silence. When they pulled up to her house, he hurried around to open her door.

"I'm fine from here."

"Come on, Madison, you know we don't do it like that in Texas. I can walk you to your door," he insisted.

"Fine," she said and walked ahead of him.

"Can I see you again?"

She froze. Why in the hell would he want to see her again? "Why? To make fun of me again?"

"Madison, I'm sorry. I know you are a plus-sized woman, and I also know that doesn't mean you eat up everything in sight. I'm so sorry for how I said what I said. I wasn't trying to be rude. It came out all wrong; please believe me. I was only suggesting that the food was so good I'd thought you'd clean your plate. I'm a lot of things, Madison, but not insensitive. And I'd never say something so mean to a woman that I'm digging."

He paused for a moment, but the look in his eyes was sincere. She believed him. She walked over to the swing and sat. He came over and sat with her. "I'm not picture-perfect, Chase. I know I could stand to lose some weight. I went through this deep depression when I lost my family." Her eyes glossed. "And now that I'm reclaiming my life, this is the body that I'm in. I don't need someone tearing me down when I'm building myself back up. It's hard enough to accept my new self for who I am, and I don't need a man to make me feel bad for how I look. If you're here because you want to prove you're not a shallow asshole who preys on women to boost your self-esteem, you're at the wrong address." She took a deep breath. "I'm sure Hope Gardner can stroke that ego of yours and do double duty as arm charm. I'm not desperate, and you are not the last man on earth, Chase Storm. I'm beautiful inside and out, and if you think I'm the safe chick to finally settle down with because no other man would want me, you're sadly mistaken."

"You're absolutely right, Madison. I know you're not a perfect size six, and I don't think you are the safe one that I'd never lose. I think you are gorgeous, and you have captured my attention with your pleasant person-ality, your melodious laugh, and you are so interesting. Tonight was the best night of my life. I've never had this much fun with a woman." He smiled at her. "I don't have any ill intentions, Madison, I promise, and I hope that you will go out with me again."

She couldn't help herself; she smiled back. "I'd like that. I mean, beneath all those layers of handsome, you do make me laugh. I enjoyed being with you tonight just as much."

He let out a breath he didn't know he had been holding and realized he was relieved at her answer. "So, we are good?"

"We are. Just watch what you say. I'm a plus-sized sister, but not desperate, Chase Storm. What you see is what you get, and if you don't like it, you have a choice."

He tilted his head and frowned. "And what choice is that?"

She cleared her throat and stood. "You can say good night and never show up again. I won't be mad, nor will I hold any ill feelings toward you."

Chase stood and moved closer to her. His lips were inches from hers. Her nipples hardened, and her center awakened.

"I don't want that option," he breathed into her mouth.

She swallowed hard, and she was sure he heard it. "What option do you want, Mr. Storm?"

"To see you tomorrow and to spend more time with you. I want to get to know you better, Madison, if that's okay with you."

"Okay," she breathed. She was beginning to sweat. She wanted him to kiss her. She wanted to taste his tongue.

"I have to work, but I can clear out as early as you'd like."

"I meet with Marcus tomorrow morning. After, I'll be free for lunch."

"Okay." Then he gave her what she wanted. He grabbed the back of her tapered head and pushed his tongue into her mouth. Their tongues danced like they were familiar with each other, as if they had kissed before. Before she could stop herself, her arms were around his neck, and his body pressed into hers. She moaned as he sucked her tongue and then her bottom lip. Her panties were getting wetter by the second.

"Chase," she whispered between kisses, "you should go, baby." He backed up, and she could see the bulge in his pants.

"Yes, I agree. Tomorrow, baby," he said, pulling her back against him.

He kissed her again, and she made herself stop him because she knew she'd asked him to come inside . . . inside of her silky center.

"Baby . . ." She backed away and smiled. "Tomorrow."

"Okay, beautiful," he said and headed for the steps.

She moved to her front door, watching Chase and smiling. He stopped and turned to look at her. "Why are you standing there?" she yelled.

"Waiting for you to get safely inside."

She laughed. "Drive safely and call me as soon as you're home."

He flashed his gorgeous smile. "I will." He paused. "Wait, I don't have your number."

She laughed. "I didn't think of that."

He headed back to the porch and handed her his phone. "Key it in," he said.

She swiped the screen. "You don't lock your phone?"

"No, I don't have a reason to."

She raised a brow. "Well, I don't either, but if you lose your phone, you give people access to your information," she said as she keyed in her digits.

"I never thought about losing my phone, but since you mentioned it, I guess I'll lock it," he said as she handed it back to him. He leaned in and touched her lips with his again, and she allowed herself to get lost in his kiss. The ringing of his phone jolted them out of their sensual fog. They both looked at the screen and saw Hope's name.

Chase hit ignore. "That's nothing," he smiled.

She returned his smile. "I know," she said, not worried about the other woman.

"So, I'll call you when I make it in."

"Yes, I'll be waiting."

He backed away, not taking his eyes off of her. When he reached his car door, he stopped, and she knew he was waiting for her to get on the other side of the door.

"Good night, Chase." She opened her door.

"Good night, Madison."

She shut the door and fell back against it. Chase Storm had her heart pounding. He was so easy to talk to, so chill, so laid-back, so damn delicious, and she enjoyed looking at him. She climbed the stairs singing, wondering where their relationship would go.

She finally climbed into bed when she finished talking to Chase after midnight. She picked up her late husband's picture from her nightstand.

"He's nice," she said. "I miss you, you know I do, but I need someone. I hope you understand. I'll never stop loving you. I just want a chance to have a family again. Losing you and the boys was the hardest thing, but I think I'm ready to love again." She smiled and kissed the picture. "Don't worry; I will never forget you guys. I promise." She put the photo down and got under the covers.

"God let him be sincere. I don't want to hurt anymore." Those were her last words before drifting off to sleep with Chase on her mind.

Chapter Ten

Chase hung up the phone wondering what in the hell had come over him. Aside from the fact that Madison was a plus-sized woman, he had never before been that attracted to one woman in his life. He had never taken the time to converse with a woman enough to even get to know her to like her. He'd meet a woman, lay out what he wanted, and she'd be willing to provide anything he requested. He had begun to believe some weren't too bright to allow such foolishness from him. Yes, he was loaded, good looking, and a beast under the sheets, but so many had allowed him to treat them like whores instead of women, and that moment Chase felt ashamed for how he had treated them. "Man, you must get yo' shit together. Madison is too good for that."

Madison Madison Madison, he thought. "What are you doing to me, woman?" he asked, readjusting his shaft in his pants. He was turned on, but he didn't just want to fuck her. He wanted to make love to her. He wanted to feel her, tease her, please her, and then hold her afterward. She'd get breakfast, lunch, *and* dinner.

He shook his head. "No no no!" he said out loud. "I'm not going there. Chase, when you marry a woman, when you fall in love, she is going to be Beyoncé-fine. No one is going to envy you with a big girl on your arm." He ordered himself not to like her.

He had followed that order until the next day when she opened the door for him. They were to have a picnic lunch by the lake. He had brought the wine, and she prepared the food.

Again, she was radiant. Her hair had a wet look, with her natural curls popping, and her makeup was again flawless. She had on a peach ankle-length summer dress that hung loosely around her curves and some sparkling flip-flops, with bright red toenail polish. He had a boomerang flashback and noted she didn't have corns on her toes, and he laughed inside.

"Wow, you look amazing," he said before he could stop himself.

She smiled. "Thank you. Come on into the kitchen. I'm almost done packing the basket. I hope you like tuna." She made a funny face, scrunching her nose.

"I do," he said and leaned in and gave her a light kiss on the cheek.

"Good, I made tuna melts. Got some fruit, and my mom provided the peach cobbler."

"Sounds good," he said. A few minutes later, they were all set to go out and enjoy lunch by the lake. "Let me carry that," he offered, taking the picnic basket. As they headed for the lake, Chase kept falling a step behind her to watch her walk. She was full and perfect.

Once they chose a spot, she laid out the blanket, and they both removed their shoes. She opened the basket and began to unload their lunch.

"Oh shit, I forgot to get the wine opener."

"I can go for it," Chase offered.

"Do you mind? It's on the kitchen island."

"No, I don't mind." He stood and hurried back to her house and went to the kitchen. He paused to look around and noticed a lot of photos of a man and two identical twin boys. *Her late family,* he thought.

He headed back and found Madison resting on her elbows under the shade tree. "Wine opener," he said and handed it to her.

"Thanks, but the flies out here are crazy. This may not have been a good idea."

"Afraid of flies?" Chase teased.

"No, not at all, but I don't want to keep fanning them away from the food."

"How about we take this inside and have a picnic on the living room floor."

"You know what? That *is* an awesome idea."

They repacked everything and trekked back to the house. It was much cooler in the air-conditioning, and they both felt better. They moved the coffee table and laid the blanket out on the area rug. Madison grabbed a couple of throw pillows from the sofa. Chase opened the wine and poured them both a glass.

"So, what made you want to turn in your player's card?" she asked, taking him by surprise.

"That's a good question, and I'll be honest," he said, hating that he was going to tell a lie. "My family kept dogging me about the company I kept, and I got tired of defending my singlehood. I just thought maybe if I did try this exclusive thing, I might get to know the right woman. When Damon introduced us for what, the third or fourth time," he chuckled, "I decided to get to know you. We talked, and you were interesting. Why you? I don't know," he lied and sipped his wine. "But I'm glad it is."

"Me too."

They ate and chatted, and then Chase helped her clean up. He helped her in the kitchen and noticed she had a piano in the corner of the formal living room.

"That's a baby grand. You play?"

"Yep. My mother had dreams of me being Alicia Keys or Chrisette Michele," she giggled. "I mean, I love music, but I'm not a limelight kinda girl."

"So you sing?" Another amazing surprise with Madison. He was starting to think this was a setup, and his broth-

ers were playing an evil trick on him for how he dogged
so many.

"Yes, and if you weren't in private schools, you'd have
seen me in all the talent shows and so forth years ago."

"What? Come on; you have to play something for me."

She dried her hands and looked at him. "Nah, I haven't
played in a long while."

"Come on, Madison, I want to see what you got."

She took off her apron, and he followed her to the
piano. She sat, and he stood near the piano. "Now, I
haven't messed with this thing in a long time," she said.
"I used to always play for my husband and sing to my boys
all the time," she said sadly. "Maybe I shouldn't," she said
getting up, shaking her head.

"No, Madison, please. I want to hear you sing. I wanna
see yo' skills, woman," he said playfully. He didn't want
her to get all sad. He knew she had lost her family, and he
wasn't trying to stir up sad memories.

She slowly returned to the bench. "It's been so long,"
she said and wiped the corners of her eyes.

"I'm sure it's like riding a bike," Chase encouraged.

She forced a laugh, dabbed her eyes again to dry them,
and messed around with the keys, then began to play
"How Come You Don't Call Me Anymore" by Prince. She
knew that one by heart. It had been one of her favorites.
"*I keep your picture beside my bed,*" she sang. "*And I still
remember everything you said. What I wanna know,
baby, if what we had was good, how come you don't call
me anymore?*" Chase applauded. She was good. He had
no idea she had that kind of talent.

"I can see why your mother wanted you to become a
singer, baby; you sound good. You can sing, girl," he said
smiling brightly at her.

"Yeah, well, I didn't want to chase any singing dreams.
Only a handful are fortunate, so I was in touch with real
dreams."

"Like?" He joined her on the piano bench.

"Business. I always said I'd be this big CEO of a Fortune 500 company. What product, I had no idea, but I wanted to be this person young girls admired and looked up to. I worked for a major electric company in Houston with advancement opportunities bursting out of the seams, but then the accident happened, and my life, all of my dreams were just snatched away from me," she sighed.

Chase caressed her face. "We don't have to talk about it, Madison. I didn't mean to make you sad, babe."

"It's okay. I'm okay to talk about it. It helps to talk about it. I mean I should have talked about it more way back then, but I shut down, Chase. I moved back home with my parents, and I was a mess. I ate my way through the pain. It's like food became my source of comfort. I missed them so much." Her eyes welled. "Now, almost five years later, I'm stuck with a bunch of unwanted pounds, and my family is still gone." She let the tears fall.

"I'm so sorry about your family, Madison." He wrapped his arm around her shoulder and pulled her as close as he could to him.

"It's okay. I know that God has this master plan, but at the time, I was angry and so confused, and for the life of me, I couldn't understand why he'd give them to me, only to take them away."

"I don't know, babe. I am not a big religious guy, but I do believe that the big guy in the sky has it all under control, even when we think things are a mess. He has a way of restoring stuff."

"How would you know, Chase? You've never lost anything in your life," she said and wiped her eyes.

"You're right, certainly nothing as big as a spouse and kids, but I'm sure I'll go through losing something. I mean, Madison, I can't sit here and tell you I know what it feels like, because I truly don't, but I will tell you that

I will do my best to help lift you up when you're down. If ever you want to talk about your husband and your boys, I promise to listen, and I promise always to try to make you smile." He kissed the back of her hand.

"Thank you, Chase. I haven't talked about them much to anyone other than Deena and my momma. I'm okay. It doesn't get me down the way it used to. I'm a lot stronger now and in a better place. I have made peace with it."

He sat with her for a little while longer in silence and just held her hand. She finally stood. "I'm going for more wine. Do you want a glass?"

"Yes," he said.

While she was gone, he examined the photos on the mantle. He saw a picture that looked like Madison, but a smaller version. She had on a fitted dress, and her body was amazing. There were more photos of the same sexy-ass Madison look-alike.

She came back and handed him a glass. "So, is this your sister?" he asked.

"Sister?" she frowned. "I'm an only child."

"Who are these photos of?"

She sat back at the piano. "All the sexy, slim pictures are of me before I lost my husband and my boys. The body before you now is my postaccident body." She gulped some wine.

Feeling like he was offensive again, he sat next to her. "Well, I think the old Madison was gorgeous, and I think the post-Madison is just as gorgeous."

"You don't have to say that, Chase. I'm fully aware that I've changed."

"I'm sure there was only a physical change. Your bright smile is the same, and I can tell that the person inside is just as smart and beautiful as you were then."

She smiled. "I'm still me," she said and sipped.

Her smile melted his heart. He wanted Madison. He really wanted her. It was early, though, and he didn't want to come on too strong, so he said, "Sing another song for me."

She put her glass down and stroked the keys. He wondered what she would sing to him next. She continued to play a melody, and he recognized it. It was Alicia Keys, "A Woman's Worth."

He listened as Madison's voice filled the room. She was breaking him down. The player in him was subsiding. He wanted to pursue this woman on his very own resolve, and he couldn't wait to tell his brothers that the wager was off. Then he thought about it. Three million bucks. Nah, he'd stick to the original plan. There were no rules about him not falling in love. That's what they wanted him to do.

A little later, after their romantic and conversation-filled lunch date, he stood in her doorway to leave. "So, when can I see you again?" he asked after kissing her.

"Wow, a third date. I must be dreaming."

"We both are, so please don't wake me."

She laughed softly and wrapped her arms around his neck. "I don't know. I'll be busy with the shop's remodel soon. I know I'm not a contractor, but I want to be a part of the entire process."

"That's right; my family is going to redo your mom's place."

"Yes, and I'm so excited." Her eyes danced as she gave him a quick description of some of the changes that would be taking place.

"That sounds nice, Madison. You should be excited."

She grinned. "I am."

"Well, it's still early. How about dinner tonight?"

"Dinner? We just had a great lunch. I can't even think of food right now."

"You say that now, but around seven or eight, your
stomach may feel different."

"Okay, I'd like to have dinner with you, Chase Storm."

"That's great. Since you've welcomed me into your
lovely home, I'd like to invite you over to my place this
time."

"You cook?"

"Nope. Can't fry an egg."

Her eyes widened, and they both laughed. "Seriously,
I don't," he said. "I'm the baby of the family and never
learned, but I think I got this under control. Trust me."

"Okay, I trust you." She beamed. "Text me your address,
and I'm there. Say, seven thirty if that's a good time?"

"Perfect." He pulled her in closer and planted another
soft kiss on her lips before he left. The first place he
headed to was Deena's office.

"Get out, Chase," Deena said. "I told you what Travis
said. I can't let you use any of the model properties
anymore, so don't even ask."

"That's not what I came for."

She raised a brow and looked up from the paper she
was reading. "Come again?"

"That's right, sis, I'm here to ask you about Madison."

"What about Madison?" Now her eyes narrowed at
him. "Chase Storm, I forbid you to go anywhere near my
friend."

"Too late, I've already gone out with her," Chase boasted.

"You're lying. She would have called me."

He shrugged. "I don't know why she didn't tell you. But
what I do know is I really like her."

"Ha!" Deena laughed. "You are incapable of liking
anyone other than the whores you keep. I'm warning you,
Chase," she threatened.

He held up a hand. "Listen, I know what you're about
to say. Yes, I know you will 'roast me like a pig,' 'gut me

like a fish,' or my favorite, make me 'come up missing.'"
He leaned forward and looked his sister-in-law in the eye.
"Deena, I like her. She is . . . she . . ." He looked away from
her, gazing into space.

"You're serious? Are you *really* serious? Chase, never
in my life have I seen you gaze at nothing. And to openly
admit that you like someone is . . . It's-it's-it's," she
stuttered, unable to find the words.

"I know, it's new to me too. I need your help. Madison
is coming over for dinner tonight, and I want to know
what her favorite cuisine is."

"Gee, Chase, I don't know. I mean, we've never discussed that before, but I know she doesn't eat shellfish.
She's allergic. She loves butter pecan ice cream." She
paused. "Who's cooking this meal? Your ass can't cook."

"I know. I'm going to call Mom or Gina. I'm sure one of
them will hook me up."

"Why don't you hire someone? That would be so romantic, Chase."

He loved the idea. "That's a perfect idea, sis." He
hopped up, went around to her side of the desk, and
planted a wet one on her cheek.

"Go on, Chase. I've told you about putting your nasty
lips on me. I don't know where they've been."

"On your best friend," he teased.

"Oh my God. Get out of here so I can call her."

"Love you, sis, and thanks."

He headed out and got into his car. "Siri," he said, "find
a chef."

Chapter Eleven

"Hello?" Madison answered.

"You are *not* seeing my brother-in-law," Deena said.

"Hello and good afternoon to you, Deena."

"Greetings, happy afternoon, and all of that shit. Now, tell me about you and Chase Storm."

Madison laughed. "I was going to tell you, honey nut; I just hadn't had a chance."

"Sure, you were. Madison, do you know who you're dealing with? Chase is no altar boy. He's broken many, many, *many* hearts. And I've never seen him with women like us."

"Women like us?"

"Don't play with me, Madi. You know, big and beautiful. He's up to something no good; I know he is."

"Deena, he's been a gentleman. He says he wants to change and try something new and different. I mean, I've had a great time with him. And, oh my God, Deena, he can kiss. Had my lips swollen and craving for more after he left me this afternoon."

"Chase?" Deena asked in disbelief.

"Yes, Chase."

"Chase? Chase Storm, a gentleman? How does he look doing that? I've never seen him in gentleman form."

Madison laughed at her friend. "Well, I've never seen this playa you and my mom have described."

"Miss Martha warned you too?"

"Yes, the very first night. She told me he had a reputation. Listen, he told me everything, Deena. And I believe he wants to change. He says he's looking for wife material, and since all of his brothers, and father, I might add, married women that look like us, maybe that's the image or example he has in his head. I don't know his motives, but I believe he's sincere. I mean, he's so sweet, and we have endless conversations when we talk. I think I like him, Deena, like *really* like him."

"Wow, a miracle is happening. Chase Storm may be turning over a new leaf. Just please, Madison, watch him and be careful. Don't be a fool for nobody, not even Chase Storm. If he's full of shit, he won't be able to keep up this charade for long. I mean, I could tell you some stories about Chase, Madi. He's a bad boy," she warned.

"No, I don't want you to tarnish the image of the Chase I'm falling for, and I think I'm beautiful enough to have a man like Chase interested. I've gained a few pounds, yes, but I've never, ever, since I was old enough to date, been with a man that wasn't easy on the eyes. What really kinda had me suspicious at first was the fact that he didn't remember meeting me before, so back then, maybe he wasn't interested, but I think he's ready now."

"Okay, Madi, date Chase at your own risk. Don't ever say that I didn't warn you, though."

"I won't, and I appreciate you for looking out for me. If he starts to act up, you know I'll cut him loose."

Deena laughed. "I know that's real. I don't recall you ever being a fool for no man, ever."

"Nope, and I'm not going to start now. I'm okay with being by myself, so for now, I'm going to enjoy myself and see where it goes. If it goes nowhere, at least I'm having fun with him."

"True. The Storm men do know how to entertain, and they are romantic motherfuckers."

"I hope so. I need a little romance in my life. And some dick, I might add."

"Oh my God, the thought of you and Chase getting it in . . . I'd love to know if he is *really* as good as these women say he is, or if it's all talk."

"Well, when I do find out, you know you'll be the first to know."

"Oooooh, Madi. This is crazy. Chase, of all men."

"Yes, Chase. And I know there are rumors, but I don't know this Chase you and my mother speak of."

"Well. Good luck with that. I'll talk to you later."

"Okay, love, bye now." Madison hung up and went back to looking for something to wear. She needed to update her wardrobe. She grabbed her phone. Her mother had tons of clothes and was always in something sexy. Now that they were both the same size, she knew her mom would help her out until she could find time to shop.

"Hello," Martha sang. Madison sometimes envied the confidence and sexiness in her mother's voice and sway of her hips. Martha Atkins was every man's dream, rumor had it, but the only man that ever made her temper rise was her father. Madison hoped she'd be as confident one day and have a love of her own again as her mother did.

"Hey, Mom, how are you?"

"I'm fine, baby, how are you?"

"I'm good. I need something to wear. Chase and I have a dinner date tonight, and I have nothing. Nothing cute, anyway."

"Chase, as in Chase Storm?" her mother questioned.

"Yes, Mother, Chase Storm."

"You're kidding me, right? You and he have another date? Unbelievable."

"Why is that, Mother?"

"Chile, Chase Storm has bedded more women than Serta mattresses," Martha said.

Madison chuckled. "Mother, I've heard this from you, from Deena, the girls at the salon, and I get it. Chase was

a playboy, a ladies' man, but I don't know that Chase. So,
please, stop reminding me of who he used to be. We all
have a past, okay, and Chase has treated me with respect.
I'm having a good time with him."

"A good time, huh?"

"Yes, Mother, a good time, and it has absolutely nothing to do with sex. We've just hung out. Chase never
lied to me, and I believe him. He says he is looking for a
mate now. He's so sweet and gentleman-like when we're
together. Please give me some credit. Let me be the adult
you raised me to be. If he is full of shit—" She stopped,
wishing she could take it back. She had never said cuss
words to her mother before. "My apologies, Mother. If he
is no good, let me discover that on my own."

"Chile, please, you can cuss. And I know you have
a good head on your shoulders. As much as I want to
protect you, baby, you are a grown woman, and I can't
judge that young Storm. Maybe he has changed, and you
are the right woman to tame him. I'll keep my opinions to
myself and let you do you. Come on over, and we'll find
something fabulous for you."

"Thanks, Mom, and thank you for supporting me in
everything. I won't be a fool for Chase or any man."

"Well, that Tony had you stuck on foolish for a second
or two."

"Keyword, Mother, *had*. I know I was wrong, Ma. That
was the biggest mistake of my life, and I'll never do anything so irresponsible again. You were right. I'll share
anything on this earth but a man. I have no excuse for
that affair, and that's not the woman I am, and I knew
better, and I've repented, and I've forgiven myself, so I
can't do anything now but move on, right?"

"Indeed."

"I'm on my way."

Later that night when Madison arrived at Chase's place, she was wowed by the beautiful home before her. She knew the Storms lived well, but she hadn't expected Chase's place to be so grand since he was a bachelor and a so-called ladies' man. She expected something quaint and cozy, not a home large enough for a family. When she parked and got out, he came out to greet her.

"You made it. Was it hard to find?"

"No, my handy GPS got me here fairly quickly. Your house is lovely. I didn't expect it to be this huge."

"Well, that wasn't my plan either, but being a Storm, we build big, and my family builds with plans for a family."

"I see."

She admired the landscaping, pavers, and fountain that decorated the front of his home and lawn before following him inside, excited to see what was on the other side of the entryway. At first glance, it was as lovely inside as it was outside. Shocked to see the décor of neutral tones, artistic accents, and soft textures, she admired the inside as much as she did the outside. Not a bachelor's pad at all. It looked as if a Mrs. Storm dwelled there too.

"This is interesting. Lovely. Not what I expected, baby. I mean, your taste is impeccable."

"Well, my mother and sisters-in-law are responsible for everything inside. I just said 'Do what y'all do,' and I liked it. I've only added a couple of masculine touches, but not much. My office space is all me, though. They didn't have any say or input on it."

"Let me guess, naked posters of women."

He laughed. "Although that's a good idea, I didn't dare go that route. Let me show you."

She followed him down a hall, and he pointed out the bathroom and the guest rooms, and then finally his office. Madison was surprised to see a Dallas Cowboy theme. He had every trinket and accessory known to man to show his team pride.

"Wow, Dallas, huh? I'm a Texans' girl."

"What? You can't be. I mean, this relationship just ain't gon' work unless you convert," he said, moving close to her. She smelled the mint on his breath and wanted to kiss him.

"So, that's it? Just because the Cowgirls are not my team, you don't want to see me anymore? I'm crushed," she faked a sigh, holding her chest.

He kissed her, giving her what she wanted. "Well, this one time, I'll make an exception, but you better be a fan. If not, I don't think my heart can take it."

She ran a finger down his chest and smiled. "Now, *that* I am."

With another soft kiss, he said, "I knew you had other great qualities."

"Yes, I have a few," she joked. He stole another kiss.

This time, she let him part her lips and dance with her tongue. The kiss was sensual, and she enjoyed it.

"I've been anxiously waiting to do that," he said, ending the kiss and giving her a couple of pecks.

"Me too."

"So, are you hungry?"

Not for food, she thought, but she nodded. "Yes, I'm starving."

"Come on." He took her by the hand and led her out to the patio. A man was cooking on the grill.

"You have a cook?"

"No, I hired him for tonight. I wanted you over, and since I normally eat out or at my parents' or Lance's, I hired someone."

"That was thoughtful. I mean, it smells divine."

"Deena told me about your allergy to shellfish, so he's grilling steak, chicken, and veggies, and we got some steamed rice, so whichever you'd like."

"I wanna try everything. It smells so good."

"As you wish."

The cook served them while they drank aged wine. Madison found herself feeling like a new woman. Chase was tugging on her heartstrings. Her husband had been a great man, and she loved him, but they hadn't had a romantic beginning, not like the beginning she was having with Chase. She and Dre had met in college and were friends first. He hadn't been able to afford to wine and dine her.

"Dinner was fabulous," she said after the server cleared her plate. She had eaten a bit too much, but it was too good not to clean her plate.

"It was, and I'm happy you enjoyed it. Let's go inside."

She got up, and he took her by her hand. Her heart was thumping out of her chest. She was too attracted to him. She knew it was date number three, but her pussy had no way of deciphering that. She wanted him to try her, to initiate their sexual dance. She wanted him to take her.

She took a seat and watched him go for the remote. Admiring his tight ass in his linen pants, she unconsciously licked her lips. Her eyes followed his every move, and when he turned around, her eyes landed on his shaft. She quickly turned her head. He laughed.

"What's funny?"

"You," he said.

Pretending to be innocent, she said. "What?"

"You were checking me out."

"I was not."

"You were," he countered.

"No, I wasn't," she denied.

"You were, and if you'd like, I can let you see what's underneath my clothes."

Her eyes got wide. "I'm good," she lied. She wanted him to strip down to nothing. She wanted to see him as naked as the day he was born.

He pulled the string on his pants with a naughty smile. She swallowed hard. "That won't be necessary, but this is your house. You are free to walk around naked if you want." The words came out in a rush, and she quickly took a big gulp of her wine. Her temperature was rising. She wanted him to take it all off, but she didn't want him to know she wanted him to.

"Why don't you come and take off my clothes for me?"

She smiled. "Ummm, you do know the cook is still here, right?" she reminded him. She took another sip of her wine and watched him fold like a chair.

"Oh, I did forget that minor detail." He came over to sit with her. "Well, until we are alone, we are going to listen to some good old R&B and sip more wine, and I'm going to give you a foot rub."

"Aaaw, snap," she said, sliding her back against the corner of his sectional. She placed her feet into his lap. "You do foot rubs? Now, I'm down for that."

"I do, so relax."

"And I haven't had one in ages, not by a man, of course, so I'm game."

"By who, then?"

"The salon. I get my feet done, and they do a little massage, but it's not the same."

"I see. Let me make your feet feel good, Madison."

With that, she relaxed and welcomed Chase's massage.

Chapter Twelve

Chase slowly rubbed Madison's feet and watched her. Her eyes were closed, and he could hear her moaning softly. He wondered if that was how she'd sound if he were massaging her love box with his shaft, or if it would be louder, more intense, more sensual. He wanted to massage her in other places. He wanted to rub his hands over her huge mounds and twist her nipples. He had been with size two, fours, and sixes, and he was so curious to know what it would feel like to nestle between her thick-ass thighs. He fantasized about putting his face between them.

He imagined she'd taste as sweet as her mouth when he kissed her, and that she'd be as passionate in the bedroom as she was when she sang to him. He was now fully open to this new and different relationship. Never had he allowed himself to like a woman, enjoy a woman, or even really talk to one. Hell, if she talked too much, that usually turned him completely off. It was always casual and strictly physical for Chase. He never even entertained sharing feelings or emotions with anyone. He'd meet a woman and say something fresh or naughty to see how she'd respond.

The ones he could fuck on a dime would find whatever clever, nasty thing he said to be amusing. The ones that required work usually called him an asshole when he'd approach her with his bedroom chat. The ones who were offended would be too much work. The ones who returned an even freakier response usually had his dick in their mouths or deep inside of them within a couple of hours. They'd have several drinks first, and they'd have him at their place, or he'd take them to a hotel or one of their properties. Either way, no one—not a single one— made it to his home.

"Mr. Storm," the cook, said interrupting his thoughts.

"Yes, Cedric?"

"I'm done, so I'll be leaving."

"Thanks for everything. My lady and I enjoyed the meal." He had just said his lady. *Is that out of line?* he wondered. He looked over at Madison, and when a smile plastered on her face, he knew it was safe to call her that.

"I'm glad. And I enjoyed cooking for you and your lovely lady. I will show myself out. Please keep me in mind for your next romantic dinner."

"I will," Chase said. He watched the man leave and then turned back to Madison. "So, babe, would you like a refill?"

"I would, and I'd like for you to show me what you were going to show me before."

His dick jumped, and the corners of his mouth curled upward. "I will if you promise to show me yours too."

"Oh no, baby. This show is all about you. I want to see what you're working with under those clothes."

"And I'm happy to show you, but I also want to see what you are working with under yours." She put her head down and bit the corner of her lip. "Don't tell me you're shy? I know you're not shy the way you were eyeing my dick down a few minutes ago, Miss Madison."

Madison looked up and smiled a sexy smile. "No, I'm not shy, Mr. Storm." She stood and slowly unbuttoned the buttons on her denim dress. It had about five buttons up top, and the bottom hugged her hips and ample ass. She opened her top revealing a set of triple Ds held up in a lace green and black bra. It was sexy. Chase hadn't known cute underwear came in that size. When she pushed her dress down from her waist to the floor, his dick stood at full attention. She wore matching green and black laced panties. She looked like a voluptuous queen. It was different for him, but not different in a bad way, he thought, putting the glass down on the coffee table. Her refill would have to wait.

He grabbed her face and then pushed his tongue in her mouth, kissing her hungrily. He wanted to know what her pussy tasted like.

He stopped and looked at her. "Can I taste you, baby? Let me taste all of you," he panted. He was anxious and so excited to have her. She nodded. He took her by the hand and led her to his bedroom. . . . The first time any woman had been given that privilege. He pulled his covers back and tossed his throw pillows across the room.

"Lay back, baby," he whispered.

When she did, he removed her panties. He pulled his V-neck over his head, removing the tee. Next were his pants and boxers. His dick was erect, and he heard Madison gasp at the sight of it.

"Baby, I'll be as gentle as you want me to be, so don't worry." He climbed into bed and positioned himself close to her side.

He kissed her lips and then went for her breasts. He rubbed them through her bra, and she raised to her elbows and unhooked the hooks. It joined her panties on the floor. He got excited just looking at her large, dark nipples. They were solid as a rock, and he rubbed his lips over one before he opened his mouth to receive it.

She moaned and rubbed his head as he twisted and massaged the other. He went back to her lips, stole a few more kisses, and then moved on to the other nipple. Hungrily, he licked and sucked, and she ooohed and aaahed, sounds of her sweet voice cheering him on. Anxious to taste her southern lips, he took his fingers and slid them down her center, stroking her clit.

Now, her moans grew louder, and he couldn't resist licking his fingers. Her scent and taste were of a woman who took care of herself. No foulness in her odor, clearance that you could eat it all night long if you wanted to. Even though she had arrived a few hours before, she still smelled of a fresh shower.

"I wanna taste you," he breathed in her ear.

Her eyes widened. "Yaaaaaaas. Taste me, baby; stroke my clit with your tongue, baby," she hissed.

"Yes, baby," he said stroking her clit vigorously with his fingers. He was in a zone and was lusting after Madison more than he'd ever craved a woman. He spoke his true feelings. "I'm feeling you, Madison," he confessed, "and I just want to please you." She nodded, giving him the go-ahead.

He made his way down to her center; then he pulled her in close and softly kissed her lips. He teased her with the tip of his tongue and the sound she released drew him in, so he dove in. He licked, sucked, and teased her lips and bulb. He pushed her thighs back and pressed his tongue against her bulb, flicking it up and down.

Madison trembled; her thighs shook. She lifted her bottom, feeding him her center, and he began to suck on her swollen clit, loving the sound of her moans. When she grabbed his head and called out his name, he knew she was there, but he continued to lick and suck until she cried for him to stop. He pulled back and watched the clear juice run out of her wet opening. The sight of it made his dick throb. He was solid and ready to feel the warmth of her walls around his shaft.

He wanted in. He wanted to feel this sweet spot. He wanted to know what Madison's flesh felt like. As badly as he wanted not to put on the plastic and just be skin to skin with this queen, he knew the rules. They were not married, and he still barely knew her. But he knew enough to know that he wanted her; he wanted her bad.

"Let me taste you now," she said in a seductive tone.

Pleased that she was willing, he got onto the bed and lay back and held his little man. When she wrapped her juicy lips around him, he groaned.

"Baby . . . Oooweee, that is good." He couldn't take his eyes off of her. She looked sexy as ever sucking his pipe. She ran her tongue down his length, and the sensations drove him crazy. "Madison, baby, you look so good pleasing my dick, baby." Her eyes were closed as she sucked and stroked and slurped on his organ. He was losing his mind.

It was intense, more so because he had a connection with Madison. This experience wasn't anything like the countless sexcapades he had shared with his one-nighters and his frequent jumpoffs. She was permanent potential. The way she pleased his dick with so much passion, he knew he'd want that feeling again . . . and again . . . and again.

He watched her as she gave his mushroom head a sloppy slurp job. When she opened her eyes and looked at him, it was over. He yanked his dick away, and a pool of hot semen erupted from his tip. It was white and thick, and it rolled down his shaft like melting ice cream. "Baby . . ." he panted. "Oh, baby, oh, baby. That was so good. I want you. I want you now."

"Don't you need a minute, baby?"

"Yes, and that is all I need." He got up. "Let me clean up, and I'll be right back."

"I'm going to go to the kitchen if that's okay. I'd like more wine."

"Yes, of course, that's okay. Would you please bring me another too?"

She nodded.

He headed to the bathroom, and Madison headed to the kitchen. When he came out, she was nowhere in sight. He looked around for her, his dick swinging as he walked. He looked out the glass slider and noticed she was out by the pool. Naked and sipping wine.

"Baby, why are you out here?"

"Because of that," she said, pointing to his hot tub.

"Yes, what about it?"

"I wanna get in."

"Right now? I thought we were going to finish what we started in the bedroom."

"Why can't we finish out here?" She got up and walked over to the dial and power switch and turned it on.

He went over to her. "So how about you let me feel you, and then we get in?"

"Get a condom," she said.

He hurried inside and was back in a flash. They stood kissing, and he massaged her breast in one hand and her ass in the other.

"I can't wait to feel you, baby," he said between kisses. His manhood had risen again, and he was ready.

They went over to a chaise lounge, and she lay back and spread her legs wide for him. He positioned himself between her thighs and slid in. She moaned and frowned. He stroked her slow at first, trying to maintain his composure. She was tighter than he'd imagined she'd be. Her tunnel felt like silk gliding up, down, and around his shaft, and he pumped harder. He pushed her legs back farther to go deeper and was amazed at how wide she had opened for him. Never would he have imagined a woman of her stature to be so flexible.

Her body looked good, and it felt good. Chase felt that he had been missing out because of being so damn shallow. She not only felt good to him, she felt better than he could remember any other woman feeling to him.

"Let me ride you, baby," Madison said.

His brows raised, and he slowed. "What, baby?"

"You heard me. Let me ride you."

He pulled out and wondered how that would work. They changed positions, and she planted her feet on the concrete ground on either side of the chair and eased down on him. She bounced up and down on him first, allowing it to go in and out of her. His dick got harder. It felt so good. Taken by her technique and how she effortlessly bounced on him, he grabbed her ass and raised his hips up and down to meet her rhythm. When she slowed and rolled her ample hips, he could no longer hold on to his nut. He exploded, letting out a groan of pleasure. He looked up at her and planted kisses on her breasts.

She had just fucked the shit out of him, he thought. "Oh, Madison, baby, what did you just do to me?"

She gave him a soft kiss. "I just made you come, baby."

"Indeed, you did."

She eased off of him, got up, grabbed her glass, and stepped into the hot tub. He went to dispose of the condom, came back, grabbed his glass, and joined her. He sat across from her, studying her face. She was such a beautiful woman. Her eyes were a pretty light brown, her light complexion was blemish-free, and her high cheekbones and heart-shaped face were undeniably perfect. Her hair was wild after their session, but the cut was so sassy it looked good in disarray.

Chase's stomach had a funny feeling that he had never felt before, and it made him nervous. *I'm tripping, right?* he said to himself. This woman is not giving me butterflies. He had a flashback of her working her hips on top of him, and again his stomach tightened. He slid over to her side.

"Madison, you're the one, baby." Speaking from his heart and in all sincerity, he said, "You are going to be my wife." He had no idea how it had happened, but it happened. He was falling in love.

She almost spit out her wine. "Chase, how do you know this?" she asked softly.

"Because I do, baby. Stay with me tonight."

"Are you sure that's what you want?"

He smiled at her and then kissed her before saying, "I've never been more sure about anything before you."

She put her head down, and he lifted it and gave her a gentle kiss. She put her glass down and straddled him, kissing deeply. That night, they made love all night long, and in the morning, Madison made them breakfast.

Chase called in to work for the very first time in his entire career saying he wouldn't be there, and Madison rescheduled her appointment with Marcus. The two of them spent the entire day talking, making love, and more talking and making more love. Since Chase had no other items in his fridge besides breakfast items, they called on Cedric again. Chase employed him for the next three days, and they stayed in, mostly naked, until Sunday. Sunday was they day they parted only long enough for Madison to pack a bag and return.

In the span of a few days, they grew closer than close, and they were falling head over heels for each other, and neither of them wanted to slow down or turn back. What they had was the start of something amazing, and neither of them ever thought they'd be that happy with someone. Madison never knew she would fall that deep for another man, and Chase never thought he'd fall that hard for anyone. They were both high off of each other and looked forward to whatever they landed.

Chapter Thirteen

The Storm family was in shock when Chase showed up at the main house with Madison on his arm. His brothers thought he was still playing the role, and his sisters-in-law thought he had been drugged or something. Either way, no one—not even his father—believed him when he said, "She's the one."

The men peered at Chase. "So, you like her? For real, for real like her?" Travis asked again.

"For the hundredth time, yes. I like her. I mean, I really, really, *really* like her. I'd say love if I truly knew what the hell love was, but I definitely like her. Not the average like her, either. I mean, I can't stop thinking about her. I love to see her smile, hear her voice, and deportment," he said because Damon was the only one still looking at him with a look of confusion. The others were shaking their heads and giving each other a look that said that Chase was full of shit. "I have spent every day with her since we've gone out. I mean, I damn near asked her to move in, guys. I want to be with her every second. She is funny, smart, intelligent, and she loves football. She's not a Cowboys' fan . . . for now," he added, "but everything else about her is perfect. Man, she can even sing. I mean, she can sing, man. Blow Alicia, Mariah, Jennifer—all of 'em out of the water. She sang that song to me, you know, that old cut by Alicia Keys," he said.

His father and brothers just chuckled as they watched the youngest Storm carrying on like a man in love.

"Singing, Chase?" Lance said between laughs. "The woman *sang* to you?"

"Yes, man. To hell with y'all. I thought this is what y'all wanted."

"We did," Damon said, "but we are still not convinced. We'll continue to play this little game with you, li'l bro. We just want to see if you keep it up. I mean, it's only been a few days."

"Yes, and in a few days, I feel like this. This has never, *ever* happened to me. Y'all know I'd never be out here singing all of this love shit if I wasn't serious."

No one said anything. They just all stared at Chase like he was a project, and that made Chase confused. They wanted him to settle down, and now that he was finally considering it, they thought he was a joke.

"Forget it. I did this because y'all kept nudging me to settle down. And now that I've found the very first woman that I allowed into my home—"

"*What?*" his dad cut him off. "You took her to your *house?*" He knew that was a violation of his youngest son's ultimate rules.

"Dad, I'm telling you, Madison is going to be your next daughter-in-law." More laughter erupted. "Fine, in six months, we'll see. I wonder if you all be chuckling it up when you have to write my checks."

"Checks?" their dad said.

"Yes, checks. These clowns said if I met a woman—of *their choice,* I might add—and gave it a true effort for six months—they'd each give me a million bucks."

"*What?*" Legend said. Their father leaned in to get more details.

"Dad, relax," Lance said. "It's just a little wager. Chase won't make it; we're sure of it."

"Yes, this thing he's doing isn't convincing anybody. I give him another month, and he'll fold," Travis said and took a swig of his beer.

"I give him another week. That itch is going to need to be scratched, and poor Chase will be on the prowl again," Lance said.

Chase grinned. "You are wrong. I already had an itch, and Madison's been scratching it every single damn day—and night—since last Wednesday."

The laughter ceased.

"You didn't," Travis said. All had disbelieving eyes, staring at him.

"I did as I said, and you idiots don't believe me. I'm feeling her. She's a good girl. She's the remedy to my promiscuity." Chase's tone was serious, but the other men didn't seem like they were buying it.

Their dad broke the silence. "Hell, I'm in. I'll match each million if that means you will take time to get to know this girl. However, I want to up the ante a little." The four guys turned to their dad. "I'll match each million if there is a wedding that follows. Meaning, if after six months you've won, and you and Madison make it to that altar, I'll give you three million for a wedding gift."

Chase looked at his father and then each of his brothers. "It's on, because as I said—and have been saying since I walked through that gate—Madison is the one, so you guys may want to secure my money now, because in six months, I'll have you three losers' money, and, Dad, I'll expect my check no later than the reception. Now, I'm going to get me another beer while you losers talk about me behind my back."

Chase went inside to the fridge and grabbed another beer and made sure he stopped and kissed Madison and whispered something in her ear to make her smile before he went back out to rejoin the men.

"Wow, you're grinning hard. What sweet nothings did he whisper in your ear?" Deena asked.

"None of your business." Madison blushed as she diced the tomatoes. The women were preparing dinner while the men did what they usually did if they weren't grilling—nothing. Madison was on salad duty, while each of the other women tended to a different dish.

"Come on, Madison, you *have* to share. In this circle, we tell it *all*," Gina laughed.

"No, I can't say what he said," she giggled.

"Don't be afraid to speak in front of me, chile," Chase's mother said. "This is the safe zone, and with the Storm men, there are always hot topics up in this kitchen."

Madison blushed. No way could she repeat what Chase said about licking her until she "came like an ocean." She continued to hold back. "I can't."

"Look, Miss Madison, you are the first and only woman who has shared this kitchen with us that is attached to Chase. Now spill!" Tasha demanded. "We want to know what he said."

Madison eyed the women, all waiting. Her heart raced. She took a big gulp of her wine. "He said he wants to lick me until I come like an ocean," she blurted with her eyes locked on the tomatoes she was dicing.

"Oh, I remember those nights of being licked until I couldn't move," Gina said.

"Shit, *remember?* What *happened* to those nights?" Deena asked. "Travis still does that and, boy, does he do it so well."

"I'm not saying that Lance doesn't anymore, just not as often or as long as he used to. Hell, we be trying to get all we can get in before one of the kids come crying at the door," she laughed.

"That's your fault, Gina," Tasha added. "I told you from day one to put your babies in a crib in their own room. All that sleeping with you only gets worse, and you'll never get it in with kids that can't sleep in their own damn beds."

"I know that's real," Chase's mother agreed and then sipped her wine. "Never did one of our boys sleep in our room. As they got older, we'd make sure there was a friend, relative, coach, or somewhere they could be on the weekends, so Legend and I could have the house to ourselves. Girl, back then, we'd stay naked the entire weekend. And when we finally got Chase off to college and them blue pills were invented, we would lock ourselves up in this house and screw all over the damn place," she shared, and they all roared with laughter. "I'm serious, and still to this day, we get it going. It may take a little longer to get it warmed up, but it be damn sho' hot by the time we get to it."

The girls were rolling by now. They were slapping high fives and clanking glasses and enjoying the conversation of love, marriage, and sex.

After a while, Deena asked. "So, do y'all think Chase has really changed? I mean, Madison, no offense, but we never thought a woman could hog-tie that one."

"Well, I don't know, Deena. We just started dating. Things are still new and good. He seems genuine enough to me, though. All this talk about him being a dog and a player, I just can't wrap my head around it, because with me, he's romantic, gentle, and attentive." She smiled, gazing off.

"Let's hope it's not an act. I mean, my brother-in-law is sweet in so many ways, but he and commitment do not live in the same space."

"Well, I don't know what to make of it, ladies. Like, can you guys tell me something good or something positive about him? I'm always reminded of this 'stranger' you speak of, but Chase isn't like that with me."

"Yes, ladies. Come on, be nice. This is my son we're discussing. I've never defended any of my children, but I've always wondered when he'd meet someone like you. Don't let them scare you, Madison. Chase has the

potential of being just as great as his father and his
brothers. It just took him a lot longer to come around. My
other sons had a little dog in them too. I used to stay on
them about finding a wife, and they just happened to find
my beautiful daughters-in-law before they turned thirty.

"Chase . . . It just took him a little longer to want to
settle down, and if he is treating you well, don't let what
everyone else say stop you from getting to know him; just
don't be a fool. If he starts to act up, kick his ass to the
curb," she said. They all laughed.

"I guess you're right, Mom," Tasha said. "Maybe he has
decided to settle down, and if not with you, Madison, I
hope this is a start for him because that playa—" She
stopped when the guys walked in. They all approached
their woman, and as a team, they all grabbed them by
the waist, gave soft kisses, and barked that they were
hungry. Mrs. Storm threw them out of her kitchen,
instructing them to wash up because dinner would be
on the table soon. All smiles at the Storm table as they
watched Chase and Madison closely. The brothers still
shook their heads and didn't believe that Chase was genuine. They knew he was a fraud.

The women were suspicious too and wondered how
long it would take before he broke Madison's heart. They
all departed, and every Storm man made love to his
woman that night, including Legend. The women dozed
off in their man's arms with smiles on their faces, and
each of them knew they were lucky to have them.

Chapter Fourteen

Three months later, Chase and Madison were still going strong. The salon renovations were just about done, and only a few minor details needed to be finished.

"Baby, this is nice," Chase said. "It turned out so well."

"It is, isn't it? I can't wait until the grand opening, baby. I'm so excited."

"You should be. You're going to have a successful place here." His phone rang, and he pulled it from his pocket. Madison got a glimpse at his screen and saw it was Hope.

Again.

"I thought you told her to stop calling you after business hours, Chase?"

"I did. Hold on." He stepped away. Madison rolled her eyes to the ceiling. Hope Gardener was a problem for her, but not for her man, apparently, because he wasn't doing anything about the damn after-hours calls.

Madison went over to the laundry area and went back to opening boxes of towels and putting them in the cabinets that hung over the bowls. A minute or two later, Chase came back.

"What was it this time?" she asked. "I mean, I know you're in charge of the budget for her and her family's new car lot, but it's getting out of hand, Chase. You don't want me to handle it."

"*Excuse* me?" he asked with a brow raised.

"You heard me," Madison snapped and grabbed the box cutter to open another box.

"Whoa, Madison. I've told you that Hope and I only have a business relationship. I'm with you. I only want to be with you, not Hope. She and I could have been together long ago. I'm a man, and I don't need you to handle shit for me."

"Fine," she said. She tossed the box cutter onto an unopened box and tried to walk away. Chase grabbed her arm and blocked her way. "Hey, wait, listen. And don't walk away from me when I'm talking to you."

"Let me go and get the hell out of my way, Chase."

"No. We're going to finish this conversation."

"We *are* finished." She yanked loose and walked away.

Chase followed. "Madison, what have I done to make you, for one moment, feel insecure?"

"Nothing, Chase, and I'm not insecure. She knows that you and I are together, yet this little dense, space-head-chick acts as if she has no respect for our relationship. She has no business calling you after nine, and if you don't see shit wrong with it, there is nothing else to say," she yelled.

"Hell, calm down and lower your voice. I agree with you, Madison, but you pissed me off with your tone and telling me that you'll handle things like I'm a kid. I don't need you to handle Hope for me. My intentions with her are innocent, and I will choose to answer or not answer my damn phone. You don't decide that for me."

She shrugged, her eyes glossy. She and Chase didn't argue much. There was only turbulence when it came to his phone, old flings calling, and when they ran into his old jumpoffs on the streets, and they tried to be all over him as if she were invisible.

"Fine," she said, "now can you go? I have things to do here."

"Oh, now you want me to go? You're kicking me out?"

"Yes, I'd like you to leave."

"Fine," he said between clenched teeth.

Madison watched him leave and locked the door behind him. She didn't want to be jealous, but that damn Hope got under her skin. She was the town's crowning glory. Folks worshiped her as she were a queen. If she and Hope stood side by side, no one would even see her, even though she was twice as big as the other woman was. Hope was known not only for her beauty but for her contributions to the community. Deep down, Madison felt she only did all the things she did for recognition and popularity, not because she gave a crap about giving back. She had never worked an honest day in her life, and she had everything her heart desired. Her family's money was as long, maybe even longer than the Storms'.

Any man in East Texas would gladly take Hope's hand in marriage, so Madison hated that the black Barbie had the potential of taking her man.

"Damn!" Madison said, balling her fists. She wanted to punch Hope in the face. She had just argued with her man, that she hadn't sexed in four days because the last-minute list of things-to-do at the salon weighed on her. She had been going home later and later each night, but that night, she had planned to wrap things up a little early so that she could service her man.

Oh well, another night alone, she thought. She opened some more boxes and organized a few more things before heading out.

When she got home, she was shocked to see an old friend sitting on her porch. He stood when she got out of her truck.

"Tony, what are you doing here?" she asked.

"I came to see you."

"At this time of night?"

"I've been waiting several hours."

"Still, this late?" she said, approaching him. "What do you want?" When she got closer, she could see his eyes were red. "Tony, what's wrong?"

"Dad passed earlier this evening."

"Anthony, I'm so sorry."

He sniffled and wiped his face.

"Come inside. I'll make some tea." He followed her, and they headed into the kitchen. "Have a seat. I'll put the kettle on; then I need to run up to change."

He nodded and took a seat on one of the stools at the island. He removed his hat and sat with his head low.

Madison washed her hands at the sink and filled the kettle. She grabbed her tea set, went for the tea bags, and dropped a few of them inside the teapot. "I'll be back down soon."

When she came back down, Tony was up and pouring the hot water into the teapot. "Thanks," Madison said.

"No problem. It was whistling for a few moments, and I figured you didn't hear it."

"I didn't," she said, walking to the other side of the island to join him. "I'll take it from here." She took the kettle from his hand. "Have a seat," she instructed.

Tony went back to his stool, and she opened the cabinet and got some cookies. She placed them on a plate and poured them both a cup of tea.

"Did you make any calls yet?" she asked.

"No, not yet. This is all just sinking in, you know. I knew this day was coming, and I thought I was mentally prepared. But I wasn't. It hurts like hell." Tears ran down his cheeks.

Madison went around to console him. "I'm so sorry, Tony," she said, rubbing his back. He turned to her and buried his head in her neck, sobbing as she held him. "It's going to be hard at first, but it *will* get better in time. The first day is always the worst day."

After a while, he pulled himself together. "Do you have anything stronger?" he asked.

"Yeah, sure." She went to the liquor cabinet and brought back a bottle of Crown Reserve, then went for a glass of ice for him. "Do you need a chaser?"

"No, on the rocks will be just fine." He took a gulp and frowned. She was about to take the bottle, but he stopped her. "No. I'm going to need more than this."

She set the bottle back down and reached for her cup of tea. "Will you join me?" he asked.

"Tony, I have to be up early."

"Madi, I just lost my father."

"Okay, let's take this to the back porch. The lake is beautiful under the moonlight. It helps me when I'm sad."

He nodded. "Okay."

She grabbed the ice bucket and lid, filled it, and grabbed a glass. He got the Crown, and she grabbed a can of Coke from the fridge.

"I can't drink it straight," she said.

He burst into laughter. "Still a girl, I see."

"Yep, I am."

They settled outside and sat in silence.

"So, when is your family coming?" Madison asked after a while.

"Tomorrow. Simone was still working when she got the call, so we decided tomorrow would be better for her. I didn't want her and the kids on the road too late."

"That's understandable."

"It's just so surreal, the fact that he is gone. I mean, yes, he was in pretty bad shape, and I knew he was suffering, but I still had hoped he'd get better."

"Well, cancer is a monster."

"I know."

"At least there is no more pain for him. And you'll be okay. You knew he was ill. Trust me, that makes a difference. It's better than getting that call out of the blue. I didn't prepare mentally for the death of my husband and twins. I mean, like, after I went down to the morgue and saw their bodies, I still went home thinking they'd come through the door any minute, asking about dinner or could they play their video games for a little while before dinner. The next morning, it was the same. I woke up thinking it was time to head down to make everyone breakfast." Her eyes glossed, but she held her tears. "But they were gone. I had to get out of that house because every moment there reminded me of them."

"That's why you came back?"

"Yes, and maybe I should not have. Maybe if I had stayed, I would not have fallen into such a deep depression. After all, my parents didn't force me or make me rejoin the real world until a few months ago. Almost four years of my life was spent doing absolutely nothing but thinking of them."

She stopped, remembering she shared the same story with Chase one night when he had asked her about her family. She could see in his eyes that he felt her pain.

"I know, Madi, and I can't imagine what that must have been like. I mean, Simone drives me nuts, and the boys are hardheaded brats, but the thought of losing them . . ." He paused. "I just can't imagine that."

"Well, I don't wish that on anyone. Sudden or not, I know losing a loved one can be tough."

"Absolutely."

When she walked him to the door, she heard her phone ringing. She had left it on the kitchen counter. "Excuse me a minute." She went to it and saw that she had missed five calls from Chase. He had sent her a text.

I'm sorry, baby. Can I come by so we can talk?

He had sent that at 12:30 a.m.

She put the phone down and walked back over to Tony. "Is everything okay?" he asked.

"Yes, I just missed a few calls from Chase."

"So, it's true? You *are* seeing him?"

"Yes, I am."

"Wow, you didn't want to continue to be my mistress, but you'd get with the town's player?"

"First, being your woman on the side was not right, Tony. And as for Chase being a player, I don't know that side of him. That seems to be the first thing out of everyone's mouth. No one ever asks if I'm happy or how things are going. It's always a comment about how much of a bad boy he is, or was, rather. He treats me with love and kindness. Whatever he was before we started dating is who he *was*. We're fine, and I'm not his sidepiece," she added as a matter-of-fact.

Tony held up his hands in mock surrender. "Hold on, Madi, relax. I'm just saying he has a reputation, so be careful. I don't want to see you hurt by Chase or any other man. Just don't be naïve, Madi. He's cunning."

"I got this. Don't worry about me and my relationship with Chase, okay?"

"Okay," he said and backed away.

He walked out, and she stood on the porch and watched him get into his truck and leave. When his taillights reached the end of the block, she turned to go back inside, but a car immediately pulled into her driveway.

"What the hell?"

Chapter Fifteen

Chase got out of the car and slammed the door. He was pissed. He had been sitting outside for two hours looking at Tony's truck in his woman's driveway. He had wanted to get out and ring her bell, but he knew that was a bitch-ass move. He had called and called, but she didn't answer. They'd had words, but having a man at her house was *not* acceptable.

He felt something he had never before felt in his life—jealousy. Before, he couldn't care less what a woman did when he wasn't around, but with Madison, it was different. He was falling full speed for her, and he didn't want to share her. It had been a shock to see Tony, a man who could give him some competition.

"What are you doing here?" Madison asked with her hands on her hips.

"No," he snapped. "The question is, what was *Tony* doing here until one thirty in the fucking morning."

"You're spying on me?"

"No, I came to talk to you about earlier since you weren't answering my calls. I pulled up and saw Tony's truck in your driveway. What the fuck, Madison? Are you fucking him now? You're cheating on me with Anthony Reed?" he yelled.

"Lower your voice," Madison hissed.

Chase's temples throbbed. No woman had ever made him feel the emotions that Madison had him feeling at that very moment, and he just wanted to punch something. He wasn't in any position to get played or compete with no man for Madison. She was his, and he wasn't going to let Anthony Reed stroll in and take his woman—and he was married—so why was he creeping around Madison's place was another question.

He rolled his neck and rubbed his head. He was frustrated, and he wanted answers. "Why was Tony here until this time of morning? What were you two doing that was so important that you couldn't answer my calls, Madison?" he said, trying to remain calm. He wanted to yell. If she had fucked with Tony, he was for sure done with her ass, and the bet would be off. He'd tried, but he wasn't going to let a woman—not even Madison—make a fool of him.

"Come inside, and we can talk."

"I don't want to go inside, Madison. If I go in and see a romantic scene, it's going to make me very angry. Now, tell me what's going on with you and Tony," he insisted.

"Nothing. I came home, and he was here. He needed to talk."

"About?" Beads of sweat settled on his forehead.

"His father died, Chase. Mr. Reed passed early this evening. That's it. I was just there for him; that's it. I offered him tea and my condolences, and he wanted something stronger. We sat out back, drank Crown, and talked about our losses. I left my phone inside on the island, and when I went to walk him to the door, I saw that I had missed your calls."

"That's it?" he said, still not convinced.

"That's it. I dated Tony in high school. A few months ago, we had a thing, but I broke it off. He's married, Chase. I was lonely, he was there, and I went there. I crossed some lines, but that was over even before we got together. Trust me, Tony and I are *not* messing around."

He looked at her. She was fully dressed, not in a tee or nightie. He needed to survey the inside; check out her bedroom.

"I need to see your bed," he said. He knew it sounded crazy, but all of this was so new to him, he didn't know what was okay or not okay. All he knew is he wanted his woman to be the woman he thought her to be and not some heartless whore as he had been over the years. He didn't want to be hurt.

"Fine, go ahead," she said, gesturing toward the door.

He rushed past her, and she posted up at the bottom of the steps. Her room seemed normal. The bed was made, and there was no scent of sex in the air. He headed to the bathroom. Her shower and tub were bone dry. He let out a breath and walked back down to where Madison stood with her arms folded.

"Believe me now?" she asked.

"I'm sorry, baby."

"You ought to be."

He pulled her into his arms. "Forgive me, baby, for everything—for Hope and for thinking you were creeping with Tony. I mean, imagine the scene. I sat outside for over *two* hours."

"All you had to do was ring the damn bell, Chase. I'm *not* that type of woman."

"I've never been in a serious relationship before, baby, so please, bear with me. I overreacted at the salon last night. You are right. Hope has no business calling my phone like that. I didn't get it until Lance broke it down to me. I wanted to come by and apologize in person. When I didn't get you, I thought you were too pissed to talk. When I got here and saw Tony's truck, all kinds of shit popped into my head, Madison. The thought of you with another man made me crazy."

"I'm with who I want to be with, Chase. I only want to be with you."

"Me too." He swallowed hard. "I love you, Madison."

She studied him. His eyes were sincere, and she knew he was telling her the truth.

"I love you too, Chase."

He kissed her, his tongue dancing around hers. "Let me make love to you, Madison," he said.

Undoing the buttons on his shirt one by one, she looked into his eyes, and his heart raced. It was like she was looking into his soul.

"Baby, I've never been in love with a woman before," he admitted. "So, I'm probably going to do something else crazy, or stupid like I did tonight before I get it right," he joked.

"Hard to believe. I'm your first?"

"Yes, you're the first, and I don't know if I'm cut out for this. What I feel is one thing, but it's still a foreign feeling, baby. I've never had a meaningful relationship, and I don't want to disappoint you. I'm new at all this."

"Follow your heart, Chase. Just treat me the way you want to be treated, and we'll be okay. I've only loved one man in my life. I thought I loved Tony, but that wasn't love. I was a kid. When I married Dre, I thought it would be forever. And trust, after losing him, I never thought I'd love again. So, we both have to do our best, okay?"

He nodded and moved his attention back to her lips. He kissed her softly at first; then it turned into a hungry kiss. He undressed her right there in the foyer, at the bottom of the stairs. She lay back on the steps with her legs spread wide, allowing him to feast on her pussy. She moaned in pleasure as he pleased her bulb and inserted his tongue inside of her. When she came, he felt her tunnel contract and tasted the juices released from her body.

He allowed her to pull him up into a kiss, sharing the taste of her sex with her. He wanted her silky walls around him. He wanted her thighs around his waist. He reached down and pulled his shaft out of his boxers; then he guided his head to her opening.

"Condom, baby, condom," she panted.

"No, not tonight. I want to feel your flesh," he whispered and pushed his way in. Her eyes widened.

"I'm not on anything."

"I don't care."

"But—"

"Do you want me to stop?" he asked. She looked him in the eyes. "Do you want me to stop, baby?" he asked again moving in and out of her wetness slowly, and she said nothing. He pumped her slow and steady, and her moans heightened the sensations. She wrapped her arms around his neck tighter, and he felt her walls tighten with every thrust.

He pushed his tongue into her mouth and worked his hips in a steady motion. She felt good, soft. Being inside of a woman without plastic was an overwhelming sensation for him. Her body, the moment, and her plush pussy were too much. He came a lot quicker than he normally would have. His body jerked, and he pushed his rod deeper as he released the best nut of his life.

"Aaah, aaaah, aaaaah," he growled.

The feeling was too intense. It was a feeling he had never experienced before. His dad had always told him never to penetrate a woman that wasn't wife without a condom, no matter how pretty or sexy she was, and he never had. He didn't want to risk making a baby—no shot could cure fatherhood—and he didn't ever want to have to get a shot for being reckless.

"Baby," he said. "That was . . . was . . . I can't explain."

"I know, Chase, but, baby, I-I-I," she stuttered. "I'm not on any birth control."

"I heard you, Madison."

"So, why did you do that?" Her eyes watered.

"Because I just wanted to make love to you, baby. I wanted to *feel* you, Madison. I love you, baby. And this was the first time I've ever felt a woman's flesh around me. I've never been skin-to-skin, flesh-to-flesh to a woman, babe."

A tear fell from her eyes. "I wanted to feel you too, but I don't know if I'm ready to have more kids. Losing my babies . . ." she cried.

Chase hadn't even thought of that. He hadn't even thought of pregnancy. He just wanted her. "Shhh, baby, come here," he said, rolling off of her. She sat up on the step, still crying. He wiped her tears away and ran his hand over her curly mane. "I'm sorry, baby, I'm sorry. I didn't think of kids or tomorrow or the cost. I just wanted to be with you and experience your body. I'm so sorry." He kissed the side of her face and tasted her salty tears. "Please, baby, forgive me. Hopefully, we are good. I mean, if we are not, it's totally my fault, and I'll accept whatever you decide. I swear."

"I'm okay; I just don't know about more kids."

"Ever?" he asked, hoping that wasn't the case. Now that he had fallen for her and started to get used to being a one-woman man, he realized he wanted to be a dad. If he and Madison married, he wanted kids.

"I don't know, Chase. I lost both of my boys at the same time to an accident. I'd be crazy, I'd be a wreck, I'd be paranoid, I would be overprotective and guard my child with my life. I'd be so insane that I wouldn't want my child to leave my sight," she cried.

He held her tightly. "Baby, what happened to the twins and Dre had nothing to do with you not being a good mother, or you not protecting your kids. I'm sure you were a great mother, and that you will be a great mother to our children. I know you will."

"Our children?" she looked at him.

"Maybe. I don't know. I know you miss your sons and that losing them was hard for you, baby, but you're here. Your life goes on, and you have to be happy again. Someday, even if it's not with me, you *will* get remarried, and you'll be blessed with more children."

Madison rested her head on his shoulder, and he rocked her. After a while, they went up to bed. The next morning, they both decided to go in late. Chase made her a late breakfast when they finally got up.

"Hey, baby," he said when she entered the kitchen.

"Hey. I see you've been paying attention to the cooking lessons we've been giving you."

He walked over and kissed her cheek and smiled. "Yes, between you, my mom, Gina, and Cedric, I know my way around a bit." He put a plate of eggs, toast, grits, and sausage on the island for her, and she sat down. "You want orange juice or apple?" he asked.

"Orange is fine." She lowered her head to say grace.

Chase poured her juice, and before he could join her, his phone spun on the island. They both looked at the screen. It was Hope. They looked at each other.

"Answer it," Chase said.

She raised an eyebrow. "Me?"

"Yes, answer it and see what she wants."

She picked it up and swiped the screen. "Hello, Hope, this is Madison. Chase is busy at the moment. Is there something I can help you with?" She listened. "I'll be sure to give him the message. Have a good one."

"What did she say?" he asked when she hung up.

"Just wanted to make sure you remembered her dad's birthday dinner this coming Sunday."

"Yes, I remember. Wasn't planning to attend."

"Why not?"

He looked at her. "You know why, Madison."

"No, why?"

"I don't like to be in the same room with Hope and her father. All he talks about is giving her away to me someday."

"Oh, so her parents want you with her too? Interesting." She bit into her toast.

"Yep, that was the Gardeners' plan."

"Well, why don't you go and take me?" She put her fork down when he laughed. "I'm serious," she said.

"Madison, it's better for me not to attend."

"Okay, since you're scared to show up with me." She picked up her fork again and took a bite of her food.

"What? You know that's far from the truth. I love you, babe. I want everyone to know that you're mine and that I'm off the market."

"Well, prove it. Take me to the party."

"Fine, we're going to the party."

She smiled. "Aw, baby, you are so sweet, but we don't have to go. I just wanted to see if you'd take me."

"Yes, I am sweet, and we *are* going, so joke's on you."

"No, seriously, I don't want to go."

"Now, I do, and you *are* coming. Your man has spoken." He went over and kissed her. "Now, finish your breakfast. I have to run home for a fresh suit and head to the office."

"Okay. Will you come by the salon later? I still have boxes to unpack, and I know I won't be done by six."

"I will, and I'll grab dinner."

"Thank you, baby."

He gave her one last kiss. "I love you. Be good."

"Love you too."

Chapter Sixteen

"So, Madison, how long have you and Chase been dating?" Shelby asked. She was one of the town gossipers who pretended to be a woman of God but was always up in somebody's business.

Madison smiled. "Almost four months now." She didn't want to be chatting with that group, but Deena and the girls hadn't made it yet, and people were pulling Chase's arm left and right.

She had gotten cornered at the bar by the yammering crew of East Texas. "Four months? Really? How did you ever tame that man?" Melissa asked.

Madison shrugged. "I didn't do anything. We met at his parents' anniversary party. We talked, and he asked me out."

"That's it?" Terri asked. "I mean, Chase Storm is not an easy win, so you had to do something."

Do something? Madison thought. There were no tricks up her sleeve, no magic wand or make-him-your-man potion in her purse.

Just as she opened her mouth to respond, Chase walked up. *Thank God,* she thought. "Excuse me, ladies," he said, "but I need to borrow Madison." He smiled and kissed her on her cheek. "Baby, I have someone I want you to meet."

The ladies gawked, and Madison felt good that they thought she had some secret remedy to snag one of the finest men in East Texas.

"Sure. Excuse me, ladies." Madison smiled.

"Bye, Chase," the women sang in unison as they eyed the couple. Chase hit them with his charming smile. "Evening, ladies."

"Thanks for rescuing me," Madison said as they walked away.

"Anytime. I know that's the gossiping crew of Tyler. What did they ask? How did you tame a man like me?"

"They did. How'd you guess?"

"Because the fellas kept asking the same thing. They want to know what you did to turn me into an honest man."

Madison stopped walking. "Well, what's your answer?"

"The answer is absolutely nothing."

"Is that right?" she asked, putting her arms around his neck.

"Well, there was that one thing you did," he joked, "but they don't need to know that."

She swatted his arm. "You are *bad*."

"No, baby, you are, and I'm ready to blow this joint and take you home and spread them big thighs."

"Calm down, baby. I'm still waiting for the girls to arrive."

"Do we have to? I've already spoken to Mr. Gardener, assured Mrs. Gardener that you were a real date and not one for hire, and I've managed to keep my conversation with Hope under three minutes. Now that I've shown my face, we can go. You know, hot tub, wine, and . . ." He licked his lips. "You know I'm dying to taste you again, and now that you're on the pill, we can enjoy each other at any given moment without worry."

"I haven't started them yet, Chase. I will on my next cycle. You are lucky those tests were all negative. The doctor said to take another one in a week, but I think we're okay."

"Again, I'm sorry. And since that night, you've been holding out on me, so tonight, I'm ready to get it in, baby."

"We will." She looked over his shoulder. "There's Deena and Travis."

He turned. "Okay, we say hello, and then we're out."

"No, Tasha and Gina are coming," she said, pulling him in Deena's direction.

"We don't have to wait for them. It's been almost a week, Madi. Let's blow this joint."

She stopped and turned to him. "How about we meet at my truck? I'll give you a little head. That should hold you until we go home."

"Oh shit, Madison, you just made my dick hard," he confessed. She laughed but couldn't respond because Deena and Travis were approaching. "Bathroom," Chase said and rushed off.

"What's wrong with him?" Deena asked when she reached Madison.

"Nothing, just something I said." She winked at Deena.

"Let me go check on him," Travis said after giving Madison a quick hug and a peck on the cheek.

"So, my brother-in-law said the L-word? Are you serious? What did you do to him, Madison?"

"I didn't do anything. Chase came by last Monday night after we had this argument about Hope Gardener calling his phone so much after business hours, and Tony was over. Instead of him ringing the bell, he sits in his car sulking for two hours. And then when Tony left after one in the morning, Chase gets out acting like a crazy man."

"Wait a minute. Why was Tony at your house until after one a.m.?"

"That was the night his dad passed. You know he and I have a history. He just wanted someone to talk to. Anyway, after Chase went through my house inspecting my bedroom and shit, he comes back and tells me the idea of me being with another man makes him crazy. Then he admitted that he loved me."

"That is fucking crazy. I never thought I'd see the day when he'd love anyone other than himself."

"So I've heard. Was he that bad? I mean, because I can't see him being that person. He is such a gentleman with me. So romantic and passionate in bed, and, girl, when he's inside of me, I forget about everything and everybody. It's like only he, and I exist. Deena, I'm in love, girl, I love Chase, and I pray that he's changed, because every time someone gets wind that I'm with him, they frown and make faces, asking me two or three times if I am talking about the same Chase Storm. Even Sister Roberts was at my parents' house one day, talking about how Chase was sleeping with two of her granddaughters at the same time, and they knew it."

"Yes, Madison, he was *that* bad. I warned you. I told you what you were getting into when you first started seeing him."

"But he didn't lie to me, Deena. He told me the first day that some would say these things about him, but he said that he wanted to change; that he was ready to change. And I trust him. He hasn't given me any reason not to. Of course, the first six weeks, his phone would not stop ringing. But those women gradually stopped blowing up his phone." She frowned. "All but crazy-ass Hope. She's going to make me check her ass."

"Well, rumor has it that she was promised to Chase."

Madison laughed. "Promised to him? What is this, the Middle East? There are no fixed unions in America."

"What's so funny?" Gina asked from behind.

"Yes, what's the joke?" Tasha asked.

Deena answered. "We were just talking about how folks swore Chase would eventually end up with Hope Gardener. You know how she would be the one Chase eventually settled down with?"

"Well, they were wrong," Gina said.

"Dead wrong," Deena agreed.

"Yes, because Madison done put it on him," Tasha said. They all laughed.

"Yes, you did, Madison. Chase was by the house the other day, and it was Madison this, Madison that. When I told Lance, he didn't believe me."

"No one thought he'd settle down," Deena said.

Snatching a glass of champagne from a server walking by, Tasha said, "I now believe that there is a God." They all laughed.

Chase walked up. "Hey, ladies, I need to borrow Madison. She sorta promised me something."

Madison winked, and the girls giggled. "And what's that, Chase?" Gina inquired.

"Wouldn't you like to know?" Deena teased. "Go and handle your business. She waved a hand at Madison.

"We'll be back," Madison yelled over her shoulder as Chase pulled her away.

They were cut off by Hope. "Chase, hold on a minute. Where you running off to? It's time for Daddy's toast. Oh, hi, Madison," she said when Chase pulled her up beside him. "I didn't see you."

Madison clicked her tongue. "I'm sure you didn't. We were on our way out. Would you excuse us?" She pulled Chase's hand to leave.

"Fat bitch."

Madison stopped in her tracks and turned back. She narrowed her eyes. "*What* did you say?"

"*Excuse* me?" Hope made a wide-eyed, innocent face.

"Yeah, that's what I thought. Baby, let's go."

"Yes, let's." Chase put his arm around Madison's waist and pulled her in for a kiss before they walked out.

When they got to her Suburban, Chase got into the driver's seat.

"The nerve of her."

"Baby, don't sweat that," he said. "Hope's a joke."

"I know, but if she thinks that, imagine what everyone else is thinking."

"Does it matter? What matters is what *I* think."

"And what's that, Chase? I've also been told you've never been with a plus-sized woman before. What made you pick me?"

He swallowed hard and rubbed his head.

"Seriously, Chase."

"Baby, what? What do you want me to say? I think you're beautiful. At first glance, I wasn't thinking 'Oh, she's hot,' but after talking to you and spending time with you, that changed."

"So, you were not attracted to me when we first met?"

"Do you want me to be honest?"

"No, I want you to lie. Come on, Chase; I want the truth. What were your thoughts of me when Damon introduced us again for the *fourth* time?"

"I was thinking 'She's pretty. A bit heavy but pretty.'"

"And that's it? Not that I was a 'fat bitch'?"

"Hell no. I will admit the truth, and this is only because I'm in love with you, Madison. You are beautiful to me inside and out, baby. I honestly had never dated, touched, or even approached a full-figured woman in my life; well, maybe back in college, once, but after just talking to you that night, after hearing your laugh, your conversation . . . And that smile, baby. Your smile is hypnotic. Your eyes, those light brown eyes . . . You just won me over. So, no, initially I wasn't attracted to you. But who cares? I'm attracted to you now, and I love you."

She wasn't thrilled with that answer, but he was with her—a plus-sized beauty—and not Hope the six back in the banquet hall. "Let's go home," she said, looking out of the window.

Chase sighed. "Baby, please tell me that you're not mad."

"No, I'm not. What matters is the here and now."

"You're right," he said and cranked the engine.

They drove back to her place in silence, and when they got in, she went straight up to her room and undressed. She was in a bad mood, but when Chase joined her in the shower and went down on his knees to lick her clit, all was forgotten. He lifted one of her thick thighs over his shoulder to gain better access, and she came at the sight of him pleasing her center.

Although he begged to penetrate her raw, she insisted that he use a condom until she started her pills.

He pleaded again, promising he'd pull out. "Baby, I just want to feel your flesh again."

"I want to feel you too, baby, but I can't. We can't get pregnant."

"Okay," he said and put on the plastic. They made love, and when they finally collapsed, Madison promised herself that she'd forget all she heard and trust her man.

Chapter Seventeen

Chase sat outside of Madison's newly remodeled salon, now also a spa, with a ring in hand. Everyone was going to be there, but he was scared as hell to ask her. Not that he thought she'd say no, but he wondered if he could actually be a husband, a one-woman man. He had made it five months with Madison, and he didn't need that last month to prove he was capable of getting to know and stay with one woman. His brothers did know what was best for him. Why they chose Madison was a mystery, but he was glad they did.

He got out, let out a deep breath, and put the ring into his pocket and grabbed the rose bouquet from the passenger seat. "It's now or never," he told himself. "I'm ready. Madison is perfect for me. Not picture-perfect to the world, but picture-perfect to me." He straightened his tie.

"Baby, you finally made it," Madison said when he walked through the door. "I was wondering what was keeping you."

"I'm sorry, babe, got a little behind." He kissed her. "These are for you. Congratulations. The place looks amazing."

"Thanks. And you are wearing that suit. Blue looks good on you, Daddy."

"Well, red does compliment your beautiful skin," he said, caressing her arm.

"Madison, can we get a photo of you and Chase?" the photographer asked.

"Of course. Let me put these down." She put the roses to the side on a little table. Chase wrapped his arm around her waist and pulled her in close to him.

"Now, face him," the photographer instructed after he'd snapped the picture.

She did as instructed, and Chase smiled at her. "You're beautiful, and I love you," he said.

The camera captured their kiss.

"Beautiful. That was perfect. Now, we need you over here," the photographer told Madison.

"You don't mind, do you, baby?"

"No, no, do your thing. I'll go get a drink."

She smiled brightly and followed the photographer.

Yes, you're doing the right thing, Chase said to himself. *She is just what I need.*

"Chase," an unfamiliar voice called out. He turned to see Tony standing there.

"Anthony, how are you? Sorry about your dad. I know it was a short time ago, but I hadn't had a chance to see you and offer my condolences."

"I'm good and thank you. It was hard in the beginning, but I'm coping."

"Good."

"So, this place turned out nice. I think Madison has done well for herself, considering all she's been through."

"Yes, she has. She's a trooper. Strong and a survivor. I think she can handle anything."

"Yeah, everything but heartache."

Chase knew where the conversation was going, so he dove in. "Meaning?"

"I know you've managed to stick around for what, four or five months, which is probably a stretch for someone like you."

"What do you mean, *someone like me,* Anthony? You don't know me like you think you do."

"No, I don't know you, but your reputation speaks for itself. Now, Madison is a good woman, a great person from a good family. If you mean her any harm, I suggest you end it now and move on."

"Are you threatening me, Mr. Reed?"

"No, I wouldn't dare do that, Mr. Storm. But if you break her heart, I *will* show up at your door."

Chase almost laughed out loud in his face. "Let me say this, and let's be clear. The only woman you need to be concerned about is your *wife.* I had my days of playing the field, but I was single. You, on the other hand, weren't when you were creeping around Madison's door. I'm not like you. I played the field when I was free to do so. I'd never do to Madison what you did to your wife, so you need not worry about me and my woman's business. The image you have in your head of who you think I am—or was—is not the man I am today. When I decided to settle down, I decided it would be with Madison. So, go find your wife and stay out of my business, because I'm sure you wouldn't want her to know just how *protective* you are of Madison."

Tony's nostrils flared, and he gritted his teeth. Chase saw his fists ball up at his side, but then they heard a female's voice.

Tony turned in that direction. "Simone," he said.

"Hey, baby," the pregnant woman approaching them said. "Can we go? My back is killing me."

"You must be Mrs. Reed," Chase said.

"Yes, I am."

"I'm Chase. Your husband was just over here telling me how happy he was for Madison and the reopening of her new place."

"Yes, it's very nice. I finally had the chance to meet her. They dated back in high school," she chuckled.

"Did they?"

"Yes, and it's amazing that they are still friends after all these years."

"Yes, it is. Most women would feel a little weird."

"Nah, I know he loves me now. That was way back in high school," she said rubbing her belly.

"Well, I agree. Tony, you should be getting the little lady home. Looks like she needs to take a load off."

"Yeah. Come on, Simone, let's go." He gave Chase a look over his shoulder, and Chase waved with a big smile on his face.

The evening continued with speeches from the different stylists that had worked there in the past and the current ones who were anxious to open. Finally, after Martha spoke, she turned it over to Madison.

"Tonight has been a night, and I thank everyone who came out to our grand opening party. I want to give a huge thanks to Storm and Sons Construction for all the hard work you put into this place to make it fabulous, and I also want to thank my mom for trusting me with her baby. This salon holds hundreds of memories for the locals here in Tyler, young and old, and we are looking forward to creating new memories in the years to come. Again, thank you all," she said.

Everyone applauded, but Chase interrupted. "Hold on, hold on, hold on," he yelled. "Everyone, hold on."

The room got quiet.

"Baby?" Madison looked puzzled.

Chase held up a hand. "I have one thing I'd like to add. I won't take up a lot of your time, I promise," he said. The crowd murmured. "My name is Chase Storm. Most of you know me as the fourth-born son of Legend and Estelle Storm. Over the years, I've been labeled as the town bad boy, a player, ladies' man, gigolo, and womanizer, yadda yadda yadda. I've heard it all." There were more whispers, but he continued. "Well, that was all true about me up until almost six months ago. My brothers and my parents and the lovely ladies of my family all suggested that I settle down and find a good woman. And let me tell you, for a very long time, I wasn't trying to hear any of them. That was . . . until I met Madison. She . . ." He paused, looking at her. "She sat down with me at my parents' anniversary party and argued with me on every subject we discussed. If I said right, she said left. If I said up, she said down. But she had this quality, this confidence, which captured me, and I just had to see her again. For the first time, I found someone I wanted to talk to and get to know." He smiled at her, and she smiled back.

Chase slowly approached Madison and went down on one knee in front of her. Her face froze in a look of shock, and he could imagine their audience looked the same. All but Madison's dad was surprised by this because Chase had talked to him before purchasing the ring.

"Madison, you've changed my life. I am the man I was meant to be because of you, and I will love you to the end of the earth if you'd accept my ring and be my wife." He opened the box.

She opened her mouth to speak, but nothing came out at first. "I-I-I," she stuttered. Finally, she gave up trying and nodded.

Chase grinned and pushed the ring on her finger before coming up and hugging her tightly. He kissed her as the room exploded in conversation.

"You mean this?" Madison asked. "You really mean it?"

"Of course, I do, Madison. You're the one. I told you that."

"I am." She smiled. "I am," she said again.

She wrapped her arms around him and gave him a slow and passionate kiss. When they pulled apart, the crowd surrounded them, and Madison was bombarded

by her mother and her future sisters-in-law, all trying to
see the ring. They surrounded her, and Chase lost sight
of her.

He started to work his way to her but was pulled away
by his brothers and father. They forced him outside.

"Dude, you proposed?" Travis asked. Chase could see
they were all thinking the same thing.

"Yes. I told you, I love her."

"Okay, Chase," Lance said. He stood stiffly with his fists
balled up at his side. He was ready to put a beating on his
baby brother if that's what it took. Chase was only in it
for the money, and he couldn't stand by and watch him
do something so horrible to Madison. She didn't deserve
heartbreak, and he hated that they had chosen her for
their wager. "This has gone far enough. We can't let you
do this to Madison. Did you see her face?"

"Guys, listen. For real, I know what I'm doing. This is
no joke; this is no game. I really love her."

Their dad paced. "Son, if you take this girl to the altar
and marry her and then leave her in a year, you will pay
back every cent."

"Dad, this is so not about the money."

"Cut the crap, Chase," Damon yelled. "This isn't funny
anymore. I mean, I don't want you to hurt that woman."

Chase was tired of trying to convince them. "Fine; fuck
it. Think what y'all want to think.

I'm going back in to enjoy my night with my fiancée.
You can sit out here and go back and forth for all I care.
I'm marrying her because I *want* to, *not* because of you."

Just then, Madison stepped out. "Baby, are you okay?"

Chase took a few deep breaths and calmed himself. He
didn't want to upset Madison or give her any reason to
question him. "Yeah, baby, I'm fine. Just having a little
meeting with the Storm men."

She looked at them. "Don't worry, guys, I'm going to take care of him and make him happy."

"I know you will, baby. Let's go back inside to the party." Chase grabbed her by the waist and escorted her back in.

"So, what do we do?" Travis asked.

"There's nothing we can do," Lance said. "Chase is going to marry her, get the money, and then dump her."

"Why did we do this, guys? Madison is a good girl. She doesn't deserve this," Travis said.

"Maybe we should warn her," Damon suggested.

Their father spoke up. "We do nothing. Let's leave him to do whatever he does. We started this, so we have to finish it. Maybe he does love her; maybe it's for the money. For whatever reason, he proposed, so we have to wait it out. Next month, you fellas give him what you promised, and on their wedding day, I give what I promised. What happens after that is out of our hands."

Lance agreed. "Pop is right. There's nothing we can do. If we warn her and he's for real, we'll ruin it for him."

"I know," Travis said. "So, we wait?" Damon said.

Lance sighed. "I'm afraid so."

After everyone was gone, Chase stayed behind with Madison so she could lock up. "Baby, leave that," he said when she started straightening the room up. "The cleaning crew will be here bright and early to handle all of this. You don't have to clean a thing."

"I know, but I hate to leave this beautiful place in such disarray. Did you really have to order two more cases of champagne? Look at all these bottles."

"I know, but I'm ready to get you home." He pulled her into his arms.

She smiled. "Why?"

"You know why. It's been a month since you've started your pills, so tonight, I can feel *all* of you."

"I know you want to, baby, but I think we should give it another month."

He frowned. "Why?"

"You know why."

"We've talked about this, Madi. I know children are not at the top of your list, and I'm not anxious to be a father, but I want to be close to you. I want that connection that lovers have when they are skin-to-skin. I can't forget that night and how good you felt and how soft and wet your pussy was. Baby, I want to feel you again. If we get pregnant, it's meant to be. You will be a great mom," he said.

She pulled away. "I don't want more children."

He thought his ears were deceiving him. "What? Say that again."

"I . . ." She spoke in a whisper. "I'm just . . ."

"Come on." He grabbed her purse and keys and escorted her to the door. "Let's go home and talk about this, baby." He turned out the lights and locked up for her. "Leave your truck. We'll get it tomorrow."

On the short ride home, they were quiet. He glanced over at her and saw her playing with her engagement ring and staring out the window.

He pulled into his drive and got out and helped her out. "Thank you, baby," she said.

Madison kicked off her shoes and headed for the kitchen when they went inside. Chase loosened his tie and went to the bedroom. He took off his suit, and when he came out of his walk-in closet, in his briefs, she was sitting on the love seat with a glass of champagne.

"Did you pour me one?" he asked.

"On your nightstand."

He walked over to retrieve it and went over to sit with her. She had removed all of her jewelry except her new engagement ring but still wore her dress.

"Baby, talk to me. Tell me the truth. Why don't you want kids?"

Her eyes welled, and she sniffled. "I'm afraid," she said.

"Afraid of what, babe?"

"Losing them. God gave me two beautiful little boys and let me fall deeply in love with them, and then he took them back." A tear fell, and she took a drink. "What if he doesn't see me fit to be a mother . . . or even a wife?"

"Wow, baby. That is a heavy thing to carry in your heart. I'm not a religious guy, and you know that, but you also know I believe in God. I don't know all the scriptures and all the things that a man of God would say right now, but I do know what I've learned over the years, Madi." He turned her to face him. "God is not cruel. My mother told me that God is a God of restoration. When you lose something, Madison, it may not be because of something you did or didn't do. You thought you'd never love again, but here we are, and I know you love me. I'll never attempt to compare your love for Dre to your love for me because the love you've given me is enough.

"If God gives you another child and something happens, God has his reasons. He's in control, baby, and we can't stop living or falling in love or having children because we lost a child or children or a spouse. It's not fair to hold up our future for things that happened in our past. It's not fair to you or me. So, please, let's go with it and hope for the best. If you prefer to continue to use condoms, I'll respect that for now, Madison, but if you go through with this and marry me, I want children with you."

She was quiet for a few moments. "What if—"

He put his finger over her lips. "What if we have five more and they all grow up and make us grandparents? We don't know, Madison, but I'm willing to go on this adventure of the unknowing with you because I love you."

She smiled. "I love you too."

He leaned over and kissed her. He wanted her. He wanted to feel her, and unless she said the word, he had no intention of wearing a condom. After intense foreplay, he was finally inside of her. Flesh to flesh, skin to skin. It was more intense, more satisfying this time. He heard himself call out her name several times. He exploded inside of her just as her orgasm hit, and she called out his name.

"Are you okay, baby?" he asked afterward.

She turned over and rested her head on his chest. "I'm perfect, Mr. Storm. Just perfect."

Chapter Eighteen

Madison sat in her closed-in porch and looked at the lake and sipped her wine. She had the soft sounds of the Isley Brothers playing on her iPod dock and thoughts of Chase running through her mind. She told herself that it was okay to love again and that having more kids would be perfectly fine.

She'd found herself talking aloud to her dead husband and sons, assuring them that no one would replace them or make her forget them. At times, she thought she was crazy, but she just felt a little guilty. She knew they were dead and gone, but she had moments when she felt like she was betraying them.

"Hey, lady," Deena, called out, interrupting her thoughts.

"Deena, you scared me."

"I was out front ringing the bell for five minutes. Since I heard music, I decided to come around and go through your French doors. You always keep them open."

"Yes, and I'm sorry. Time got away from me, and I forgot you said you'd be by with the bridal books."

"Yes, ma'am, and after I fix a glass of whatever you're drinking, we can look through some of these. Carla is a great planner. She did all of our weddings. You're going to love her."

"I hope so. I'll go in and get you a drink. Have a seat. I'll be right back."

Madison went inside and poured Deena a glass of wine and brought it out along with a tray of fruit, cheese, and crackers for them.

"Oh, thank you, girl. I need a snack like nobody's business."

"Me too. So, what do you have for me?" Madison asked.

Deena handed over the magazines. "Go through them and highlight some of your ideas. When you meet with Carla, you can show her your taste. You know, give her something to work with."

Madison put the books to the side. "I will." She looked out at the lake.

"So, are you sure you're ready?"

"I guess. Honestly, I have my moments when I feel like I should stay single and never have another child, but then I think that if it were me who had died, I'd want Dre to find someone else."

"Yes, sad but true. Life goes on. And you are still young. You need love in your life, and a couple more kids will make you happy, Madi."

"You think so?"

"I know so. But who'd have thought it would be Chase? I can honestly say that I've seen a change in him. He really loves you, Madi. When he talks about you, his eyes sparkle. He wears a smile all the time. I've never seen him like that, ever. Travis and I still debate about it."

"Debate? Why?"

"Well, Travis thinks he's going through a phase; doesn't think he's sincere. But I told him that Chase of all people would not have turned in his player card if he wasn't truly ready."

"Well, I sure hope you're right because if he is playing, I'm going to gut him like a fish," she joked. They both laughed.

"I know that's real." Deena held up her drink, and they clanked glasses. "I'm just happy for you both. You needed a love, someone exciting and with character. Chase certainly has character, and he needed someone like you to bring him down a notch, to show him real, wholesome love. Them hoes he was running behind back in the day were no good for him."

"Still, I can't see that Chase. Lord knows I'm glad I didn't know him, because if I had, I might have never gone out with him."

"That's for damn sure," Deena said and sipped. "Oh, before I forget, Gina is giving Lance a birthday party Saturday after next at her house. I'm not sure if Chase mentioned it. I'm not even sure if he knows, but we need all the sisters, including you, now that you're going to be one of us, to make a couple of dishes. You need to call Gina and asked what she needs you to make. Be prepared to make two large pans of whatever you're assigned because the Storms do nothing small. The guys are going to grill."

"Okay, let me call her," Madison said. She dialed the number and put Gina on the speaker. "Hey, Gina, I'm sitting here with Deena, and she was telling me about Lance's party. Do you know what you need me to make?"

"Oh, girl, I'm so glad you called. I'm sitting here with Mom and Tasha now. Why don't you and Deena come over?"

Madison looked at Deena, and she nodded. "Okay, we're coming. See you in a bit." They hung up, then headed out to their cars and hurried inside when they got to Gina's. "Hey, ladies," Gina called out when they walked in.

"Hey," they said in unison. The women exchanged hugs and kisses. "Madison, let Momma see that ring again."

Madison held up her hand. "This is a ring. You ladies ought to be on your men for an upgrade. Chase put all of them to shame with this one."

"Well, I happen to love my ring," Tasha said.

"I love mine too. . . . But an upgrade wouldn't hurt," Gina said.

Deena agreed. "You ain't never lied. I mean, Chase did do it big. That ring is gorgeous, Madison."

"That means she got some good coochie," Mom kidded. They all laughed.

"Hold on, hold on. *I* got some good coochie too," Deena said.

"So do I," Tasha and Gina echoed at the same time.

"Well, I don't know about all of that, Mrs. Storm," Madison said. "All I know is I ain't mad at him, because this ring right here is gorgeous." They all giggled and high-fived.

They poured wine, discussed party plans, and everyone's dishes were assigned. When Lance walked in, they all got quiet.

"Don't get quiet because of me. I'm going straight to my man cave." They all snickered. "Baby, come here," Gina called out.

"Yes, dear," he said, pretending to be annoyed.

"Have you gotten a good look at Madison's ring?"

"No, can't say I have."

"Show him the ring, Madi," she said with a little smile. Madison held up her hand. "Do you see that stone, baby?"

"Yes, I see it. If I was across the room, I could see it."

"And Chase got that ring; Chase, your *baby brother*. How long we been married?"

"Almost ten years. Baby, where is this going?"

"You know how you go and get a new car or buy a new television because you want to move with the times?"

"Yes," he said, raising a brow.

"Well, I think you need to hit the jewelry store tomorrow." She threw her left hand up in front of his face. "I think I need an upgrade," she said. The women laughed.

"Baby, your ring is fine," he tried to protest.

"And so is the bed in the guest room," she countered.

"Point well taken," he said. He kissed her forehead and hurried out of the kitchen.

"Oh hell, I'm getting an upgrade too," Tasha said, grabbing her handbag and keys. I gotta get home and inform Damon that the guest room will be his *permanent* room if I don't get more bling on this finger."

"You guys are so wrong," Madison said. "Now, they are going to be mad at Chase."

"No, they won't," Mom said. "Hell, they ain't broke. They spend money easily on cars and golf clubs and stupid shit like that, so a bigger diamond is in order."

"I know *that's* real," Deena said and stood. "I'm going to head home too and make *my* demands." She and Tasha left, and Madison walked out with Mom.

"Madison," Mom said.

"Yes, ma'am?"

"Thank you."

"What for?"

"For whatever you did to win my baby over. I was beginning to worry that he'd be out there for the rest of his life, but you . . . I don't know what kinda coochie you got, but it locked my boy down. He loves you, Madison. A mother knows. I've never seen a look of love in my son's eyes until you, so thank you." She gave Madison a tight hug before they separated, and Madison headed to her car.

Chapter Nineteen

Chase paced back and forth, wondering what in the hell Hope was talking about. He had just sent her a revised budget report for the upgrades and changes she and her family had made. She said that the numbers didn't match the quote and that her figures didn't agree with his. That was bullshit. Chase was a lot of things outside of the office, but when it came to numbers and his job, he was a whiz. What she was saying wasn't making any sense.

"Hope, I'd love to go over this line by line and item by item, but I can't tonight."

"Well, maybe we should take our business elsewhere, Chase, since your clients are not important to you," she griped.

Chase's nose flared, his jaws clenched, and he balled his fists. He wished his family would have never taken on the Gardeners' project. Working with Hope was like working with a horny mule. She wanted him and tried to seduce him every opportunity she had. She was too heartbroken and astounded that he was with Madison, and there was no chance for them. He knew that was her lifelong dream since college, but it wasn't going to happen, and he wished that she and her family would accept that he had proposed to Madison.

In some conversations with the bitter one, she'd talk shit about Madison and Martha like they betrayed her family in some way or she'd make mention of how Madison was always jealous of her since they were kids.

She'd go on and on about Madison only wanting what belonged to her, and he couldn't comprehend for the life of him how she thought his and Madison's love and marriage was a big scheme to get back at her over some childhood vendetta. Only he knew why it was Madison and not her, but he didn't care to enlighten her on his family's business, so many times, he'd just let her ramble on like a fool while he chuckled inwardly.

"Hope, you know that's impossible, right? Construction is already underway. If you pull out now at this stage, your dad's company will lose more money than it's worth. Now, I want to figure this out, but I can't do this tonight." He looked up when Madison walked in. She smiled and kissed him on the cheek. "If you come by my office in the morning, we can go over this line by line."

"I have to go to our finance board in the morning, Chase, so this has to be done tonight," she pressed.

He sighed with much frustration. Hope Gardener was definitely his least favorite person in the world. "Fine, meet me at my office in an hour."

"That's more like it," she said. He hung up.

"What's wrong, baby?" Madison asked.

"Hope Gardener. She's a pain in my ass." He threw his phone on the sofa.

"What does she want now? That chick is relentless."

"She swears the numbers I sent her are not matching up, and this . . ." He paused. He wanted to say bitch, but he'd never call a woman that in front of another woman. "She wants a line-by-line."

"Okay, so we go and give her a line by line."

"We?"

"Yes, *we*. Do you think for a second I'm going to allow you to go in at what, eight forty-five at night alone?"

"Yes, that's exactly what I was thinking."

She raised both brows high. "So, I can't go?"

"I prefer you not to go."

She put her hands on her hips. "And why not?"

"First, because you should trust me. If you go rolling in there with me, Hope will know she has you shook. Second, as a man, I don't need my woman tagging along to make sure I behave. You're going to have to trust me, Madison. I don't roll like that. I go alone. I will handle my business and then come back and handle you."

"Oh no, wrong answer. Either I go, or I go home."

"Seriously? Madison, I don't do chaperones or babysitters. If I tell you I'm going to handle business, that's what I mean."

"Really? And with your track record, I'm supposed to believe that?"

Stunned by what she said, he laughed a little. "You're not serious, are you?"

"Dead serious."

"Okay. Well, if that's what you think of me, go home. After all this time, my past has never had any effect on our relationship, but now you want to hit me with that bullshit. Do what you gotta do, Madison!" He walked away and headed to his room to get dressed.

She ran after him. "Chase, you're blowing me off because I don't trust you going to see Hope alone?"

He stopped and turned to look at her. "Nope. I'm just not dealing with this bullshit, Madison. I've never cheated on you. I'm with you because I want to be with you. I put a fucking ring on your finger, and I've committed myself to this relationship. You didn't even know me in my running days, but you come at me with that? Like I've ever given you a reason not to trust me?" He shook his head. "I'm just not that guy to deal with bullshit. I cater to you; I love you; I shower you with love and affection. What you are doing right now, I don't deserve it. Now, I'm going in to work to handle Miss Gardener's account, and as I said before, then come home and handle you. If you are here when I get home, we'll make love, sleep well, and wake up in each other's arms. If you want to leave, leave, and I'll see you later." He brushed past her.

Madison stood in one spot and listened to the water run as her man brushed his teeth for his meeting with the other woman. She wanted to move, but her feet were frozen. He came out a few moments later, dressed in a pair of slacks and a V-neck shirt, smelling as good as he normally did.

He walked over and planted a kiss on her lips. "I love you, Madison, and only you. I'll be back as soon as I can."

Even after he left, Madison was still planted in the same spot. She was angry as hell, but everything he said was right. Chase had been a gentleman from day one and had only shown her kindness, love, and affection. She stepped out of her shoes and undressed, then went into the master bath and started the water in the tub. She wanted to be hard core and leave like she didn't give a damn, but the truth was, she did. So her ass knew leaving wasn't an option. She was going to welcome her man home and give it to him all night if he wanted it.

She went into the kitchen, poured a glass of red wine, and used the remote to turn on the speakers in the master bath and bedroom. She put her favorite station, Joe's, on Pandora. Back in the bathroom, she stepped down into the tub and relaxed and waited for it to fill.

"Please, Chase, don't let that bitch come between us," she said out loud. She had a great relationship with Chase, she had no reason not to trust him, but that damn, sneaky-ass, man-chasing bitch Hope was an entirely different story. Hope was just one of those types that had no problem doing whatever it took to get whatever she wanted. "You conniving whore. If they all only knew your family's secrets and why our mothers stopped talking years ago when you stopped being my best friend, no one would respect your ass anymore," Madison said and took a sip of her wine. She had sworn to her mother that she'd never utter a word to a soul because Martha was a woman of grace and didn't believe in slinging mud.

When her mom decided she wouldn't speak to Hope's mother again, Martha said that no matter what, she'd never tell anyone what she knew. Her mother knew Mrs. Gardener had her reasons for staying with her husband, but her word was her word. "Hope, you are such a fraud," Madison said and then decided to put Hope Gardener to rest. She wanted to enjoy her wine, bath, and R&B and be ready to please her man when he got home. "No matter how many tricks you have up your slimy sleeve, Chase is in love with me, so I'm good," she declared and then relaxed in her bath.

When Chase arrived at his office, he went inside and powered on his computer. Hope walked in ten minutes later. She looked as good as she always did, and her dress looked as if she planned to hit a night spot after their meeting.

"Okay, Hope, it's after nine, and I don't want to be working this late. Show me the reports."

"All business and no play makes Chase—"

He cut her off. "A dull boy," he finished. "I've heard that before, my dear. Let's go over these numbers so I can get home to my fiancée." At that point, he didn't give a rat's ass about her feelings. It was late and dragging him down to the office at that hour was just it for it, and he was on the verge of telling Hope to pull out and let her family lose whatever they'd lose.

She pulled a file out of her bag and spent thirty minutes rambling and complaining. Forty-five minutes later, he found the error.

"Okay, here is where the discrepancy is. This says one hundred grand when it should be ten grand. That's why you're coming in over budget. I'm not sure how this happened, but if it was our mistake, I apologize. We will get it taken care of first thing in the morning."

"But I need the report tomorrow."

"Hope, just point out the discrepancy, and we will have new files sent over ASAP."

She stood and smiled. "Fine, but if I get shit for this, I'm going to blame you."

"Fine, I'll take full responsibility." He stood. "Now, can we go?"

"Not so fast," she said.

"Hope, it's after eleven. I promised Madison that I'd wrap this up fast. What is it?"

"Why did you lie to me?"

"Lie to you? I've never lied to you. What in the hell are you talking about, Hope? I've never lied to you about anything."

"You did, Chase Storm. You said that you'd wife me when you were ready to settle down, but I hear that you've proposed to Madison after all of these years that I've waited for you."

He let out a breath. "Hope, I said that when I was twenty-four or twenty-five years old. No way did I think you'd hold me to it, let alone take me seriously."

"Well, I did. I've held out and waited for you, Chase, and Madison, of all people in East Texas. I'm not saying she's not a good woman, but she's not me, and she's fat as hell. I mean, when did you start loving the big girls? I know your family loves them brick house women, but *you*, Chase? Why are *you* doing this?" Hope cried.

Chase knew Hope was upset, so he didn't check her on the name-calling. It was an immature statement, but he understood why she was upset with him. "I'm sorry, Hope, but I fell in love with Madison. I didn't plan to fall in love with her, nor did I think it would be her, but it's her. I'm sorry for feeding that crap to you back then. I knew it was bullshit when I said it, but I honestly didn't think you'd hold me to that. We were young, and I wasn't thinking about my future or actually having a future with you, and I'm so sorry."

"So, this is it? Are you *really* in love with her? It's not a rouse or a joke?" she asked with tear-filled eyes.

Chase didn't want to be cruel or hurt her, but it was a done deal. "It is her, Hope. There is no chance for us. I'm marrying Madison. She is the woman I fell in love with. She is my choice, and I am not ashamed of it or embarrassed. Yes, my baby is a 'big girl,' as you say, but she is so gorgeous and sexy to me, and no matter what you or anyone else in this town thinks of her or me, we are in love, and we're getting married."

Tears fell, and she swiped them with the back of her hands. "Well, you've been heard. Loud and clear, Chase Storm. Goodbye, Chase." She grabbed her files and hurried out.

Chase powered everything off and rushed home. Madison's truck was still parked in his driveway, and he was so relieved. He hurried inside and was happy to find her naked under the sheets.

He climbed in bed and held her tightly from behind. "I'm happy that you're still here."

"Me too," she whispered.

"I'll never hurt you, Madison. I'm not that guy anymore. You have nothing to worry about. You can trust me with your heart. Hope is old news, and I don't want her. Even before we met, I didn't want her, Madison."

"I know."

He squeezed her tighter. "I love you so much."

"I love you too, and I'm so sorry, baby."

"For what, Madi? Why are you apologizing, baby?"

"For how I treated you earlier. You have never given me a reason to doubt you or to feel insecure, and how I acted, and the things I said were unfair, and, Chase, I'm sorry. I know you love me, and I know you'd never hurt me like that, and I'm sorry for how I acted."

"I accept your apology, Madison, and I'm glad you truly know me better. My past isn't far behind me, but I've never wanted the old me to interfere with the new me. I fell in love with you so quickly, and things moved so fast that sometimes, I have to stop and breathe and pinch myself. A year ago, nobody could have told me that I'd be in love, engaged, or even be with a plus-sized woman. I don't hate who I was, because I did me, and I never lied or pretended to be someone I wasn't, but I'm glad I changed when I did, and I'm glad Damon introduced us again, Madison. Tonight, I had to apologize to Hope," he said, and her head popped up.

"For what?"

"For lying to her. Madison, I know it was stupid, but I did promise her a ring and marriage. I did tell her years ago that it would be her when I was ready to settle down, but I swear that I never in a million years thought she'd believe me, but according to her, she did. I can tell you, that I never meant a word of it, but I shouldn't have said that shit."

"I can't believe she thought you were serious," Madison said, resting her head back on his arm.

"Neither can I; but she did, and I told her tonight that you are my choice, my love, my heart, and my wife."

"How'd she take the truth?"

"Better than I expected. I mean, she didn't cuss, fuss, or break anything, so I'd say it went well."

"I hope it went well enough to leave us alone. Our town is small, and every time I see Hope, she gives me a look or a snarl. Hope and I were inseparable once, and to think we can't be in the same room now is just crazy."

He pulled her to his chest and held her closer. "What happened with you two?"

"When our moms stopped talking, Hope's mom decided that Hope and I would no longer be friends. Shortly after that, they went away for a long summer out of the country, and Hope and I never spoke again. Years later, after my family died, Hope came by my mom's to offer her condolences, and after that, we went back to being strangers. I hadn't seen her again until our first date, and since then, it's like I see her crazy ass everywhere I go," Madison said with a chuckle.

Chase was silent for a moment or two and then said, "Well, Hope is not a thorn in our sides anymore. I don't want to talk about her any longer. I just want to make love to my fiancée."

"And your fiancée wants to make love to you," she purred.

He planted kisses on the top of her head and then face, moving down to her neck, massaging and pulling her nipples. She turned over to her side, and his dick swelled, and he slid in easily from behind. They had lazy sex that night, and he came inside of her again.

The next day, he tossed out his jumbo box of Magnums. His condom days were done.

Chapter Twenty

"Go outside and quit running in and out of this house," Gina yelled at the kids again.

"I am *not* looking forward to *that*," Tasha said.

"Me either," Madison agreed.

"Well, I love being a mother," Deena replied. "When I had T.J., my world became complete."

"Well, I did enjoy motherhood." Madison smiled, thinking back. "But I had my moments when I needed a break. My boys were very active."

"I'm sorry," Tasha said. "I didn't think when I made that comment, Madison. I wasn't trying to be insensitive."

"It's okay, girl. I'm fine. I miss them, but now I smile more when I think of them."

"Well, I wish I could have gotten to have known them. I mean, you came home, but not often enough back then."

"Girl, you know how it is. Life. Work. Routine. And we get less and less personal time," Madison said.

"True. Travis and I haven't had a vacation in forever."

"Oooooh, we should plan something after the wedding. Or a girls' trip before the wedding. That would be awesome," Gina said.

"That is a great idea. I think we should go to Las Vegas for your shower," Tasha suggested.

"It would be so much fun. Without the guys, of course."

"That does sound fun."

Chase walked in. "Madison, come out here for a second, baby, and tell these fools that I cook." The ladies laughed.

"Yes, you've learned how to cook, baby," Madison confirmed.

"Would you come out here and tell *them* that?"

She stood. "I shall return, ladies."

When she went out, she found the guys all engaged in a debate about Chase being a house husband.

"Now, ask my baby," Chase said. "Ask her."

The men looked at Madison.

"Does this Negro know how to cook?" Damon asked.

"And we're not talking about no eggs and toast. I mean, can he cook a *meal?*" Lance asked.

"Yes, Chase does cook now. Between me, Mom, Gina, and our chef, he knows a little something."

They all laughed at the same time.

"Thank you, baby." Chase pulled Madison in and kissed her. "Now what? See, I take care of my lady," he boasted. "Don't none of y'all cook for y'all women, so I got y'all beat."

Madison went back inside.

Gina was fussing about the kids again. "Girl, Brandon is so damn lazy. His room stays a mess, and he's always begging for a new video game or the latest tennis shoes. That boy gon' make me put his nine-year-old ass out."

"Girl, let me have him for a week," Tasha said. "He'll come back reformed."

"See, that's why you need to go on and have a baby because you think this is easy," Gina said, refilling the ladies' glasses.

"Girl, I grew up with seven siblings. Kids were the last thing on my mind. I was happy when Damon agreed to wait, but now I think I'm ready."

"Well, you are close to forty now, Tasha," Deena said.

"Oh no, I'm only thirty-six. I *just* turned thirty-six, so *forty* is four entire years away, boo," Tasha snapped. They laughed.

"You're a mess, Tasha, I swear," Gina said. The doorbell rang, and she glanced at the clock.

It was close to four, so her guests were starting to arrive.

"Okay, ladies, it's showtime. Y'all know the Storm party rules: keep an eye out for spills and folks' kids standing on my furniture. If someone even *dares* to go near the stairs, stop them in their tracks. There is the spare bathroom down the hall, and the guest bedroom on this floor has a bathroom, so if people are in both, the other party has to hold it. I don't want *nobody* on my second floor."

Chase introduced Madison to his cousins and aunts and uncles and friends of the family. There were so many she couldn't remember everyone's name. She held babies, fixed plates, wiped noses, and blended in with their family. Her parents came, and her mom and Chase's mom teamed up to tell them love secrets, recipes, and ingredients for a successful marriage. They weren't shy about sex talk, either. They were both old-school wives who knew what they were talking about. They both had kept a happy home and husband for over forty years.

As the crowd began to get smaller, the women found themselves inside, while the men remained out. They had talked about everything and somehow talked about the same subjects again.

"Enough talk about these crazy kids of ours," Gina said. "Let's talk about this wedding."

Tasha chimed in, "Yes, Madison, how nervous are you? I mean, you *are* marrying the infamous Chase, the East Texas Ladies' Man." She grinned, and the other ladies exchanged high fives and chortles.

Madison took a sip of her drink and smiled. "I'm fine. I'm not nervous at all. And for the record, Chase has changed. He loves me." She blushed.

"True," Deena said, agreeing with a nod.

"Well, if I would not have witnessed this with my own eyes, I'd tell you to run as fast as you can," Gina said.

"Well, that was my initial reaction when he first asked me out, but after I accepted, he was serious. I discovered he was a great guy," Madison smiled.

"I guess. In all honesty, I think you changed him. The more he hung with you, I noticed a change in him," Deena said.

"Well, as you all know, it took me a little to take him seriously after I heard the rumors."

"Well, good luck, because I'm still not convinced," Tasha said.

Madison ignored her comments about Chase and got up to refill her glass. They didn't know him as she knew him, and she believed that their union was real. After all she had gone through and then to meet Chase, she felt blessed. He was not only wealthy, and from a line of great men, but he was also, without a doubt, fine as hell. He stood at six feet, with a set of sexy lips. Eyes dark and brows thick, and long, beautiful lashes. He had a strong jawline and always kept his mustache and beard lined to perfection. Body, right and tight, and he dressed like a million bucks, even on a casual day. Confident was an understatement if one would describe him because when Chase walked into a room, he owned it. He had been with every gorgeous gal in East Texas, one could say, so imagine how the majority of them felt when he settled with Madison Atkins-Morgan. Even Deena, her best friend, thought it had to be a joke when Madison told her he had asked her out.

Now, after only a little over six months, Madison's left hand housed an engagement ring. And they had set a date for only three more months out. The city of Tyler was still gossiping about the two of them, but finally, the unbelievers were starting to believe.

***

"So, this is really it?" Lance asked his little brother. The large crowd had gone, and the only ones left at the party were the brothers and their mates. The women were now outside on the deck off the kitchen, while the men claimed the deck off the den. Lance and Gina had a huge custom-built home with a wraparound porch and three decks. One off their master, one off the kitchen, and the third one off the den.

"Yes, this is it, man. I mean, Madison is the one."

Head tilted and a brow vaulted, Damon asked, "Chase, seriously, you're not going to pull a crazy stunt or dump her the night before the wedding, or leave her at the altar, are you?"

"No. Damn, man, why can't y'all believe me when I say I'm in love with her? I mean, do you guys think I'd go to this extreme if I *didn't* love her?"

His three brothers looked at each other and burst into a roar of laughs. "Yes, you would," Travis continued to laugh as he spoke.

"Common on, li'l bro, you won the bet. You don't have anything else to prove," said Damon.

Lance added, "Yes. We all know that Madison is not your type, so you can drop the act."

Getting serious, Travis said. "Yeah, Chase. You're going to hurt that woman. She loves you, and you took this bet thing way too far. We expected you to flee after the first date, but here we are, wondering why you took it there. Why did you ask that woman to marry you?"

"Yes, the three million is yours. I'll write you a check tonight before you leave," Lance said.

"Yes, and I'll have one ready for you tomorrow first thing," Damon added.

Travis took a swig of his beer. "Yes, I'll drop my check off tomorrow before I go home."

"Listen, keep your money, okay? The bet means nothing. I know that was the initial agreement. I know I was an ass, and for you three to bet me a mil apiece to date Madison for six months was a bit much, but—"

"So, it *was* a joke?" she said.

All the men turned to see Madison standing there with four cold beers locked in between her fingers. The women had taken turns going to check on the guys, and it was her turn. She headed around the porch smiling but paused when she overheard them talking. She shouldn't have eavesdropped, but when she heard Travis say, "*Yes! Unfortunately, you did what we challenged you to do. Going out with Madison is something we all thought you'd never agree to, so you won the bet, bro. I'll drop my check off tomorrow before I go home.*"

Her voice jolted Chase, and he stood up quickly. "Madison!" he said. "Baby, hold on, it's not what you think."

"Really?" she said and walked up to him. She put the beers on the table and slid the ring from her finger. "You won the bet, so you might as well collect your cash. Stay the fuck away from me, Chase!" She dropped the ring in his drink and hurried off.

"Fuck!" Chase roared and ran after her.

She passed by the women in a rush, with Chase after her. "Wait, Madison. Wait, baby, hear me out, please."

She grabbed her purse and headed for the front door. He grabbed her arm, and she yanked away.

"Get away from me!" she roared. Her face was full of tears. "You're *exactly* who they said you were, Chase Storm. Everybody warned me, even told me that you were a fraud, but I thought they were all wrong. I let you in. I trusted all the things that you said because I thought you changed. All of those nights when you wooed me, I thought they were real. I fell in love with you," she cried.

She wiped her tears. "But you are a snake, and I want you to stay away from me. You are a liar. You are *exactly* who everyone warned me about. You haven't changed one bit."

"I have, Madison. At first, it was a bet, a wager, but now, I'm for real about you. About us. I love you, Madison. I fell in love with you, and I want you. How things began, I'll admit, was crazy, but I'm so glad it happened because I'm madly and deeply in love with you."

She wiped away more tears. "Somehow, I don't believe that bullshit. Now move, Chase." He didn't budge. "Move!" she yelled.

"Chase," Deena called out. "Just let her—"

He raised a hand, cutting her off. "Madison, I love you. I started this under stupid intentions, but what I shared with you is real. What we have is real. I love you so much, with all of me," he said. "Please, let's talk this out. Don't leave like this. I'm so sorry for hurting you, Madison. I love you. Just, please, let me explain. This is real. Where we are right now is real. Please, I love you. Just let me explain."

She looked at him and then slapped his face so hard it sounded like a tree branch breaking. He didn't move, and she turned and rushed out of the kitchen door. She ran to her car, opened the door, and threw her purse so hard it missed the seat and landed on the floor. She pressed the start button and peeled off.

She was humiliated and embarrassed to know that she was a big fat joke. She wondered if the wives were in on it too. "I fell for all of those lying words. All the bullshit, all the lies. You said I was beautiful," she cried.

When she pulled into her circular drive, she sat in her car and cried before getting out. She felt so damn foolish for falling for his game. Just as she got out to go inside, Chase pulled into her driveway.

"Fuck!" she said.

Chapter Twenty-one

"Go home, Chase; get the fuck away from my house!" she yelled.

He ran after her up on her porch. "No. Will you stop for a second and listen to me?" he asked, blocking her front door.

"It was a lie, Chase. You hooked up with me over a stupid wager. How much was I worth, huh? How much did my heart cost? How on earth did you put a dollar amount on love?" she cried. Her eyes filled with tears.

"Madison, baby, please. Let's go inside, and I'll tell you the truth from beginning to end. I swear, if you want me to leave afterward, I will, but you have to know the truth."

She studied him for a few seconds, then moved by him and opened her door. She walked in, and he followed closely. She tossed her purse and keys onto the sofa and leaned against the wall.

"Can we sit?" he asked.

"Talk, Chase," she barked.

"Madison, please, we need to sit."

She hesitated but moved over to the sofa, and he took a seat next to her.

"It all started out as a wager, Madison. I was out of control. I was all over the place, and I wasn't nowhere near the point of settling down. I was everything that they said I was, baby—a man whore, a womanizer, and a player. I owned up to that, and I walked in that role proudly. I thought I could do what I very well pleased because I was single and, most of all, honest. I didn't lead any of them on. I told them the deal, and most of the women I involved myself with were cool with that.

"My family was always on me about my behavior and stressing how I should man up and settle down and be the honest man that my folks raised me to be. I guess the only way to get my attention was a challenge. My brothers knew I'd only do exactly what they'd challenge me to do and to make the pot sweeter, they threw in the cash bonus. I had to get to know one woman and be faithful to her for six months.

"I'll admit, my first thought was this was going to be a piece of cake, but then they threw in that it had to be the woman of *their* choice and no sleeping with other women on the side. I thought, 'Hell no, that's not going to work,' but then I thought, 'Why not?' With that, I agreed, knowing my brothers wouldn't do me wrong. They chose you. At first, I was like, 'Hell no, she is not my type' and 'I'd never go for a woman like her,' but Damon introduced us, and after just five minutes of actually holding a conversation with you, Madison, you drew me in.

"You were the first woman that I paid attention to above the neck. I actually listened to what you had to say. Your conversation was engaging and interesting, and I would have talked to you all night because you were just different. You were the smartest woman that I'd ever talked to, and even though I tried to convince myself that I'd never fall for you, it only took one date to realize I was wrong. After our picnic, your singing to me, I went to them and told them that I really liked you, Madison. But I was so bad back then that they didn't believe me. Every time I tried to convince them that I was falling for you, they'd mock me. Even when I proposed, they still swore I was playing games and that I was going to drop you after I got the money.

"Right before you overheard everything, I swear to you I told them I didn't want the money, and that none of it mattered because you are the one, Madison. Things started out with the wrong intentions, sweetheart, but I promise you, I've changed.

"All I want is you. I need you. I love you, Madison. Six months ago, I didn't think I was even capable of loving a woman, but that all changed. You changed me." He paused as if he wanted her to say something. When she remained silent, he said, "Madi, baby, please say something."

She stood. "Get out, Chase. This so-called truth or confession of yours should have come months ago. I can't even recognize who you are right now, and I have a very hard time believing that I was just so intriguing, so beautiful, and so irresistible, that you fell so deeply in love with me. I don't trust you. What you and your family did to me was bogus. I can't marry you knowing that I was a ploy in some brotherly wager. Now that you're reformed, go and find the woman of *your* choice."

"No, Madison, no. I choose you. I love you. I'm telling you that you are it. I want to marry you. I want to be with you, Madison. What we did was jacked up, and, baby, I feel you, but what about us now? You can't stand here and look me in the eyes and tell me that you don't know that I love you.

"When I make love to you, when I hold you close, when I see your smile, Madison, that is my world. And I need you. I need you. I can't leave here without you telling me that we can work it out. Baby, I'm sorry about how we started, but I'm not sorry I fell in love with you.

"Please. Madison, baby, I'm sorry. I'm sorry for not telling you. I'm sorry you found out this way. I planned to tell you the truth, but after we were married. Baby, please, don't call this off. You are my world, Madison."

"I thought I was. Now leave."

"No."

"Come again?"

"I'm not leaving until you say you forgive me, Madison. I've never been afraid of anything in my entire life, but right now, the thought of losing you . . . The thought of you and me not being together is scaring the fuck out of me, baby. Please, Madison." He moved closer to her and grabbed her as if to kiss her.

She pulled away. "You know what, Chase?" she scowled. "I used to defend you every time someone threw your doggish ways in my face. Used to feel like I was the luckiest woman on the planet to have roped this man that everyone thought was impossible to rope. Everyone said that you were incapable of loving someone other than yourself, and I'd say, 'No, you're wrong. He is gentle, loving, and kind, and he treats me like silk.' I thought your actions were truly genuine." She paused. "How much?"

"Madison, baby, what are you asking?"

"How much was I worth?"

"Madison, please, that has absolutely—"

"How much, dammit!" she yelled.

He let out a sigh. "Three million." He left out the bonus his dad had added.

"At least I wasn't cheap," she sneered. "Get out, Chase. Go and collect your money. Enjoy it, because I'm done with you. For the record, I was fine. I was fine with being single. You and your brothers treated me like a charity case. No, they pimped me out to you, like I'm worthless. Did it ever occur to you that you may not have fallen for me, Chase? Did they consider that you'd break my heart in the process of you becoming a reformed player?" She laughed bitterly and shook her head. "Just leave, Chase. I don't have anything else to say to you."

She turned and headed up the stairs. He called out for her, but she kept going.

Chase's eyes burned with tears. He was hurt. Heartache was a new emotion for him, something he'd never experienced before, and it hurt like a bitch. He left Madison's and drove straight to Lance's.

"Chase," his oldest brother said when he opened the door and let him in.

"Don't fucking 'Chase' me. How could y'all pick Madison? Huh? Why her?" He paced. "I've lost her, you know? She's never going to speak to me again."

"Chase, she's just upset. She loves you. Give it time; this will blow over."

"Fuck that, man. I mean, that's all you got for me? I tried to tell you guys after I started feeling her that my feelings were sincere, but all of you, even Dad, acted as if I were a joke. My life was fine the way it was. I was happy. I didn't have to care about who or what, and now, the first woman I love suddenly fucking hates my guts, L! She never wants to see me again."

Chase fell back on the couch and sobbed. He put his face in his hands and cried.

Lance came over and hugged his baby brother. "We'll help you get her back," he said in a low voice.

"I love her, L. Madison is my baby, my heart. I've never loved a woman in all my life. If I don't get her back . . ." He sobbed.

"Chase, you *will* get her back. I'm so sorry. I know we went about it all wrong, but we thought we were doing what was best. We thought we were helping you."

"Best for who? Now that I've given my heart to someone for the first time, just like that, it's over. Do you have *any* idea what this feels like?"

"No, little brother, I don't. I'm so sorry for what I've done to you and Madison, but I swear I'm going to do my best to make things right."

"Is he all right?" Gina asked in the darkness.

"No."

"I can't believe what y'all did, Lance. What in the hell were you guys thinking?"

"We were thinking of our baby brother."

"And apparently not thinking of Madison."

"Gina, please, I feel horrible enough."

"And you should. If they don't get back together, Lance, both of them are going to be messed up for a while. Chase loves that woman, and this is his first heartbreak. Y'all think he was bad before this. If y'all don't fix it, he's going to be worse than he was before Madison."

Lance processed what his wife said. He prayed he could help to get them back together because he was afraid she was right.

Chapter Twenty-two

The next morning, Madison woke up and looked around her room. She looked down at her clothes and realized that the night before wasn't a dream. She and Chase were truly over and done. He had gone out with her on a $3-million wager, and her eyes welled up all over again. She didn't know how she was going to make it through a day without him because she had fallen so deeply in love with Chase, she felt she couldn't breathe without him, and she was experiencing love loss all over again. She went to the bathroom to relieve her bladder; then she turned on her shower. She slowly peeled off her clothes, and it felt weird, even like make-believe because she'd never *ever* imagined herself to be played like that. She felt like a fool, like she was so worthless that the Storms would play such a game like that with her heart.

After she showered, she went down and got a glass of orange juice to coat her throat, because it felt dry and scratchy. She gazed out her window and looked at the gorgeous lake view and her eyes welled up. She trusted them; she trusted them all, and they'd do that to her. "Sons of bitches," she said and put her glass down. She went for a tissue and dried her eyes. "Just wait until Hope Gardener hears about this one," she cried. "Why would you not tell me, Chase? I thought we were close, and I thought-I thought-I thought," she continued to sob. "I'm going to be the laughingstock of East Texas," she said, then blew her nose.

She got herself together and then went to open the door to get her paper. When she opened the door, she was surprised to see Chase sitting in one of the wicker chairs. He had on the same clothes he wore the night before, and she wondered how long he had been out there on her porch.

"Chase?" she whispered.

He looked up and noted that he looked just as horrible as she did. It looked as if he slept right there on her porch, but she didn't have any compassion for his ass after what he had done to her.

"Can I please come inside and talk to you?"

"We said all there was to say last night," she reminded him.

"No, we didn't, Madison. This just can't be it for us." He stood up from the chair and moved toward her. "I can't accept that we're over. Don't you know how much I love you? Don't you love me?"

"Of course, I do, Chase, but that doesn't mean shit right now. You played me," she shouted.

"Baby, I didn't play you. I was all in, I swear. It started off with the bet for us to meet, Madison, but after our very first date, Madison, the bet didn't mean anything, and I wish you'd stop being so stubborn and forgive me, and let's get back to being who we are," he said.

"And *who* are we, Chase? *What* are we? We are a *sham*," she spat and threw her paper at him. "Don't you get what you Storms did to me is belittling and more than that, childish? If you hadn't agreed to do it and dated me on your own, I'd let it go, but you went along with them, Chase, and we are over. Done. I trusted you, and you played me for a fool!" she cried.

"No," he protested. "We are *not* ending it this way, Madison, and you can't stand here and act as if what we had wasn't real, so stop being so stubborn and forgive me.

I'm so sorry for how this all started, but I'm not sorry that we turned out like this. I love you, Madison. I've never been in love with a woman in my life until you," he cried.

"We're a big fat joke," she continued.

"No, baby, no!" he shouted.

"It was a fucking bet, now get off my damn porch, Chase Storm, before I call Tyler's finest to come and escort you off," she barked. She was too angry and disappointed with him at the moment, and there was nothing he could say right then to make her feel better. She didn't want to see him or be near him.

"Call them. I don't care, Madison, because without you, I'm broken, so call them!" he yelled. "Let them come and take me in because if I can't fix this and make things right, my world is over anyway," he declared.

She looked at him and wanted to reach out and touch him. She wanted to say, okay, I accept your apology, but she wasn't going to be nobody's fool, so she stormed into the house and went for the phone. She came back to the porch to let him know she was for real. "I'm not playing games with you, Chase. Please leave me alone right now. I can't talk to you, and I can't hear you right now, and I need you to leave."

"No, I'm not leaving until you tell me that you forgive me and that you still love and want to marry me and that we can work this out!" he fired back.

"Are you fucking kidding me right now?" she yelled back. Just then, before she called the law, a car pulled up. It was Lance, Travis, and Damon. They all quickly got out and headed up to the porch. She figured a neighbor must have called because of the commotion she and Chase were causing. Their town was big but small, and every-one knew who the Storms were.

"Get your brother off my damn porch," Madison hissed.

"Come on, Chase, let's go," Lance said.

"No, I'm not leaving until we fix this," Chase disputed.

"Get him off my porch before I call the law," Madison threatened.

"Madison, that's not necessary. We got him, and we all owe you a sincere apology," Travis said.

"Don't," she barked. "I don't want to hear an apology. I had so much respect for you all, and this is what y'all do. I mean, if this is what the Storm men are about, I'm glad I dodged this bullet," Madison spat gesturing to Chase.

"Listen, Madison, we honestly meant no harm. We were trying to do something good, for you both, but we just didn't think of the consequences if things didn't work out. We just stupidly never factored that in, but believe me, Chase told us several times that he was in love with you. He told us that all bets were off, I swear, but we're the ones who gave him a hard time," Damon tried to say.

"That's right, Madison, it was us," Travis said.

"Madison, believe me, we had only good intentions for you and Chase," Lance spoke up. "And we are so sorry. You and Chase belong together. Please don't hold it against Chase. He loves you, Madison, and everyone knows it. Please don't let what we did ruin things for you two. We can forget about the six million and put this all behind us," Lance said.

Madison's head tilted to the left, and her eyes widened like saucers. "*Six* million? Chase, you told me three. What is he talking about?"

"Oh shit," Damon said.

"Baby, please, that's not important."

"No!" she yelled. "It's all out in the open now. How in the hell did three mil turn into six mil in less than twelve hours?" she demanded. They all were stone-faced.

"You lied to me again, Chase? Was the marriage double or nothing?" she said trying to piece things together. She was no idiot.

"No, nothing like that," Chase said.

"Listen, Madison—" Lance started.

"No, I want to hear this from Chase. My future husband, the man that loves me so much," she spat and folded her arms across her chest.

"My dad matched the three million if we were to get married," Chase said in a nervous rush. The look of defeat on his face showed Madison that he was well aware that that was the straw that broke the camel's back.

She was done with him and his entire family. "Get off my damn porch and please don't ever come back." She went inside and slammed the door so loud it sounded like a gun going off. She listened to Chase call out for her and beg for her to come back while he banged on her door. She knew his brothers had to physically drag him out to the car because she heard the rumble of their actions from her stairs where she sat for what seemed like hours. She felt numb all over and couldn't feel anything. She didn't want to cry or want to feel anything. She wasn't a drinking woman, not the hard stuff anyway. She had it for guests, but she went for the vodka. By two in the afternoon, she was sloppy drunk and in her worst moment. Her phone was in the lake because she got tired of Chase calling back to back. Sloppy drunk, she was on her living room floor when she heard keys. The only person it could be was her mother, so she shut her eyes real tight and thanked God. Her momma had finally come to comfort her. As soon as Martha joined her on the floor, she cried in her mother's lap until she passed out asleep.

Chapter Twenty-three

It had been nine days, and Chase was in a world of depression. He had called Madison and texted her so many times, and she never answered nor replied. He drove by her house twenty times a day, and she wasn't home. He knew she had gone back to her parents and no way would he be granted entrance past their gate, so he had no idea when he'd see her again because she didn't go into work either.

Chase prayed that she was okay, but if she felt anything like him, he knew deep down she was doing terrible because he barely even recognized himself in the mirror. His place was a mess, and he hadn't washed his ass— *everything* was a funky mess. The doorbell rang, and Chase didn't budge. It rang again. "Go away," he growled, but the person on the other side of the door rang the bell again. "Fuck! Leave me alone," Chase roared, but the persistent person or persons on the other side of the door refused to leave.

Chase didn't bother to get up from the sofa; then he heard his garage door opening. "Who the fuck!" he cussed, rising from the sofa. By the time he was on his feet, the door from the kitchen had swung open, and four well dressed men walked in one by one. It was the Storm men, and they came to get Chase's ass back in gear he figured. Chase was in no mood to hear what any of them had to say, so he looked at them and then flopped back down onto the couch. "Y'all wasted a trip because I have nothing to say to any of you."

Lance spoke first. "That may be true, but you have a job that you've just abandoned, Chase. When do you think you're going to get back to it?"

"You think I give a damn about work right now, Lance?" he yelled, and they all came to the other side so they could stand before him and not behind him. Travis swiped the empty pizza boxes from the sofa and took a seat. Damon posted by the fireplace, and Lance sat on the arm of the sectional. As tailor-made as Legend was, he sat right next to his son.

"Look, Chase," Lance said, but Legend raised a hand to silence him.

"From the looks of things, I'd say that you're not interested in joining the world right now."

"How'd you guess?" Chase said smartly.

"Because you and this place are funky as hell. Now, I know love has whipped your ass, but you are a Storm, and you are going to have to get yourself together, son."

"Really, Dad, really? It's been a little over a week since she left me, and I'm supposed to bounce back just like *that?*" he snapped his fingers in the air. "You tell me how long it takes to heal a broken heart. I mean, y'all come up in here in your tailored suits, fresh to death, expecting me to be okay because I'm a Storm. Well, news flash, I'm *not* fucking okay.

"Look at you, Lance, and Damon. Just look at yourselves, Trav. All of you are fine. You know why? Because none of you have been where I am today. Tell me which one of you has lost the only woman you've loved? Huh? Go ahead, big bro. Tell me in what state of mind you would be if Deena, Gina, or Tasha left?" he barked. "Oh, and you, Dad, how long have you and Mom been together? If you went home, and she was gone, would you just get yo'self together?" he blasted; then he put his face in his hands. "Y'all wanted this, not me. I was happy.

I was happy. I didn't have a care in the world. I only had me to worry about," he sobbed.

His brothers and father were all silent. His father then pulled him into his arms. "You're right, son, and we *are* sorry beyond words. We should have listened to you. We should have believed you, and we're going to do everything we possibly can to fix this."

"How? She won't even talk to me," Chase cried. All of the Storm men's shoulders dropped, and Lance slid onto the sofa from the arm. Damon took a seat on the ottoman, and they sat in silence for a few moments until Lance said, "We came up with a plan to get her; now, we must come up with a plan to get her back."

"No, no more plans," Legend said. "We have to stop trying to move things like chess pieces. As you all can see, it doesn't work like that when it comes to matters of the heart. I'll talk to her, son, and ask her to have dinner with you, and we see if you and Madison can work things out on your own. I owe her an apology just as much, and once I give her my apology, it will only take time for her to forgive what we've done and then decide if she wants to start over with Chase. We can't go in with schemes and strategies. We can only apologize and wait."

"*That's* the master plan, Dad?" Chase asked in disbelief.

"Yes, my son, that is the master plan, and for the record, I will tell you that I know how you feel. Way back in the day before Estelle and I got married, we had a hiccup in our relationship," he said, and Chase sat up straight. All eyes were now on Legend.

"What kind of a hiccup?" Chase asked.

Legend stood and undid his suit jacket and then removed it before sitting back next to his youngest. "Well, back when your mother and I were dating, there was this other gal name Corrina, and, boy, that Corrina was a brick house, you hear me; something sexy, and she knew it. Well, Corrina was working down at the desk at the supply dock, and she had every man's nose opened wide, but she wasn't interested in any of them. That woman wanted me. Now, I was young and stupid. Yo' momma told me that Corrina was just a little too friendly, but me, 'Aww, no, Estelle, she's harmless, and she's just a nice gal,' but yo' momma knew she was up to no good."

"So, what happened, Pop?" Lance asked.

"Well, I was a young nineteen-year-old guy, and I was trying to be cool, and Corrina asked me over to watch TV one night when her parents were going to be gone. Now, I was in front of my boys, right, and didn't want to look soft, so I told her sure, I'll come through. So I went over, and this gal was all over me, and I was scared to death because I was courting your momma. When I say I got the hell up outta her house, I got up outta there and *ran* all the way home. The next day, rumors were going around about how me and Corrina had made out, and yo' momma got wind of me being at her house. She walked up on me in front of everybody and called me a cheating, lying dog and slapped my cheek so hard, you could see the smoke rise off my face," he said, and they all burst into laughter.

"Momma did that?" Damon asked between laughs.

"She sure did and told me she never wanted to see me ever again. And you talking about a broken heart. I wrote her letters, brought her flowers, and followed her around, begging her to take me back."

"How did you get her back?" Chase asked.

"Yeah, Dad, what made you two get back together?"

"Well, I finally gave up trying. It was four months later that your mother decided she loved and missed me enough to accept me back. When she came back, she asked me again, did anything happen between me and Corrina, and I told her that I never touched that girl, and I only loved her, but it was the worst four months of my life."

"So, you know how this feels?" Chase asked.

"Yes, I do, son, and your mother is the only woman I've ever loved this deeply. If she hadn't come back to me, well, let's just say, we wouldn't be sitting here today."

"But what if she never comes back?" Chase asked sadly.

"I think she will. What we did was crazy, but it's nothing you two can't come back from, li'l bro," Damon said.

"If she truly loves you, she'll forgive you at least, and if you two never get back together, Chase, well, we'll have to cross that bridge when we get there, li'l bro. We had good intentions, but we just did it in a fucked-up way," Travis said.

"Yes, we did," Chase said. "I should have just told her the truth when I realized how important she was."

"Well, son, let's move forward. I'll call Mr. Atkins and see if he will allow me a word with Madison. Hopefully, she'll hear me out; then, hopefully, you two can put this behind you."

"I hope so," Chase said. They all stood.

"Now clean up this place."

"Don't push it. I have to get Madison back before I can get back on track."

"Whatever." Lance shook his head. "You stink like hell," he said as they all headed for the door.

"Whatever," Chase said. He took a whiff of his underarms and decided he could at least shower.

Chapter Twenty-four

Madison headed toward Houston, thinking she'd never return to Tyler again. Everywhere she went, people whispered about her and Chase. She was the laughingstock of the town now that word had gotten out, so she figured she would lie low for a while. Besides that, she was tired of running into Chase and people advocating on his behalf. She had visit after visit from someone trying to convince her to talk to him. His brothers came by every day, so she moved back to her parents' just to not have a Storm ring her doorbell every five minutes. They told her Chase really loved her. Hurt and embarrassment had destroyed her world, and she wanted to get away from it all. Then when her father came to her and spoke to her about seeing Chase's father, she refused. She didn't want to see another Storm. Her dad told her that she was being a bit stubborn, and for a moment, she considered what her daddy said, but decided it was her life, and she'd be as stubborn as she wanted to.

She'd had an encounter with Hope, and the only thing that kept her from ripping the other woman's eyeballs out was Deena, who happened to arrive just in time to break them up. Hope had said that now that Chase was a "free man," she'd make him hers, and Madison wanted to beat her to a pulp. Deena couldn't confirm whether Chase was seeing Hope or any other women, because he was barely speaking to his brothers and hadn't been to his office since the breakup.

Madison couldn't get out of town fast enough. She had hired an assistant manager before the salon's reopening. She could handle the day-to-day management, and whatever Madison needed to do could be done from her laptop or tablet.

"Why are you running away, chile?" her mother had asked while she was loading up to leave. It had been three weeks of ducking and dodging Chase, his brothers, their wives, and Chase's parents. After the flowers, phone calls, text messages, and Facebook posts from Chase had ceased, she guessed he had given up trying to win her back and was with Hope, the sexiest bitch in Tyler, or back to his old whoring ways.

"Momma, please. You know why. We've been through this. My relationship with Chase was a joke, a big fat lie, and now he's with Hope. I wish them well."

"Madison Grace, now I know you don't believe that bullshit. From day one, you were caught up in a magical romance with Chase. As I've told you, it doesn't mean a hill of beans how you two came together. What matters is how you end up. And, Hope . . . You know she only said that to get under your skin. Humph, with her family's secrets, she need to go and sit down some-damn-where. Hope Gardener has nothing on you. She's a spoiled bitch, and you're doing *exactly* what she wants you to do. It's okay to take him back if you truly love him, darling, and I know you miss him. It doesn't matter about the bet. You fell in love, something you thought you'd never do after Dre," Martha said tenderly.

Madison paused and thought about what her momma was saying. She did miss him, and she did want him back, but how could she go back to him after what he and his family had done to her? Why didn't he just tell her? Would it have changed things, or would she have still left? Madison was even more confused about what she should do. She needed to get away from Tyler. Clear her mind, sort things out, and reevaluate it all. The answer about what to do wasn't going to come easy. She blew out a breath.

"Mother, what you are saying is right, but I don't know. All I know is that we ended up here, Mother. We are done."

"Because you won't take him back. Chase has done everything in his power to win you back, but you won't budge. I know you're hurt, pissed off, and feel like this was all a joke, but it wasn't, baby. Yes, this all started with a bet, a stupid bet. Men do dumb shit like that, Madison. They think they're clever, but we both know that they're not, and in the process, you put a move on the man's heart, and he loves you."

"Why didn't he tell me, Ma? He could have told me."

"And would you have stayed, Madi, or would you have done what you're doing now? You kicked the man to the curb. I know you love him, baby. He was a jerk for agreeing to something so foolish, but that wager, that bet, or whatever his brothers put him up to, put two hearts together. Chase is not that same old playboy that he was. When he talks about you, Madi, his eyes dance. His words are sincere, and if he didn't give a damn, he'd have said fine and not even attempted to win you back. Don't leave like this. You and Chase can start over. I know you love him."

Madison was quiet. She did love him, and her heart ached for him. She was just still so damn angry.

She felt like a project or a specimen. She was the ugly girl someone paid $6 million to date. The feeling was awful.

She had thought their romance was genuine, but it was a setup. She couldn't get past that. "I gotta go, Mother. I'll be in touch," she said. She grabbed her last bag and put it in the truck and then shut it. She got in and cranked her engine as her mother stood on her porch and watched her get into her car. "All of my bills are set up on autopay. The only mail I should get is junk. I love you, Ma," she yelled and waved bye.

"I love you too. You're making a big mistake, Madison Grace."

"Oh yeah? It's *my* mistake to make. I'll call you when I get there."

She pulled out and headed toward the highway. She drove telling herself she was doing the right thing. Something in her wanted to go to Chase's and tell him she would take him back, but she drove on.

"Nakia," she yelled when she saw her friend. They hadn't seen each other since the death of Dre and the boys.

"Look at you, girl," Nakia said. "I thought I packed on the pounds."

"Don't even start that shit."

"You know I ain't trippin'. Come on in." Madison followed her inside.

The two women sat up all night drinking and catching up. The next morning, Madison woke up and found herself alone. She figured Nakia had gone to work. She showered and decided to get out. She visited some of her old stomping grounds, her old job, and caught up with a few old coworkers, and then hit the grocery store before heading back to her girlfriend's place.

"Hey, girl, you're cooking?" Nakia said when she walked in. She went to the fridge and grabbed the wine to pour herself a glass.

After taking a sip from her glass, Madison said, "Yes, I wanted to fix something nice for you to say thanks for letting me come out here to clear my head."

"Girl, we've been friends since college. You know better. I'm here when you need me."

"I know."

"So, you're really done?"

Madison sighed. "Yes, love is no friend of mine."

"Don't say that."

"I'm serious. As soon as I got out there to love again, I got a fraud. A fake."

Nakia stood and walked around the counter. "Listen, Madi, you need to stop doing this."

"Doing what?"

"I've heard all you've said about Chase, and what he and his family did was a bit odd, but look what happened. You two fell in love. What's the harm in that? And to be the recipient of a few millions ain't a bad rap to me—"

"Chase turned down the money."

"That's even more of a reason to take him back. I'll admit, it was a jacked-up way to hook up, Madison, but after you started to date him, I heard from you more, and every time you sounded superhappy. It's okay to take him back, girl. Especially after everybody has had their two-cent opinions. To show them, marry him and live happily ever after. Trust, there will be no more chatter once you two exchange vows. I mean, you sound crazy as hell up in here complaining about a stupid-ass bet. I mean $6 million, Madison. Hell, introduce me to one of those Storm men. Some men do way worse shit than that. He didn't cheat on you, hit you, nor does he have a secret crazy-ass fetish. The man loves you. He's apologized. His family has apologized. You gon' walk away from love over *that*? Girl, bye!" Nakia said and polished off her wine. She got up to refill her glass. "By the way, when you get married, send yo' girl some of those millions that makes you feel uneasy. I'll spend it," she joked, and they laughed.

Madison gave it a little thought. Chase had been the
perfect gentleman, and he treated her more than well.
And the lovemaking was insane. Was she overly dra-
matic? What is all that serious? Now, she felt a little crazy
for reacting as she had. "Why are you always making
sense of shit?" she asked Nakia.

Nakia smiled. "Because I'm your voice of reason. Just
like in college."

"Yes, you are, but still, I'm going to visit for a little
while, if that's okay. I have to process things. I'm still
mad at him."

"Really, Madison? Seriously?"

"Okay, I'm not mad. But I am embarrassed. I'm no
charity case."

"Girl, the man bet six mil on your ass. And didn't lose.
Hell, call me charity. I'll be like here," she joked raising
her hand. "So, go get your man and make his family pay
up. Hell, send me a couple of million for this session, and
you still have to name your daughter Nakia."

Madison laughed. "Oh my God, I forgot about that."

"Well, I didn't. You just had two boys first, but you
promised you'd name your daughter Nakia, and if you
don't get back to Chase and work on that little girl, it will
never happen."

Madison swatted her arm. "Oooooh, you make me sick,
but I love you."

"I love you too, girl."

"You *are* going to visit me in Tyler?"

"Yes, I promise this time."

"Good, now let's eat. My appetite hasn't been this good
since the breakup."

"Well, your crazy ass should have came here day one of
the breakup, and you and Chase would have been back
together already."

"I guess you're right."

"Hell, I'm always right. Let's eat," Nakia said.

That night, Madison lay in bed dreaming of Chase and making love to him. She woke up and realized the moans she thought were from her dream were not. In the next room, Nakia was making things happen. Madison got up to go for her headphones and then remembered she hadn't packed them.

She went into the kitchen, poured a glass of wine, and sat outside on Nakia's patio. She looked out at the city and thought back to her life with Dre.

He had been a simple guy; nothing fancy about him, and he hadn't taken much time or pride in his appearance. He was a jeans-and-Polo-type of guy, and since they got church from TBN, he didn't have anything fancy to wear. They'd always find themselves hitting the stores for weddings, graduations, or Dre would be the repeat outfit guy.

She smiled because, although he wasn't GQ, he was her friend. He was a great father, and he always managed to take care of business. But he wasn't spontaneous, and he didn't turn it out in the bedroom. She sighed.

Was I really happy, or did I just settle? She loved Dre, there was no question, but after experiencing a whirlwind romance with Chase, she realized things with her husband had been dull. Her relationship with Chase was magical, romantic, and full of sweet surprises. And Chase made love like he invented the Kama Sutra.

"God, please, I don't want to compare them. I didn't want Dre dead," she said, feeling guilty that her relationship with Chase was more romantic, more exciting, and just mind-blowing. He was gentle when he had to be, and he fucked her senseless when she needed him to. She missed him.

"I don't love him more than you," she said, looking up, speaking to Dre. "I would have lived a million years with you just how we were. Things with Chase are different, but I loved every moment of my life with you."

Dre was a great man, a man she'd always love, but Chase was *the* man. The man she craved. Brilliant, cocky, and stylish. If she invited him somewhere, he could hit his closet, not the mall. She'd hardly seen a repeat outfit on him, and he smelled good on every occasion.

He took pride in his appearance, and his cockiness turned her on. Her thighs trembled. She took a sip of her wine and rocked from side to side, because her entire being missed Chase, and she wanted to be back in his life, back in his arms, and *definitely* back in his bed. "I miss you, Chase," she said out loud. She admitted it. "Why didn't you tell me, baby? Would I have left you?" *Would it have made any difference?* she asked herself again, still not knowing the right answer to that. If he had told her sooner, would she would have acted differently?

"No, it would make no difference, because regardless, I'm in love with you, and I know you are in love with me."

She got up and went inside to refill her glass and was greeted by a naked god. "Oooooh," she said, covering her mouth.

"Madison, right?" he said casually like he wasn't in his birthday suit.

She nodded.

"Funny meeting you like this. I'm Charles, Nakia's boyfriend. Good night," he said. She eyed his tight end as he headed back to Nakia's room.

I am going home soon. Hearing Nakia and her lover had made her realize just how much she missed her man. She got her refill, went back to her room, and prayed that they were done fucking for the night.

The next day, she got a room at an upscale hotel to have a few days alone before heading back to Tyler. It didn't matter what Chase was doing or who he was doing it with. . . . She was going to reclaim her man.

Before she left, she hung out with Nakia, and they promised to visit more. The drive home was the worse because she couldn't get home fast enough. She was more than ready to reunite with her man. "I'm coming, baby, and I still want to be your wife," she smiled.

Chapter Twenty-five

"Chase," Hope yelled.

"What?" he snapped.

"Didn't you hear me? I just asked if you're coming with me to Shelly's annual barbecue. I've only told you this five times."

"Nah, I'm good."

"Chase Storm, you're going to have to snap out of this funk. And shave, for crying out loud. I mean, a beard is sexy, but you got a Paul Bunyan thing going on. So not attractive."

"Hope, you and I are not 'you and I.'" He paused. "You know what it is. I told you where I stood, so if you can't deal with it, please, go. I don't need you or want you here."

"Listen, Negro, I'm the only one who wants your ass at this point. Word on the street is you are a joke, so you ought to feel privileged to have someone like me. She's gone, Chase. *Gone.* That fat bitch wasn't cut out for people like us. We do what we have to do to get what we want, so suck it up. I expect you to be at my parents' at seven for dinner tomorrow night. It's my little sister's birthday. And for crying out loud, go and see a fucking barber and shave that shit off of your face. It's not cute anymore." She slammed the door on her way out.

He cringed. Why did he let her in? Why did he let her comfort him after accepting he and Madison were done? He had let her suck his dick because he needed the release, and now, they were supposedly back together. *Damn.*

He got up from the sofa and looked around. His place looked like shit, and from the reflection in the mirror hanging on the wall, so did he. He grabbed his phone and dialed Madison's. Again, it went straight to voicemail. She still blocked him. His eyes watered, and he wondered what his next move would be.

He drove out to her house again. Normally, he'd sit on her porch for hours, wondering where she had gone, but this day, he saw her mom coming out of the house.

He got out of his car. "Mrs. Atkins, hi. How are you?"

"I'm fine, Chase," she said. The look on her face confirmed he looked like hell.

"Listen, Mom . . . Can I still call you Mom?" he asked.

"Of course, darling. I never told you not to."

"Where did she go? I miss her, and I'm, like, insane at this point. I just want to see her face. I come by here every day and no Madi. Please tell me where she's gone. I'll go there. I need to bring her home."

"Sit down, son," Martha said. He sat on the steps, and she joined him.

"I'm so sorry for hurting her," he said. "I didn't mean to. I'd give up everything to have her back."

"I know, and I'm sorry, Chase. Madison is strong-willed when she wants to be and weak when she shouldn't be. Right now, she's just angry. Trust me, when the anger passes, she's going to be lonely and realize how much she misses you. Now, I'm no expert, and we've talked about this before, but just give her more time. And being with that Hope Gardener didn't help the situation, fool," she shot and popped him on the back of his head.

He grabbed the spot she hit. "Mom, I'm not with her. I mean, I am, but it's not what you think. She's like the rebound stalker chick. She thinks she's helping me, but she's only helping me realize how much more I miss Madi and getting on my damn nerves at the same time."

"Well, Madison went to Houston. She's spending some time away. In the meantime, come with me. You need a shave. If she were to come home this moment, she'd never take you back."

"But I *want* her to see me like this. To show her how lost I am without her."

"No, she'd think you're touched in the head. Come on, follow me to the salon. Let me get you back to normal."

He hesitated. "Okay," he finally said.

An hour later, he looked like himself again. "Thanks, Mom, I look like me now."

"Yes, you do. Now let me give you a word of advice." Chase raised an eyebrow. "I can't predict the future, but after so long, it will be okay to move on, son. You're still young."

"I know, Mom, but I won't. I'll wait for her."

"Chase, be realistic."

"I am. I love her. I'll wait for her to come around. I know she loves me. It was in her kiss, her touch, and the way she smiled at me. That's what I hold on to in my heart. I didn't imagine that. And one day, she'll remember and come back to me."

"You're a good man, Chase. A bit dumb, though," she joked, "but a good man. I wish you two well."

"Thanks, Mom." Chase stood and gave Martha a tight hug. "When you talk to her, tell her I love her, and I miss her, and I'll never give up on us."

"I will, son."

"Thank you." He kissed Martha's cheek and then went home, but not before driving by Madison's. He knew her mother said she had gone to Houston, but he went by her place anyway. He walked around to the back of her house and pulled the door handle on her screened-in porch and was happy to find that it was open. He went inside and took a seat and stared out at the lake. He looked down and noticed all the bride magazines that Madison had stacked on the wicker coffee table. He grabbed the one on top and thumbed through the pages.

He looked at some of the posted notes that were on pages of things that Madison liked, and his eyes welled. "I'm sorry, babe, and this wedding *is* going to happen, I promise. I don't know what it's going to take, but I'm going to get you back." He looked through several more magazines, and by sundown, he headed home. The only thing he had on his mind at that point was getting Madison back.

When Chase got home, he dialed the cleaning service his family used and set up an appointment for his place. The next morning, his staff was shocked to see him back in the office, looking sharp like he did before.

He met with his assistant, and she brought him up to speed on all the projects that had been delayed during his absence and brought him up to speed on what projects were on time or ahead of schedule. Chase fell right back into the flow of work, and that day did help him to not think of Madison every second of his day. Before he left for the day, he called for his brothers and his father to meet him in the conference room.

"Look, Chase, again, we are sorry and so happy to see you back to work," Lance said.

Damon spoke next. "Yes, li'l bro—"

Chase cut him off. "Look, there is no need to apologize again, okay? I've had enough apologies to last a lifetime. I've called this meeting to redeem my winnings. Although I said no to the monies earlier, I've changed my mind. Since I've lost Madison, I might as well enjoy something. I want every dime that's due to me. First, though, I want a check for the cost of Madison's home and the renovations to her spa refunded back to her. You can forward the checks to her or handle it however you want, but after that, I want the remainder of it transferred to my account."

No one argued.

"So, all is forgiven?" Travis asked.

"Yes. It is what it is, right? She found out, and she left, but I never broke our agreement. I did what I was dared to do. In the process, I fell in love and got my heart broken. This is where I stand now and until she comes back to me, and I want to move on."

"Son, I'm truly sorry," his dad said.

"Dad, I'm good. My focus now is just on giving her time. I busted my brain on things I could do to win her back, and I can't do anything but give her time to realize how much she loves me and wants to be with me."

Lance jumped in. "Are you sure? Because we all know about this thing you got with Hope. What's up with that?"

"Hope and I are nothing, and as soon as I leave here, she'll know it too. I don't love her. Hell, I don't even like her, and why I allowed her to come within five feet lets me know that the breakup with Madison put me in a very bad place, but I'm ready to move on, and Hope will get this news tonight, I promise you."

"Do you plan to go back to the way you were?" Damon inquired.

"What does it matter, Damon? I mean, seriously? When I was playing the field, I was honest, and I didn't hurt a soul. I didn't front. I was free to move around, go as I pleased. You guys were the ones who didn't like my lifestyle. So, what'd you do? You dangle this proposition in my face, allowing me to fall in love and get my fucking heart broken. I destroyed the only relationship that ever meant anything to me, and broke Madison's heart in the process." He struggled to keep his cool. "So, does it truly matter, Damon? Huh?" He felt his eyes burn, and he didn't want to cry in front of them. "Just please take care of those two things and give me the rest of my winnings." He stormed out.

He hurried to his car, upset, hurt, and confused. He missed Madison so much. He just wanted her back. He didn't give a shit about the money, about Hope, or even his position at the business anymore. He just wanted her, but what could he do? There was absolutely nothing he could do at that point.

Please, Madison, he prayed, unable to hold back his tears. *Please, baby, come back to me. I love you; I love you; I love you, baby. I've never loved anyone, but I love you.*

He dried his eyes, got himself together, and headed to Hope's parents' place for dinner.

There, they greeted him with smiles and hugs. He sat at the table in silence picking at his food, ignoring the uppity, fake conversations that went on. All Hope's family talked about was money and business.

"So, Chase, what do you think?" her father asked.

He hadn't been listening. He swallowed hard and asked. "About what, sir?"

"Another dealership in Longview. I mean, that would make lot twelve, and since you and Hope are going to marry soon, I think you should consider taking over as the GM and relocating to that area to start fresh and new."

His eyes bucked. There were no marriage plans. And what would make Mr. Gardener think he'd leave his family's company to work for him?

He cleared his throat. "Well, sir. I have a solid position at my family's company, and the thought of leaving Tyler has *never* entered my mind."

"Well, Hope told us about the little feud you guys have going on, so I thought a change of scenery would do you some good. And my baby girl is not getting any younger.

You've been the topic of my angel's life since when? The seventh grade?"

Chase had had enough. It was time to set the record straight and be done with Hope Gardener. He dropped his fork and stood. "No disrespect, Mr. Gardener, but I would never consider relocating or leaving my family's business. Ever. As far as any personal issues going on in my family right now, they're none of anyone's business. We had a hiccup like most families do from time to time, but we are fine. There is no feud, so whatever you heard about me and mine, forget it. My family and I are just fine.

"I was foolish to make promises to Hope about us one day getting married. Although I've been a topic in your home since junior high, she hasn't been a topic or even a thought in mine." He turned to her. "Hope, you are a gorgeous woman, and any man would be lucky to have you, but I don't love you. I don't want you, and I will never marry you." He looked back at Mr. Gardener. "Sir, I'm sorry, but Hope knows where we stand. She's known it for a long time. I was hurt by the woman I love, and Hope pretended to be a friend to aid me through my tough time, but she was only up to the same old tricks. Mrs. Gardener, I'm sorry. I know you and my mom are friends, but I don't want to be with your daughter. I'm in love with Madison Atkins-Morgan, and that's who I'll marry one day."

Hope looked furious. "You asshole!" she yelled. "You are the stupidest man on this planet. You'd leave me for that fat bitch? That's why you're lonely now because she *left* you. Yes, let's be real, Chase Storm. Your brothers put a wager on that hog for you to even go anywhere near her, and when that pig learned the truth, she left you!" she spat with venom.

"Hope," her dad said, holding up a hand signaling her to stop.

"No, Daddy, I need to tell this second-rate Negro about himself. Don't nobody want you, Chase Storm. You are *used* goods, and you'd be *lucky* to marry me. If you walk out now, you will be alone forever. I'm the best woman for you. Madison is a miserable rhino who only wishes she could be me. She has since we were kids. *I'm* the one who has loved you forever. Walk out that door, and you're done," she threatened.

Chase managed to muster up a smile. "Good night, Mr. and Mrs. Gardener." He headed for the door.

Hope yelled profanities and threats behind him, but he didn't stop. He got in his car and sighed. He felt better but still not good.

When he got home, his mind went into overdrive, thinking how he'd go to Houston and bring Madison home. He'd have to work on Mrs. Atkins to find out her location, but he had to get his woman.

Chapter Twenty-six

Madison drove with her stomach in knots. Traffic was crazy, and she thought she'd never make it to Tyler. By the time she pulled into her driveway, it was after eleven. She wanted more than anything to go to Chase but decided to wait until the next day. She went into her house. She had missed her space. She had missed her bed. And she had missed her man.

She grabbed her cell phone and unblocked him. She hadn't wanted to see his calls or texts, but now she wanted him—all of him—and she couldn't wait to see him. She would go early before he left for work. If Hope was there, oh well, who cared?

Her alarm sounded off at six, and she hopped up like a Pop-Tart, showered, and dressed. Then she drove to Chase's place, anxious and excited, and she couldn't wait to see his face, kiss his lips, and wrap her arms around his neck. She was so happy to see that he hadn't left yet.

Taking a deep breath, she got out and went to his door. She had a key, but using it after they had broken up would probably get her shot, so she rang the bell.

After a couple of moments, he opened it. "Baby," he said. He looked shocked to see her.

She smiled. "Hi. Can I—"

"Sure, sure. Come on." He stepped aside to allow her to enter. "I know I should have called first."

"No, Madison, you never have to call. You are welcome here at any time."

"Where's Hope?"

"Home, I assume. Why would I know where Hope is?"

"Come on, Chase. I know you two are together."

He moved closer to her, got so close she could smell the mint on his breath. "I'm not with her. I've missed you so much, Madison. Please tell me you're here for us."

"Yes, I—" His tongue was down her throat before she could say any more.

"I love you, baby," he whispered between kisses. He held her so close, and she felt her heartbeat beating to the rhythm of his.

She moaned from his kisses. She had missed him. Truly missed him. "I love you too," she breathed into his mouth.

He broke from their kiss. "I want you back. Madison, I love you. Please take me back. I messed up big time. I own up to that. I started out on the wrong foot, but I fell in love with you. Please?" he said. His eyes watered, and the sight pierced her heart.

"Chase, I'm not second rate, or a charity case, or so undesirable that nobody wants me."

"Baby, I know," he cried.

"No, Chase, listen to me. Seriously. I have to say this before we can move forward. What y'all did was foul. You fucked with my self-esteem and my mind for a moment and had me second-guessing myself, and that was so unfair to do that. The way I found out devastated me, Chase. That's why I left. That news was like a gut punch or a kick in the damn head, and it was so embarrassing, Chase. I mean, people pointing and laughing and whispering behind my back was humiliating."

He stepped back and rubbed his head. He let out a sigh and took a seat on the little bench in his foyer. "Madison, you have every right to be mad, pissed, angry. . . . Whatever you want to label it. I never told you that your emotions, or how you felt about what went down were irrelevant, and trust me, I totally understood your reaction to something like that. All I've been doing since you've been away is praying for you to focus on us and our time and everything that we have built during the time we were together.

"Truth, the raw truth is, I'd have never approached a plus-sized woman. No, I would have never chosen you out of a crowd. I was shallow as hell and not focused on looking for a wife or anyone to spend the rest of my life with back then. To be honest with you, Madison, I'm glad I wouldn't have chosen you before the bet because you would have been just another notch in my belt, another bed buddy, and I wouldn't ever have tried to get to know you or even hear you. Truth, all the times that we were introduced, I never noticed you because I was on some other shit, Madison. But that is not who I am today. I'm a changed man, and I owe it to you, and, in an odd way, my brothers, for seeing something in you that I may have never noticed in a lifetime on my own.

"What my brothers and I did and what I agreed to was foul, Madison. Yes, it was low but as wrong as it was, it brought us together, and I found the love of my life. No matter how we got to today, this is where we are, baby, and I love you, I adore you, and I still want to marry you. None of that has changed. I've been miserable without you, Madison.

"Please, don't just throw everything we have now away. You know me. When I'm with you, I'm the man I'm supposed to be. You bring out the best in me, Madison. Please tell me you're here to work it out."

She looked him in the eye. "Yes, Chase, that is exactly why I'm here. I wanna work it out. I'm here right now, because I want you, Chase. I love you, and I missed you so much, and I don't care where we started anymore. I just want what we have right here and now. Where we are now is the only thing that matters to me, baby, and I do forgive you, Chase, and your family for what y'all did. I don't give a shit about the wager, the money. All I want is you. All I need is to be with you."

"Madison, baby, please be sure. My heart can't take you walking out on me again. You have to be truly over it and honestly forgive me, because I don't want this to be an argument next month, next year, or when you're on the delivery table wailing in pain while you're giving birth."

She giggled. "I'm so for real, Chase. I love you, and all is forgiven. I was so sad and lonely without you."

He stood, walked over to her, and gently kissed her again.

"Thank you, Madison, for forgiving me and coming back to me. I was so scared that I had lost you forever, and I didn't know how I was going to make it for the rest of my life without you."

"Well, I'm here to stay, and I'll never leave you again, Chase. Just don't do anything crazy to drive me away."

"I promise I won't," he said and kissed her.

She pulled away. "And Hope Gardener—is she an issue?"

He laughed. "After the scene at her folk's house last night, I can promise you that she will never be an issue for us ever again."

"What? What happened?" she inquired.

"Later, baby, I just want to reunite with you. We can talk about Hope later. She isn't important. Reconnecting with you is all I want to do right now."

They moved to the living room and on the sectional, they reacquainted themselves with each other. She moaned, he groaned, she shook, and he smiled. He could still make her tremble.

"Chase, baby. Oh, Chase," she moaned when she climaxed a second time. "I love you, I love you, I love you," she sang.

"You like that, baby? Does that feel good?" he breathed into her soft spot.

"Yes, yes, yes, yes. Chase, oh, baby, I've missed your tongue, baby. That feels so good," she moaned in pleasure. Chase licked and sucked and used his fingers to penetrate her opening until he made her come. "Oh my God, Chase, baby, oh my God, baby. I'm there, I'm there, baby. I'm coming for you," she uttered.

He kissed her inner thigh and came up with his erection in his hand. He stroked himself, while she regained her composure. "Turn over and let me slide in from behind," he demanded.

She turned over on her stomach and pushed her ass up in the air. He slid in easily. No condom, no barrier, and the familiar feeling of his rod had Madison squirming and singing his name. She closed her eyes and visions of her wedding, lovemaking, and having his babies invaded her mind. Those thoughts made her happy, and she couldn't wait to start a new life with Chase. He was the one, and she was happy to be right there with him.

"Ooooh, baby, do me. You know what I like. You know what I like, Daddy." She pushed back, meeting his thrusts, and he pumped harder and faster.

"Aaaaaah, baby, aaaaaah," he roared. "I love you, I love you, I love you. Madison, be my wife. Be my wife," he moaned.

"I'm yours, Chase. I'm all yours, baby, forever," she cried with him as he released inside of her. They only waited a few moments before they were at it again. They took a short break, ordered food, drank wine, and talked as if they had never had a second apart. They made it to his bed, and she gave him her body for the rest of that night, making up for lost time.

Chapter Twenty-seven

Chase's phone ringing awakened them. He sat up and picked it up. It was his father. "Wait, Dad, what? Please explain to me what's going on."

"Well, since you've ignored our million and one calls yesterday, Hope Gardener has filed a suit against us," he blared.

"What suit? What for? What grounds? That's absurd."

"Sexual harassment, inappropriate conduct—you name it."

"Dad, you know that's crazy. You already know the deal with Hope and me."

"Son, I know, and I'm not calling to shit in your corn-flakes. I'm calling to warn you about this fiasco. I know you, son, and I know Hope isn't the woman you wanted, so she's acting out and taking this bullshit too far. Evidently, you pissed her father off too for him to move forward with this bogus shit."

"No worries, Dad. Madison is right here next to me, so absolutely nothing can dampen my mood today. I'm not worried about Hope or her ridiculous lawsuit. Everyone in this town knows that Hope has had it bad for me for years. No judge is going to believe her. Anyone that knows anything about my and Hope's history knows that this is some old bullshit."

"You are absolutely right, son, and did you say Madison is there with you?"

"Yes, sir, I did," Chase smiled.

"Good to hear, son. And everything you instructed has already been taken care of. Two to three days tops, the transaction will be completed, and I am so glad she came back to you."

"You know that wasn't personal, right? And even though we don't need it, we deserve it for everything we've been through."

"I know. A wager is just like business, and a man's word is his bond. I wish you and Madison the best, son."

"Thanks, Dad."

"You're welcome. Now, I know you want to lie up all day with your fiancée and reacquaint yourselves and all that jazz, but you need to get your ass in gear. We have a meeting with our attorneys at eleven. Don't dare think of being late. We must put the Gardeners to bed as quickly as possible."

"Dad, I'm there. I'm going to feed my woman, and then I'm there, and this is going to be a walk in the park; trust me," Chase declared with confidence in his voice.

"Good." His dad hung up.

Madison rolled over to face him and asked. "Baby, what's wrong?"

"Fucking Hope strikes again. She filed a harassment suit against me, saying that I acted inappropriately and whatnot. She knows I've only been professional with her, well accept when we . . ." He went quiet.

"When we did what?" she questioned, but he said nothing, just dropped his head. "Tell me everything Chase. We weren't together, and I want to know the truth. I don't want to be blindsided ever again, so tell me what went down while we were apart."

He sighed. "She gave me head, Madison; that's it. She caught me at a moment where my head was fucked up, and I let her, okay? But I promise you, baby, that's it. Nothing more. I didn't do anything with her, and trust, my only crime is allowing her to think that we could be together. No warm exchange, no kisses, no affection. I never touched her.

"Baby, I know I should not have allowed Hope to come around, but it was crazy when you left. I wasn't myself, and I allowed it, and I will understand if this changes things. I made a vow to never lie to you again about anything. You know my past. You know I've been a dog. I've been with a lot of women and done a lot of shit, but you are my future, babe. Please tell me that what I did doesn't change anything, Madison. If it does, I won't like it, but I'll respect it."

"It changes nothing, Chase, baby; relax. I'm not going anywhere, and although I don't like that that bitch touched you and pleasured you, I believe it meant nothing. I know you love me, and I know Hope doesn't mean anything to you, Chase."

"Thank you so much, baby. For my future, and once we are married, I'm going to spend the rest of my days making up for my mistakes and making you happy."

"No making up required, my love. I forgive you. We move on. I'm looking forward to our future, Chase. I was angry, but the bottom line is where we are now. I'm not a joke, because, in the end, you're me. That's all that matters, and, technically, I did leave."

"You did, but I shouldn't have gone anywhere near Hope's ass. She's just full of drama, and every time I turned around, there she was, trying to be nice, a friend, and I just should have stayed away from her, and I'm sorry."

"Chase, we're good, baby," she smiled.

"Thank you, Madison. Now, get up. I'm going to make you breakfast, and you and I are going to the law office so we can take care of this Hope situation."

"Baby, I have a better idea. How about *you* go talk to the lawyer, and *I* pay a visit to my childhood bestie, Hope?"

"Nah, baby. I don't want things to get worse. You go up in Hope's face, she'll provoke you to bust her head open. Then you'll get the cuffs on you."

She burst into laughter. "Trust me, baby, I got this under control. All I need is two minutes, and this here lawsuit will go away."

"Okay, give me more. How can you be so sure that you don't plan to go down there and beat Hope to the white meat?" he joked.

She continued to laugh. "Okay, baby, come on now; be serious," she said and sat up. "Now, I'm going to tell you something, and as my fiancé and soon-to-be husband, you have to promise me that you will never tell another soul what I'm about to tell you."

"Okay, I promise."

"Now, Chase, you have to make a vow to me, that you will never, *ever* repeat this, not even to your brothers."

"Okay, okay, woman, I vow that I will never tell a soul, now out with it," he pushed.

"Well, my mother and Hope's mom were tight when we were kids. I mean thick as thieves. They were friends since first grade, all through high school, and even college. So, Hope and I were friends since the crib. We were like sisters . . . up until high school."

"What happened?" he interrupted.

"Well, one afternoon, Hope's momma came to our house crying her eyes out. I overheard her tell my mom that Hope was pregnant, something that Hope never even shared with me. Hope was slim, so at first, no one could tell. By the time she started to show a little, it was summer break and close to her due date. The truth is that her little sister, Constance, is *not* her little sister. Now, I don't know who else her momma confided in, but as far as I know, Mrs. Gardener hasn't shared that information with anyone other than my mother. I pretended not to know. The only reason why our mothers stopped talking is because my mother wanted Hope's mom to expose the father, but she refused, so my mom didn't want to have anything else to do with the Gardeners. When I remind Hope of her secret, trust, she'll back off."

"Damn, I had no idea. That's crazy. Constance is her daughter?"

"Yes, Chase, but you cannot say a word."

"I won't, but who's the father?"

"Now, that is something I don't know. I didn't hear his name."

"Damn, well, I never even suspected."

"Of course, you didn't. It's a secret, Chase. I don't think anyone else knows. I'm sure my mother will take this to her grave."

"You think you can fix this?"

"Baby, trust, this will be another thing we put in our past bucket."

"Okay, Madison." He kissed her. "Oh, and one more thing." He pulled her ring from the nightstand's top drawer. "You're going to need this back."

"Yes. Gimme, gimme, gimme," she bounced on the bed like an excited kid.

"And you have to give me more before we go."

"I can do that."

He kissed her, slid the ring back on her finger, and she gave him just what he wanted one more time before they got out of bed.

Chapter Twenty-eight

"So, to what do I owe this meeting?" Hope asked with attitude.

Madison didn't wait for an invitation; she just strolled into Hope's office. "I just wanted to catch up, Hope. You know, chat a little, old friend. As long as we've known each other, you've never acknowledged that we were friends. . . . I mean best friends at any time of our lives. My mom and your mom were thick as thieves back in the day. I mean, up until you got pregnant, you and I were best friends. But you come at me crazy after Chase and I broke up, and if it weren't for Deena, I would have kicked your bony ass. As soon as I vacated, you tried to move in on my man again, and now you are screaming *harassment?*"

Hope hurried over and shut her office door before she continued to speak. "I'm not sure why you wanna bring up my pregnancy after all of these years, Madison. You know I was only fifteen, and you also know I was raped. Why are you bringing up my family's secrets?" she asked in a panic.

"Why are you suing my fiancé, Hope? Seriously? You know this is some bullshit. I told Chase a little bit about this secret of yours, but I didn't tell him you had gotten pregnant by your stepfather. You can save that rape crap because I know what went on back then, Hope. And if you don't drop this asinine lawsuit, I will tell *everyone* the entire truth and not leave out *one* detail."

"You wouldn't." Panic set in, and Hope was noticeably shaking.

"For Chase, I would, Hope. I love him. I got over us no longer being friends long ago, Hope, and I promise you, I *will* tell it all if you don't back off. Chase isn't the man that you and everyone else has labeled him to be, and, yes, he is in love with me. You are not going to ruin his family name with this bogus lawsuit. I would have still been your friend back then, Hope, no judgment, but you just stopped talking to me, *not* the other way around, and you walk around Tyler with your nose up in the air looking down on me, telling whoever will listen that I'm jealous of you and I just want your life and what you have. No, baby, I think it's just the opposite. Even before I met Chase, I got married before you, I had kids before you, and you think that I'd want *your* life? Please," she spat. "Today is where all of this madness ends, or I'm just getting starting. I'll tell anyone who will listen about your stepdaddy and your 'sister,' I mean daughter," Madison threatened.

Fear was written all over Hope's fair-skinned face. She nearly fell into her chair and said, "Fine, Madison, I'm stopping the suit. Just don't air my family's business. This will kill my sister, and destroy everything."

"I'm sorry you went through something so horrific, Hope, but I was your friend. Being molested and raped is so horrible, and as I told you back then when we were friends, none of it was your fault. My mom wanted to help you and told your mother to file charges against him, but your mother didn't want to give up her lifestyle with the Car King. She didn't want anyone to know, so my mom and I never told a soul. But if you don't drop the charges against my fiancé and his family, as you said, I *will* go public. Chase loves me enough to keep what I told him this morning about Constance a secret but don't provoke us. Drop the charges and let us be."

Hope looked at Madison. Her eyes welled. "I've loved him since middle school, and he told me that he'd married me, Madison. Chase Storm was supposed to marry me, not you. He said he loved me," she sobbed.

Madison's eyes watered for her. "I'm sorry, but I love him now, and I'm not letting him go.

No lawsuit, no lies. Nothing will keep us apart."

Hope wiped her eyes. "I'll call off the suit. You have my word."

"Thank you." Madison stood.

"My family's secrets are safe, right? My sister would be hurt the most; you know that, right?"

"Trust, when I leave this office, I won't think of you at all, Hope Alexandrea Gardener. Your life means absolutely nothing to me. All I care about is me and mine, so, yes, your secrets are safe. And please don't hesitate to make that call. Chase is meeting with his attorney at eleven. Good day, Hope."

An hour later, she was at the salon trying to get up to date on everything. Her assistant had done a great job holding everything down, but she was back, and everyone needed to know who the real boss was.

Her phone rang, and she smiled when she saw it was Chase. "Hey, baby."

"Hey, my love, where are you?"

"At the salon. What's going on? How did everything go with the lawyers?"

"Baby, I don't know what you did, but the Gardeners dropped all complaints. There are no more suits, and we are all clear."

"Chase, baby, that's great. I'm so happy to hear that."

"Well, my family is itching to see you and to celebrate us reuniting, and the whole fiasco with the Gardeners is buried, so you gotta come to my parents' for dinner tomorrow night. Everyone is going to be there. They're all excited for us."

"I'm there, baby. I'll always be here for you."

"Promise?"

"Chase, I promise."

"So, tonight, my place or yours?"

"Yours. I just need to run home for a few things, but definitely yours."

"I love you, babe."

"I love you too."

"I'll be there in, like, twenty minutes."

"Chase, seriously? You can't wait to see me later?"

"No, I can't wait until later to see you."

"Well, I'm working, babe. You know I have to get up to speed on everything, but I'm anxious to see you too."

"I'll see you in a minute."

They hung up, and Madison smiled. Chase was it. Her lover and her new best friend. She never thought she'd love again or be close to another man like she had been with Dre, but God blessed her with Chase, and she was elated that they were back together. She tried to wrap up her paperwork as quickly as possible and afterward headed out to the floor to catch up with her staff to see what she had missed when she was out. She was in a conversation with one of the stylists; then he walked in. Unable to keep her composure, she raced into his arms, and they shared a sensual kiss.

He smiled. "I've missed you."

"I've missed you too."

"So, can we get out of here? I can follow you home, and you can pack a bag, or we can just stay there."

"Either way, babe; let me grab my purse, and we can go."

"I'll be waiting," Chase said and watched her hips sway as she walked away. He took a few steps backward because he couldn't take his eyes off of her. Just as she turned the corner and was no longer in sight, he heard someone say, "Damn, Chase, how much would you bet for me?" He turned to three of Madison's staff members; all were giggling.

"Excuse me? What was that?"

"Well, everyone knows that you made a bet to date Madison. I mean, she's a great boss and all, but she ain't got shit on me," one of the stylists said striking a sexy pose. "Now, if she's worth three, I know I'm about a ten." She continued, and her giggling friends found her to be cute, but Chase didn't.

"Listen, Joss," he said reading her name tag that was pinned to her smock.

"You can call me Jocelyn, baby, and for ten million, you can even call me Madison," she joked, and her coworkers found her to be hilarious because the soft giggles were nonstop and louder.

"Joss," he said again with a little authority, "I don't know who or what gave you the courage to step to me with this juvenile behavior, but I'm not a toy, and I don't play with little girls. What you heard about Madison and me is true; it's no secret, but if you and your little fans think it's okay to make jokes or come at me sideways about me and Madison, think again. Stay in your lane, or you'll find out how many millions I can spare to make sure you never work in East Texas again—not even bagging groceries," he said, and all giggles and banter immediately ceased. Chase was bluffing. He didn't give bread crumbs about this little low-class chick, but he wanted them to know that he wasn't the one to be played with, even though he could care less about gossip or ridicule. The entire town was whispering, but they were not going to make him walk away with his tail between his legs. "Are we clear?" he asked, using his boss tone.

"As a bell," Joss said, and the little smirk she had on her face before had disappeared. They all scattered when they saw Madison coming out from the back of the salon.

"You ready, baby?" she asked.

Chase locked her arm into his. "Yes, I'm ready to go home and pamper you," he said and gave her a soft kiss. He and Madison proceeded to the door, and he looked back to see the envious ones watching, and he smiled. Madison was his arm charm, and he felt like the luckiest man in East Texas.

Chapter Twenty-nine

Madison was sitting at her desk in her home office, logged into her bank account. She sat bobbing to the music that played through her speakers enjoying an old, smooth jam, "Simple Things" by Glenn Jones. She had her eyes closed while the page loaded because she felt so good that morning, and her life was perfect. Everything about her life felt so good, and she wondered why things with Chase were so great. "Lord, you gave me love again after all the pain I went through with losing Dre. Am I supposed to feel this good, Lord? Is something wrong with me, because I missed them so much every day, but I couldn't imagine not having Chase in my life? Like am I wrong for feeling this good with this man, when I loved Dre?" she asked out loud talking to herself. She decided to shake off those guilty feelings that she would get from time to time.

"If I had died, I'd want you to be this happy," she said and moved the mouse because in her brief moments of deep thoughts the screen went black. When she saw her balance, she blinked and quickly hit the account summary icon. She looked at the transaction and wondered why she had over five hundred grand deposited into her account from Storm and Sons Construction. That had to be a mistake, she thought, but then she looked at the number and subtracted the price of her home, and the balance was the amount equal to the amount of the spa renovations to the penny. She snatched her house phone from the desk and dialed Chase, and when he didn't answer, she didn't leave a message. She grabbed her phone to Facetime him. After a few moments, he answered her call.

"What's up, babe? I'm on my way in to the office, and I swear I'll be back before lunchtime," he said. It was a Saturday morning, and Chase never worked the weekends, but since he had just recently gone back, he was trying to get back on track.

"That's not why I called you, babe. I had a deposit to go into my account yesterday for $590,000. The exact amounts for my home and my spa renovations from your company. Is this some kinda mistake? Did something happen with the checks that I wrote to your family's company?"

"No, it's not an error or anything like that. I went to my family and told them that I wanted the money that they owed me," he said.

"Why would you do that?"

"Because, Madison, it was a solid wager, and, technically, we won."

She was quiet. Something about that made her uneasy again, like it was really about the money. "Chase, I thought you said the money wasn't important."

"It's not important, Madison. I don't need it, but I won it fair and square."

"Unbelievable," she expressed and shook her head. "I don't want this money back, Chase. I don't want any part of the bet that was placed on me like I was a charity case."

"Madison, please, don't say that. We both know you're not some charity case, and I don't need the money, but they owed it to me—owed it to us. I told you that I had plans to tell you everything after the wedding, so, please, take it. It's the least my family can do for all the craziness they put us through," he pleaded.

Madison said nothing; she just looked at him. He looked so sexy in his shades, and his charming smile almost made her say okay, but she said, "I don't want it."

"Madison, you're ridiculous. You know my family has money—lots of it. You are marrying into a pretty wealthy family, and we do things like bet millions, go to Vegas or New Orleans, and wild out. We work hard, and we play hard, and either you have the money back in your account this way, or you have it back when we get married. Either way, it's yours."

She bit the corner of her lip. "This just makes me feel like . . ." she said but had no words.

"You will soon be a millionaire's wife, Madison. You see how we live. So, please, keep it."

She didn't say anything at first, but then she said, "I will keep it, but I plan to give it away . . . well, after I give my mom back her portion."

"It's yours to do whatever you want."

"Whatever I want?"

"Whatever you like, and I know we don't carry on like superstars, nor do we take anything for granted. My brothers and I can never step foot up in our company's walls, but we appreciate everything our grandparents started for us, and we'll never let anyone outside step in and do what we do. Our children will be the next generation to run this company, and we all pray that our offspring will love and dedicate as much love, blood, and sweat as my brothers, cousins, father, uncles, and I have. I believe we are as successful as we are now because we work hard every day."

"Well, I suggest you go in and do what you gotta do because I want to make a change in plans."

"What do you mean?"

"I'm going to call your momma and the girls and see if we can have brunch today because you and I need to take a trip."

"A trip? Where do you want to go?"

"You'll see. Let me check on some flights. I have some-one I want you to meet, and I want to give her this surprise in person."

"I'm game. How should I pack?"

"Just casual. If we need anything, Mr. Millionaire, we'll just have to buy it."

"I'm in," he said, and they ended the call.

"Siri, call Nakia," Madison said. The phone rang, and she picked up.

"Hey, girl, how are you? How did it go with Chase?"

"Honey, we are good. I'm calling to see what you have planned for this weekend."

"Girl, not too much. I'm just doing some charts for work. Some of my clients get on my last nerve."

"I hear ya, but I was thinking we should take a trip."

"Take a trip? Take a trip where, girl? I can't afford no getaways right now. You know I'm saving to move to Cali."

"I know, but just a couple of days. I want you to meet Chase; besides, I'm paying."

"Just say when and where."

"Hold on, love. I'm going to make the arrangements and send you an email. Just pack a bag. I'm going to try to get us flights for tonight."

"I'm game, girl."

"Good. I'll call you back in a few." They hung up. Madison began to search for flights, and then it hit her. . . . She should make it a couples' thing. Do a girls' getaway, and let Chase and his brothers do their thing at the same time. "Yes!" she said.

She dialed Deena, filled her in, and asked if they could get away. Deena said they were in, and then they called Gina, Gina called Tasha, and they all decided to meet up at the main house to discuss it and book their flights together. Before heading to Chase's mom's, Madison made a pit stop to her bank and transferred funds into her parents' business account, then got a cashier's check for $300,000 that was eighty grand less than the cost of her home, but she figured it would be a generous enough amount to give to her closest friend other than Deena.

Even though she had sent Nakia a few hundred here and there over the years when she was in a bind, this would ease a great deal of her friend's financial strain. She smiled when she walked out of the bank and couldn't wait to see the look on Nakia's face when she opened the envelope that housed the check.

She made it to the main house, and they all pulled out tablets and gadgets to book flights. The other wives informed their husbands of the last-minute getaway, and since it was four couples going, they had to take two different flights to score four first-class tickets to leave that night. Estelle declined the trip. She said Vegas was too fast for her and Legend, but she wished them all well as they departed. They all met up at the airport together in two cars and then parked. Deena and Madison and their mates were on one flight, and Gina and Tasha and their mates were on the other. All were leaving on the same airline, but leaving two hours apart. Madison made sure that Nakia had a first-class ticket out of Houston, and she'd arrive shortly after she and Chase would.

Madison fastened her seat belt. "You good, baby?" Chase asked.

"Better than good."

"This was a great idea, you know. To get away for a couple of days."

"Yes, indeed. I love Tyler and its Southern charm, but it is some messy folks in our town."

"Yes, and I can't wait until we're married, and everyone sees that our union is real."

"You know what, babe? I don't even care anymore what folks think. I mean, every damn body always got to have an opinion or two cents or a say-so in someone else's life when they need to tend to their own house. I go out to the store and even at my salon, I know they are still whispering and laughing behind my back."

"Yes, they are. I had to say something to that chick Joss yesterday. It's just petty."

"Yep, we live in a petty world, so we have to stay in Chase and Madison's world. A place where drama doesn't exist."

"Exactly," he agreed.

"Would you like a drink?" the attendant asked.

"Yes, we would," Chase answered. "What would you like, babe?"

"Chardonnay would be perfect."

"And I'll have a vodka and cranberry," Chase said.

"No problem," the attendant replied; then she turned to Deena and Travis. They put in their orders, and the two couples drank, laughed, and chatted until they landed in Vegas.

They arranged for car service and were taken to The Palazzo where they had two, two-bedroom-connecting suites on the same floor and a one-bedroom suite a couple of rooms down for Nakia.

Shortly after they got settled into their room, Nakia called and said she had just landed. Madison told her she had a car there to pick her up and to call her when she was in the lobby. Once Nakia arrived, Madison insisted that Deena accompany her to greet Nakia. She and Nakia only met once at her family's funerals, and she was hoping they'd hit it off and get along.

"Nakia," Madison yelled when she spotted her. She had just seen her a few days ago, but they hugged like it had been ages. "You remember Deena," Madison said.

"Of course, I do," she said and reached in to hug Deena, which took Deena by surprise.

"Oh, okay, hi, Nakia. Lovely you made it," she said, and Madison raised a brow. Why was Deena acting all stuffy all of a sudden?

"Come on, girl, let's get you checked in. I have you a suite not too far down from us, and we are going to have a blast, girl."

"Oh, hell yeah," Nakia cheered, and Deena sorta frowned, but Madison took Nakia by the hand and went to get her checked in.

"Once you get settled, come down to our suite. I'm dying for you to meet Chase."

"Okay. Let me take a tinkle, check out the wet bar, and I'll be right over," she said.

Deena and Madison headed back to their suite, and as soon as they walked in, Madison asked, "Deena, what's up with you? Why were you giving Nakia the side eye?"

"A little rowdy, isn't she?"

"Oh no, Deena, don't you get all Hope Gardener on me. Where is this stiffness coming from?"

Deena let out a sigh. "A'ight, a'ight, I'm a little jealous. I mean, on the way to the airport, you were like Nakia this, and oh, Nakia that, and I can't wait for Nakia this and Nakia that."

"Aaaaaaw, honey, stop. I've known you since middle school, and when I went off to college, Nakia was my roommate and the only friend that I left college with, but I love you two equally."

Deena swatted her arm. "See what I mean?"

"Okay, I love you more," she said and opened her arms to hug her. "But don't tell Nakia," she whispered, and then the men walked in from the terrace.

"Baby, you have to see this view," Chase said.

"Yes, baby, it's spectacular," Travis added, and before they walked out, there was a tap on the door.

"Wait, babe, that has to be Nakia," Madison said and rushed over to the door. She opened it and pulled her in. She introduced her to Chase and Travis, and they all enjoyed drinks and the view until the rest of the Storms made it to the hotel. Then they all decided to split up. The guys were all set to go their way, and so were the girls when Chase stopped them and pulled Madison into his arms.

"Really, Chase, don't you ever get enough?" Deena said.

"Yes, Chase, the way you two have been carrying on, y'all might as well stay here," Gina said and then polished off her glass of wine.

"I want my baby to know how much I'm going to miss her tonight. Y'all know it wasn't my idea to split up," Chase griped.

"Look, baby, give me your phone."

He reached into his pocket and handed it to her. "Why do you need my phone?"

"Type in your password," she instructed, and then he did.

She took the phone. "Now, I'm going to turn on my location for you on my phone and turn on your location for you on your phone, so when you wanna know exactly where I am, just check it."

"Y'all give me a break," Lance moaned, and they all burst into laughter. "This is Las Vegas, not North Korea. We don't need to trace y'all location."

"Shut up, Lance. This is between me and Chase," she barked at him, and everyone continued to laugh.

"Yes, this is our thang," Chase defended.

"Oh, how I miss that newness," Gina sighed.

"Yeah, yeah, whatever, guys; let's do this," Damon said, and they all began to file out of the suite. Chase and Madison tried to exchange one last kiss, but the girls and the guys pulled them apart in two different directions.

Chapter Thirty

The next day everyone slept in. The first one up was Madison, so she crept out of bed and allowed Chase to continue to sleep. She kissed him softly on the forehead and then grabbed her robe and purse. She went out into the living room and looked toward the other end of the suite. Deena and Travis's door was still closed. She made her way to the front door and went down to Nakia's room. She wanted to give her the check before they started their day, and she wanted to give it to her in private. She tapped on the door lightly, but there was no answer, so she figured she was also still asleep. Next, she rang the bell. After a couple of moments of nothing, she dug in her purse and pulled out her phone. Before she could dial Nakia, she heard. "I don't need service!"

Madison laughed softly and then rang the bell again. "Are you sure, madam, because we must give service every day," Madison faked in a foreign accent.

"Oh Lord, hold on," she heard Nakia grumble. A moment or two later, the door was snatched open. "Ma'am, please, I—" she paused and laughed. "Madison, what in the pure hell! Do you know what time it is?"

"I do, and this couldn't wait."

"Somebody better be bleeding or on fire," Nakia said and dragged herself to the sofa and flopped down. "Girl, it's, it's, it's . . ." she said squinting at the digital clock on microwave which they had a view of from the living room.

"Almost one p.m.," Madison said. She could see twelve forty-eight.

"Well, I don't have my contacts in, heffa. What are you doing up? Goodness, we shut it down at what . . . seven this morning?" Nakia yawned and stretched.

"We did," Madison said and then took a seat on the sofa beside her.

"Then why aren't you still laid up with Chase, who is fine as all get out, Mrs. Madison? And he is so sweet. Just the way he looks at you. Oooooh, I can't wait to have *that* with someone."

"What about Charles? I thought you two were doing well."

"We are, Madison, but you know how I am. I mean, he's supersweet, gives me any and everything I want, and I know he's crazy about me, but—"

"But what, Nakia?"

"It's like he's too good to be true, and I'm so scared, because I've never felt this great in a relationship before, and you know I can be a major bitch. I'm scared I'm going to run him off."

"Now look who sounds crazy."

"I'm serious, Madi. Listen, let me give you an example. I wanted to go to this vineyard the other weekend with two of my coworkers, but he had made plans for us to go to Dallas and meet his daughter. I knew he wanted me to go, but the company was footing the bill for me, and I didn't want to miss the opportunity. So I go to him, right, and I was like, 'Babe, I know we were supposed to go to Dallas, but blah blah blah came up at work, and I wanna go.' And he was like, 'That's cool, baby, go. We can reschedule Dallas.'"

"Really? What an asshole," Madison said sarcastically.

"He didn't dispute it; he just went with it."

"And please tell me what is wrong with that?"

"I don't know. It's just if he had done that to me, I'd be pissed, and I would have cussed his ass out."

Madison laughed. "Now look who sounds crazy as hell. Nakia, you finally met a nice guy, and I'm so sorry all the ones before him gave you such a rotten experience that you can't accept that he's the real deal."

"Girl, I guess you're right. I really like him, Madison, like I like him, *really* like him. Like I think I love him like him."

"Well, just accept you've found a sweet guy who is willing to put up with the bitch in you and be happy."

She nodded her head. "Yes, you're right, because I've clowned him, and he still takes good care of me and makes me laugh. And, oh, Madison, when we're together, he makes me laugh, and even when I attempt to lose it, he has this way of calming me down. I think he's made me soft," she laughed.

"Thank God for Chuckie. Let's please keep him around. Don't let your inner bitch tarnish him."

"Okay, okay, I hear you."

"Good, now, let's get to why I woke you."

"Can we order up some breakfast first? I am starving," Nakia said, getting up and going for the hotel's menu.

"Nah, you go ahead. I want to wait and have breakfast with Chase."

"Suit yo'self."

"Well, anyway," Madison continued, and Nakia took her seat back on the sofa, "you know about the whole entire story with the bet and all that jazz."

"Indeed," she said scanning the menu.

"Remember when I told you Chase declined the money?"

"That was a dumbass move for sure, but, yes, I remember."

"Well, it turns out he changed his mind, and he refunded me the cost of my home and the renos on my mother's salon."

"Get the fuck outta of here, Madison! That is awesome. You are too blessed. Is this why you brought me out here to Vegas? This was a much-needed trip, and I just wish Charles was here; then all would be perfect. He'd die if he saw this suite," Nakia said, excited for her friend.

"Yes, that's just one of the reasons why I brought you out here."

She put down the menu. "Bitch, you better not be pregnant," she said with her eyes and mouth wide open. "Oh my God, Madison, you *are* pregnant." She hopped off the couch in excitement and started doing her happy dance. "I'm going to be an auntie," she sang, and Madison had to reel her back in.

"No no no, Nakia, girl, I'm not pregnant. Sit your crazy ass down. You think if I was pregnant, I'd be throwing back shots last night with y'all?"

"Aw," Nakia slid back onto the sofa. "My bad. Hell, I didn't even think about last night. Shiiiid, we got our drank on!"

"We did, now calm down, chick, and here," she said with an outstretched arm. "I brought you here because I wanted to give you this in person."

"What is it?" Nakia said taking the envelope.

"Open it, silly. I hate when folks do that. Just open it."

Nakia's hands trembled as she opened the sealed envelope. She slid the check out of it, and her head fell backward. "No no no, you didn't. This does *not* have my name on it."

"Yes, it does. Now you can pay off all of your student loans and get you another car, because that Honda is on its last leg. I was shocked to see you were still driving that hooptie."

"No, Madison. Man, this is too much. I can't accept this. I mean, what kinda prank is this? Is this room set up with hidden cameras? You want me to jump up and down and scream, so somebody can come out and say I've been punked?"

"Nakia, no, this is a gift to you from me, because I was blessed with it. I paid for my house with this, and my house is paid in full, thanks to my settlements. And now, thanks to Chase, it's yours, even if Chase and I didn't make it. I still have a good amount to keep me for a while, so it's yours."

Nakia's eyes welled. She leaned in and hugged Madison as tightly as she could. "Thank you, my friend. I never expected something this grand from anyone, and this is more than generous of you, Madison. Thank you," she cried.

"Well, my parents are good. I'm an only child, and even if Chase and I have children, believe me, they will be well taken care of. I just want you to not stress about so much financially. You have said a dozen times how you want to go out on your own and start your own agency, and now you can do that, Nakia. I believe in you."

She pulled back. "Oh my God, I can't believe my eyes. I've never seen this many zeros on the same check as my name."

They laughed. "Well, hopefully, in the future, after you get your business going, this won't be the last time. Now, go online and see where the nearest Bank of America is and deposit your money, and then make your trip out here perfect. . . . Fly your man out here."

Nakia jumped up. "Girl, I'm on it," she said and raced into the bedroom and came out with her phone. She dressed quickly, and the car service took her where she needed to go. Madison made it back to her room and was surprised to see Chase was up, out on the terrace with a cup of coffee.

"Hey, baby, how long have you been up? Why didn't you call me?"

"Well, I checked my phone for location and saw that you were right here in this building, so I knew you were with Nakia. Did you give her the check?"

"I did."

"How do you feel?"

She smiled. "I feel great. I mean, I never thought I'd ever live like this," she said with a hand gesture to the view. "My parents did well when I was growing up, and I never lacked for a thing. I had piano lessons and ballet and a singing coach and so many things in a huge gated home. Even at our public school, most kids were well-off, and because my parents paid for my education, I didn't know about scholarships and grants and loans until I met Nakia. That girl came into the dorm with the bare minimum of things with her aunt, not her mom. My parents were there, setting up my room with fancy bedding and curtains, and I had brought so much stuff that my parents had to take some of it back home. I had a brand-new Nissan Sentra that I had gotten for graduation, and when my parents left, I remember Nakia saying with attitude, 'I didn't know I'd be rooming with a rich girl,' and I replied, 'Who me? I'm not rich,'" and she just laughed.

"I asked, 'What's so funny?' and she just walked out of the room. I stood in our common area and looked into my room, and then I looked into hers. She didn't even have a TV or curtains, not even a tenth of what I had, only a used-looking comforter and one large suitcase that she didn't bother to unpack.

"The first few days there was tension, and she barely spoke to me until one evening I was in the bathroom doing my hair, and I was doing my regular Mariah Carey thing, and I burned myself with the curling iron. My high note turned into a high-pitched scream. She ran to the bathroom to see if I was okay. My neck was on fire, you hear me? And she told me to put butter on it. I laughed, of course, and she laughed, and that was the first time we had a conversation, all over a burn on my neck. I learned that her aunt raised her because her mom left one day and never came back. Some of the things she told me were so terrible I couldn't believe my ears. That winter break, she went home with me, and here we are now.

"She's a good person and a beautiful friend, and I feel so good that I was able to do that for her."

"I'm happy too, baby," he said and stood to wrap his arms around me. "This view is so amazing. I'm glad we came. To get a break from Tyler makes me feel like we're in an entirely different world."

"Yes, and it's certainly gorgeous out here."

"Gorgeous enough to get married?"

"Oh no, oh no, we are *not* getting married out here, Chase Storm. I want to get married at home with my parents and family and friends attending."

"We can still do that, baby, but think of how cool it would be to do it here and now."

She turned to him. "Are you serious, Chase?"

"Yes, why not? Look, my brothers are here and their wives. Nakia is here."

"Aw, baby, as tempting as that sounds, I want to wait."

He frowned. "Okay, I understand. My parents would probably tie me to a tree if I didn't do it the Storm way anyway."

"So, what's up, family? What are we getting into today?" Travis interrupted. He and Deena came out on the terrace to join them.

"First order is food, guys. I'm hungry as hell," Gina said and then sat.

"Me too," Madison added.

"Let's check and see if Lance and them are up. We can order room service or go out."

"I say room service because I don't want to get dressed just yet," Deena said. The guys went inside to call Lance's suite, and the ladies stayed out and just enjoyed small talk. By five that afternoon everyone was dressed and ready to have fun. The couples decided to split up and do couples stuff, and Madison was so happy that Charles was able to catch the next flight out, so he'd be there later on that evening. Nakia decided to get a massage and do some shopping so she wouldn't be a third wheel with Chase and Madison. They stayed in Vegas until that Wednesday, and then it was back to Tyler, back to work, and back to wedding planning.

Chapter Thirty-one

"Madison, you can make potato salad for Sunday, right?" Chase's mother asked.

"Yes, ma'am, I sure can."

"And make sure you get here on time. We want to get dinner started."

"Well, that's your task. Deena, you got veggies, so the corn and broccoli are on you. Gina, please say you made the desserts."

"Yes, ma'am. Lance is bringing them in now."

"Momma, what's wrong?" Tasha asked. All the women had noticed Mrs. Storm seemed out of character.

"I'm fine. I'm just overjoyed that this gal," she said, holding a hand out toward Madison, "has come back into my son's life." Her eyes welled, and she wiped them. "My baby," she cried. "My baby wasn't himself." Madison stood frozen. "Madison, I know you and Chase have work to do on y'all's relationship and all, but when you left, there were times that I didn't recognize my boy." She paused and grabbed a dishcloth. "I'd go to check on him, and it's like nothing I could say or do would comfort him. But when he walked in tonight with you, he was my Chase again, my baby. And I know it's because you came back." She lowered her head. "My boys messed up; thought they were doing more good than harm."

"Mom, I'm fine. I was angry at first, but now I'm fine. I know what they all did was out of love, not to hurt Chase or me. The way it started and how it came out was just terrible, but love . . . Love is so strong, Mom. Love wouldn't let me stay away from him, and I'm glad to be back. I'm not mad at my brothers-in-law anymore, because if it had not been for them, I would have never fallen in love with Chase. The here and now is all that matters."

The women listened to Madison as they all chatted and prepared the food. It felt like old times.

"Baby, how long?" Lance yelled, walking in and interrupting the girl moment. "I'm starving,"

"Baby, get out of here. Dinner will be ready soon," Gina promised.

He backed out, and the ladies got back to work. Five minutes later, Chase came into the kitchen and whispered something in Madison's ear. She smiled, and he kissed her on the neck before walking back out.

"Okay, spill," Tasha said.

Madison blushed. "I can't this time, for real."

Deena held up a knife. "You know there are *no* secrets in this kitchen."

"For real this time, I can't tell. It's too, *too* personal."

"Do you want to be kicked out of the circle?" Gina asked.

"Okay okay okay. He said to meet him upstairs in his old bedroom so he can taste my bud," she confessed. The other women laughed.

"Well," his mother said, "you'd better hurry. Dinner is almost done."

Embarrassed, Madison put the lid on her bowl of homemade potato salad. "I'll be back." She hurried up the steps. As promised, Chase was there to service her. Twenty minutes later, after she came, she rejoined the ladies in the kitchen. "What did I miss?"

"Nothing but a bunch of horny Storms," Gina said. "Two seconds after you left, Deena met Travis outside in the guest house, and, Tasha, let's just say she didn't share. She just disappeared."

"Damn, I miss those days," Chase's mother said. "Back in the day before these boys came along, Legend and I would do it anywhere," she blushed. Tasha and Deena walked back into the kitchen, both giggling like schoolgirls.

"Okay, what are we chatting about?" Deena asked and grabbed her wineglass and went to refill it.

"The good old days, before my boys were conceived."

"Speaking of," Gina interrupted, "Lance told me something about you and Dad breaking up back in the day over some hottie name Corrina."

"What?" she laughed. "Legend told them boys about that story?"

"That's what Damon told me," Tasha said.

"Oooooowwwwweeeeee, let me tell you girls about this man-stealing tramp, that's what I used to call her back in the day. She was stacked, you hear me. Big boobs, tiny waist, round hips, and an ass that was so natural, not all man-made like this crazy plastic surgery generation today. Corrina was 'Sexy Red,' them boys used to call her back then. She had all eyes on her everywhere she went. I think I was eighteen, and Legend was around nineteen, and it was right around the time he started working at the warehouse.

"They hired that old man-stealing heffa as a clerk, you know, to file and keep records of stuff. Any who, word got out that she had an eye for Legend, and I told him too. I said, 'Legend, that woman is interested in you,' and he replied like all simple men with no clue, 'No, Stelle, she's just a friendly gal.' Yeah, she was damn sure friendly, all right. She invites him over to watch television one evening while her folks were away, and that gal was all over him."

"What did Dad do?" Gina asked.

"Ran up out of there like a scared little girl— as he should have. See, at first, I didn't know what happened because the word was he was now courting her since a neighbor saw him hightailing it out of her front door."

They were all laughing. "What did you do, Mom, when you found out?"

"I dropped his ass like a hot potato. Yes, I did and told him I don't have no time for two-timing dogs."

"Then how did y'all end up back together?"

"Well, what Legend doesn't know is I overheard Miss Corrina at the local café telling her girlfriends how he behaved, how he was scared to touch her. She said she wanted a real man, not a little boy who don't know what best for him. So, I marched up to her and demanded the truth. I asked to her face, 'Were you messing around with Legend when he was courting me?' and she told me no, that she had tried and nothing happened.

"It had been four months, so with that news, I rushed back and got my man," Estelle said proudly, "and been with him ever since. Madison, ask your mom about how Corrina tried to get her hooks in your father too. Martha dragged her ass in the middle of the street and whipped her tail!"

"My mother did *what?*" Madison asked, stunned. Martha had never told her about the Corrina story, so she was dying to hear the details.

"Dragged her in the middle of the street and told her if she didn't stay her ass away from Will, she was going to give her a good old East Texas ass whoppin', and we were in our twenties then. Martha and William were newly-weds, and that girl used to go by your daddy's auto shop pretending something was wrong with that old Nova she drove, and one day, she told yo' daddy if he ever needed something *extra* on the side, to call her. Well, he threw her out and made the fatal mistake of telling Martha, and yo' mother drove up in her driveway with her shiny Cadillac, banged on Corrina's door, and dragged her off her porch and into the middle of the street. All of the neighbors were on their porches watching, and the whole town got wind of it. Not even a month after that, Corrina moved outta East Texas and didn't come back till many years later after her parents passed, and people still would remind her of that ass whoppin' that Martha put on her."

The women were laughing so hard, they didn't notice Lance walked into the kitchen.

"Ladies, ladies, what's so funny?"

"Oh, nothing, baby, just girl talk," Gina said.

"Well, we are starving out here. How much longer? Dad sent me to get the 411."

"You tell your father it will be soon. We'll call you fellas shortly," Estelle said, and Lance hurried out of her kitchen. The women finished up and then set the table. Finally, the entire Storm clan and their wives and the new fiancée were at the dinner table again.

"Let us all bow our heads. Father God," Legend began. He blessed the food and was sure to add a word to God for his sons and their families. The group laughed, ate, and had a good time as they normally did when they got together. After dinner, the women cleared the table and cleaned while the men found their way to the den to smoke cigars, have drinks, and discuss sports and cars. Madison felt like she belonged. She was happy not only to have Chase but to have her soon-to-be mother-in-law and sisters.

They were all so loving, so giving, and their bond and circle was a place where she felt warm and at home.

"You're ready, baby?" Chase said.

"Yeah, I think so. Mom, is there anything else you need?" Madison asked Chase's mother.

"No, baby, y'all did it all. You two go home and enjoy each other." She winked.

Madison shook her head. Chase's mom was just as freaky as her mom. She hoped she and Chase would have the same fire at that age.

Chase and Madison talked nonstop on the ride back to his place. He was grateful to have a lady like Madison in his life. He'd never thought he would stop chasing women, but Madison was the cure to that addiction, and he vowed to love her and treat her like a queen for the rest of his days. They got home, made passionate love, and fell asleep holding each other. Things couldn't be any more perfect than that.

Chapter Thirty-two

Madison was in a horrific mood. It was only two days before the wedding, and too many last-minute things needed to be done, and the forecast was calling for rain on the day they had planned an outdoor wedding. They had the civic center as a backup, but she had been so excited about getting married outdoors. Now it looked like that idea was a bust. Family and friends from out of town were blowing up her phone about reservations and details that had already been emailed to them weeks ago, and Madison was about to pull out every strand of hair on her head. She was happy that Nakia had finally arrived so she could help Deena with the things she didn't want to handle.

"Madison, where are you going?" Nakia yelled behind her. She was moving as quickly as she could to get outside and suck in some air. They were at the convention center getting ready to start rehearsal soon, and Madison was on the verge of having a nervous breakdown.

"Air, Nakia. I need air," she yelled back and kept on walking. Chase hadn't arrived yet, and she was pissed because no way was he under as much stress as she was.

Nakia jogged to catch up. "I'll go with you," she said.

As soon as Madison stepped outside, she looked up at the overcast sky. "See, this is *exactly* why I didn't want to set myself up on hopes for an outdoor wedding."

"Well, at least we have a beautiful alternative. Now, everything will take place here, so no one has to leave after the ceremony."

"There's an upside," she laughed lightly.

"Madison, come on; level with me. What's *really* going on with you?" Nakia asked, taking her hand. "I was with you on your wedding weekend with Dre, and you were not acting like a bridezilla. Tell me what's wrong."

"I have a really bad case of the jitters, Nakia. This wedding . . . A wedding is like the most special and blameless vow between a man and a woman, and I keep thinking about my wedding day with Dre, and how I was so happy and how things were so perfect, and then God took him away, just like that," she snapped her fingers. "Now that I'm in love, and I'm so deeply in love with Chase, I have this crazy fear that something terrible is going to happen, like God is setting me up again. I know it's crazy, Nakia, and I promise you I've tried to convince myself that I'm wrong and that this foolishness is all in my head, but I have this crazy feeling that something horrible is going to happen."

Nakia grabbed her friend by her shoulders. "Listen, stop it. Stop it right now, okay? Enough with this melo-dramatic bullshit, Madison. I know it was tough and a very hard thing to go through when you lost your boys, but life is so full of *what-ifs* and *maybes*. No one knows what tomorrow holds. All we can do is wake up and deal with it. If you base your decisions on what-ifs, you might as well live in a damn bubble. You are marrying a young, sexy, funny, loving, and compassionate person. Chase is your tenfold."

"My what?"

"Your tenfold. Whenever God takes something from you, his reward to you is tenfold. There is a time to lose, and there is a time to win. You have suffered your loss; now, it's time to win, so dry those tears. You are a bride, and you should be just as happy and excited as Chase. Hell, he's probably on his way, smiling from ear to ear, and you're over here all depressed and bringing me down." She reached into her purse and pulled out a flask. "Here, take a drink of this," she said and handed it over to Madison. Madison took it, drank, and threw her head back and frowned.

"Damn, Nakia, that was straight."

"And that was *exactly* what you needed, now get in gear, Atkins. Let's get back in there and get ready for this rehearsal. And tell that wedding planner of yours she needs a larger crew because maid of honors don't do the shit she's been asking me to do. I'm supposed to be catering to you, not helping her with centerpieces and shit."

"Okay, I'll talk to her," Madison said, and they headed back inside.

The rehearsal went well, and Madison was not as jittery as she was earlier that afternoon, but she was not settled with the wedding taking place indoors. Her wedding planner had managed to deck out the banquet room where the ceremony would take place, and the last-minute décor ideas came together perfectly. At the rehearsal dinner, Madison had a blast, and some of the encouraging words that friends and family members had for them were comforting. Madison was so relaxed and finally at ease.

"So, babe, I'm going to head to my bachelor party, and I promise it's going to be small, not too rowdy, so you have nothing to worry about. Just some cards, cigars, and drinks. No wild women or strippers, so don't worry," Chase assured her.

"Well, you do that simple and quiet and cards and cigars, but I know me and my girls are about to turn up," she yelled. "*Wooohooooo!*" she continued. "And there may even be strippers, Mr. Storm, so don't wait up," she said dancing in place.

"You know The Robot is no longer in style, right?" he teased.

"Don't hate because I got moves," she joked.

"Yes, *terrible* moves. Keep up that routine, I'll have nothing to worry about," he laughed.

She paused and put her arms around his shoulders. "I love you, baby, and you have absolutely nothing to worry about. Now give me my sugar, and I'll see you day after tomorrow at the altar."

"I'll be there, and on time." He gently kissed her. "I love you so much, baby, and I can't wait until we say I do."

"Come on, Chase, damn!" Damon yelled out.

"Yes, let's get it started," Travis said pumping his pelvis like an old man.

"Now, see, he need to quit," Madison laughed. They said their final goodbyes and I love yous; then Chase went to join the guys while they barked like dogs, and Madison went to join her girls. She didn't know what was in store for that night. All she knew was it was going down in a club in Longview. The girls had a party bus, and even though it was a bit much, Madison climbed in and was ready to get her party on.

The girls made it to the club a little before eleven, and Madison wasn't the only one wearing a tiara and bride-to-be tee shirt in that strip club, but she felt like the most important bride in the building. They all got lap dances, Madison was picked up like she was as light as a feather, and she threw back as many shots as the alcohol limit could take. She was definitely wasted by the time they made it back to her house in Tyler.

All the girls agreed to stay at her place. That was where they would all dress and leave from in the morning. They had the entire spa to themselves the next day to get manis, pedis, and facials, and the staff was scheduled to come to Madison's home the next morning to do makeup and hair. Time flew by, and Madison woke up the morning of her wedding with those same jitters, so she called her momma.

"Good morning, my daughter. Happy wedding day," Martha sang.

"Good morning, Momma, are you up?"

"Yes, I've been up since six this morning."

"Why so early, Momma?"

"Well, I wanted to go by the civic center to take a look at things one more time. I checked the reception hall and made sure everything was right."

"Momma, that is why we paid the wedding coordinator the big bucks, and besides, how did you get in so early?"

"Chile, you know Lamar Jr. is security up in that. He knew not to tell me no."

"Wow, Momma, thank you. If I didn't know any better, I'd say you were just as nervous as I am."

Martha laughed lightly. "No, baby, I'm not nervous; just happy that this day has come. I remember the day when you came home to bury Dre and the boys. . . . That look on your face, the sounds of your wails when you cried was something that tore my insides to pieces. I remember nothing could comfort you, and how you would be up in your room holding Dre's shirt and those boys' night blanket. It broke my heart to see you in so much pain, and now, here we are. A new day, a new love, and another chance.

"I remember telling you over and over again that the pain would get easier, and you'll love again, and I remember your little stubborn voice, just like William, 'No, Momma, never. I'll never love again,' but ole stud muffin Chase swept you off your feet," Martha teased.

Madison giggled. "I know, Momma, and today is going to be a good day, and I'm going to live my life without fear. I spent the last few days with this overwhelming feeling that something was going to go wrong, and you know what? Everything is perfect. Even this morning, the clouds have somehow vanished, and the sun is shining so brightly. I have jitters, but the same jitters I had with Dre, you know. Those happy jitters."

"That's good, Madi, and I'm so proud of you. I'm so happy for you and Chase. It was a bumpy road, but you know my famous line," she said.

"Yes, Mother, I know. 'It's not how you start; what matters is where you end up.'"

"Exactly. I wasn't too thrilled about baby Storm in the very beginning, but he proved all of us wrong."

"Yes, indeed, and you know, Ma, if it weren't for me leaving and going to Houston, I still may not have listened to reason. Everyone told me to forgive him and to not worry about the wager, but Nakia showed me how silly I was not to forgive him."

"Well, I'm glad you came around."

"Me too."

"I reckon it time for you to be getting up and hitting the shower. I know the girls will be there soon to glam you ladies up and get you all ready."

"Yes, I'm up in my room, but I hear the girls moving around downstairs, and I smell bacon, so I know Gina must be whipping us all up some breakfast."

"For sure, the Storm men did pick some winners. Good girls from good families. Like my daughter."

"Ma, there is something I've been meaning to ask you."

"What is it, baby?" she asked with concern in her tone.

"Who is Corrina, and why did you drag her out in the middle of the street?"

Martha burst into laughter. "Chile, who told you about that? That old, crazy Estelle?"

"Yes, ma'am. She told us all about it a few Sundays ago."

"Well, I'll tell you a later time. Just know this, I got that 'don't mess with my man' mentally, and after what went down with me and that Corrina, every woman in East Texas knew not to push up on William Atkins, baby. I had them women scared to take they car into yo' daddy's shop."

She and Madison got in a good laugh, and then Madison got up from her bed. She grabbed her robe, and after she brushed her teeth, she headed downstairs. Everyone was gathered together in the kitchen eating and passing serving dishes.

"Good morning, ladies. How did everyone sleep?"

They had every inch of Madison's five-bedroom home covered with clothes, accessories, and you name it.

"We slept well, lady. How did *you* sleep?" Gina asked after all the ladies said how well or not well they slept. Tasha was the only one to complain because she ended up on the sofa in the living room.

"I slept so good, and I am ready to walk down that aisle and marry the finest man in East Texas," she smiled.

"Hold up, now. Chase looks like Lance, so he can't be the finest," Gina said and then bit a piece of bacon.

"And Damon looks like an older version of Chase—so boom," Tasha said.

"Wait one minute. If they all stood next to each other, you'd think they were quads," Deena added.

"Okay okay okay, damn, ladies. Let me rephrase. I'm ready to marry one of the finest men in East Texas. Is that better?" she joked.

"Much," Deena said.

Madison took a seat at the island. "Please, can you fix me a plate, Gina?"

"Sure, love."

"So what time will the ladies be here for hair and makeup?" Nakia asked.

Madison looked at the digital clock on the stove. "In about an hour and a half, so after we finish eating, we should all get our showers in."

"I know that's real," Nakia said.

"So, Nakia, you haven't said much about Charles. He's a looker too, and he seems supernice," Deena said. Madison smiled because Deena was being nice. Before, Nakia sensed her icy tone, but by the time they departed Vegas, Deena and Nakia were getting along just fine.

"Well, I didn't want say anything until after the wedding, because y'all know I don't want to take any attention off of my girl Madison, but he proposed a few days ago before we drove out here, and when we get back to Houston, we're going to get a place together."

"Nakia, why didn't you tell me, girl? Congratulations," Madison said and got up to hug her. "Where's the ring?" she asked looking down at her finger.

"Here it is," she said reaching for her phone. She went to a picture of it. "It was too big, so we're getting it sized."

"Aw, that is pretty," Madison said, and they passed the phone around so each lady could take a look.

"Thank you," Nakia said to the ladies as they complimented her on her diamond. It wasn't as big as the ones the Storm wives were sporting, but it was beautiful enough for her.

"When we come back from our honeymoon, we'll visit Houston and have a proper celebration," Madison said as she took her seat. Gina handed her a plate, and the girls continued to carry on endless conversations.

They took turns in the shower, and Gina and Deena made sure Madison's kitchen was spotless. They took the trash out right away so they wouldn't forget. Madison and Chase were scheduled to leave that night for Bora Bora for a one-week honeymoon.

A beautiful, white SUV limousine was awaiting the women outside. The sun was shining so brightly, Madison wished she would have gone with her original plan of an outdoor wedding, but the decorations turned out so beautiful at their venue, she just thanked God for a beautiful day. No umbrellas and worrying about dirty rain spots on her gown or her bridesmaids' gowns, and Deena and Nakia, her matron and maid of honor, looked stunning in their purple gowns. They laughed and sang songs until they made it to the venue.

The planner came out to show the ladies inside, and they all went into an empty banquet room not far from where the main event was doing to happen. It was going to be a good forty-five minutes before the wedding was to start. Madison was so happy that her wedding was going to start on time. The lot was full, so many folks had already arrived. Nakia and Deena stayed with her while the other sisters went to check on things.

When it was close to time, Madison's dad looked in on her. "Are you about ready, baby girl?"

"Yeah, Dad, give me a moment. I'll be right out."

"Sure, pumpkin. You know they can't start without you," he smiled.

"I know," she smiled back brightly.

He walked away and left her to be alone. She turned her back to the door and looked at the portable mirror that her planner had in there for them. "Okay, it's showtime, Dre. This is it!" she said and fought her watery eyes. "I hope you and the boys are happy for me. I will always love you guys," she said and took a deep breath. She nodded at her reflection and was about to turn around, but a voice made her jump.

"Oh, how sweet. Talking to your dead husband and kids before you walk down the aisle to marry *my* man," the voice said.

Madison turned, and the first thing she noticed was the silver piece of metal in her hand. "Oh my God, Hope. What are you doing here?"

"I'm here to make sure you understand that you ruined everything for us, for me and Chase. How is it that you come back here to town after your husband dies and end up with the man who was meant for me? Do you know I've been planning our wedding since I was 18?"

"Hope, come on; put that gun away and please stop this. Just leave. I won't tell a soul that you were here."

"No! No! No! That *isn't* how things are going to happen," she cried.

"Hope, what do you think will happen if you kill me?" Madison trembled with fear. "You will go to prison," she said.

"Prison? Bitch, are you serious? Do you know how many judges in this town that my father knows who'll let me walk for a little money? Do you know not a juror in this town will convict me? I *will* walk, and you will *not* be missed. It was a game, Madison, a fucking bet, and you are about to lose," she said and pointed the gun at her.

"Madi, are you ready, baby?" her father's voice sounded on the other side of the door. He jiggled the handle, but Hope had locked it.

"Daddy, call the police!" Madison screamed.

"You dumb bitch," Hope said and aimed. Madison didn't know what to do, so instantly, she rushed Hope, knocking her down. The gun flew from her hand. Madison struggled to keep her down, and they tussled on the floor. "Daddy, call the police!" she continued to yell, fighting for her life. It was such a struggle for Madison because her tight undergarments and all that dress was making her have to fight ten times harder. Hope scrambled away and tried crawling toward the gun, but Madison grabbed her ankle and pulled her back from it. She kicked. Her foot landed on Madison's nose, and that dazed her. Blood quickly trickled down onto Madison's gown, but she had to regain her composure and keep Hope from shooting her. Before Madison could reach Hope, she had the gun, and as soon as she pointed it at her, she was tackled to the floor by Chase. Madison hadn't realized that they had unlocked the door and come in. Chase held Hope down on the floor, and his brothers rushed in and managed to get the gun out of her hand. Hope lay on the floor whimpering like a child. Then Chase rushed over to Madison's side.

"Baby, are you okay? Are you shot or hurt?" he asked in a panic touching her all over.

"I'm okay, I'm okay," she cried out of breath.

"Come on, baby, stand up; come on," Chase said helping Madison from the ground. She had a couple of drops of blood on her gown, but her coordinator rushed over with tissues and grabbed some spray from the pocket apron she wore around her waist. She quickly sprayed and dabbed while Madison held the tissues to her nose. Within minutes the police were there and handcuffed Hope.

"Madison, we're going to need a statement," one officer said.

Madison sat. "Not until after my wedding," she replied.

"But, Madison, this is an urgent matter," he said.

"And so is my wedding, Frank. She is *not* ruining my day, okay? Chase and I are getting married, so you are welcome to stay, but I will not talk to you until *after* Chase and I exchange vows. Now, you are welcome to stay, but I'm getting married today—right now," she declared.

"Honey, are you sure you don't need a moment?" Chase asked.

"I do, Chase." Her eyes welled, and her mother squeezed her hand. "But I will have my breakdown *after* we're married. Mother, please fix my hair and make sure my nose is clean, okay? Just cover it with makeup, and, Clara, can you get the blood out?" she said.

"I'm doing my best," Clara said as she focused on the stains.

"Madison, honey, I really think you need a minute," Martha suggested. Madison nodded and agreed with her mother.

"Please, everyone, give me a second with my daughter. Chase, go out and calm your guests; Deena, Nakia, will y'all help him out?"

"Yes, ma'am." They all filed out, and Clara told her to stand up. She helped Madison out of her dress.

"This solution gets red wine and blood right out. Take your time, I'll be back, and your dress will be good as new," she said as she left the room.

"I'll wait outside," William said.

"No, Daddy, please stay," Madison said, and he shut the door. He pulled up a chair beside Madison and took her hand while her momma just held her close. Madison cried a good cry while they sat in silence. Her dad dabbed tears from his eyes, and Martha used her handkerchief to dab at her tears.

Usually, it would be her mother to speak first, but her daddy had words at that time. "You know, baby girl, what doesn't kill you makes you stronger. This was a day, but God kept you, and today can still be great and a wonderful day to remember. You're walking away with a bruised nose, but a beating heart, and I know it's going to be hard to put that gown back on and walk down that aisle, but your mother and I will walk you down all the way. And when we give you away to Chase, he will carry you for the rest of your days. We'll worry about Hope Gardener tomorrow. We can rearrange your honeymoon, but for now, let your momma fix your beautiful face and touch up those pretty curls. We're going to turn a bad situation into a joyous occasion, okay?" he said and smiled at her. She smiled back. "That's my baby girl. We've defeated bigger demons than Hope Gardener, and she is going to pay, darling; trust me. I got this," he encouraged her.

"Thank you, Daddy. I love you so much," she said and hugged his neck tightly.

"I love you too, baby girl. I'll find Carla and one of them girls from the spa. I know they got all that fancy makeup stuff in their trunk; if not, I'll send someone to pick you up something. This is your day," he declared and stood.

He kissed his wife, and she gave him a comforting nod. Then he left. Several moments later, the ladies were back, and Clara had worked her magic on the gown. The glam squad touched up her face. Although her nose was a bit swollen, she still made a beautiful bride. Martha and William both walked their daughter down the aisle, and after all the photos were taken, Madison and Chase took time away from their reception to talk to the police. Even after the events that went down before the wedding, Madison and Chase held it together and managed to have a great wedding and reception.

After some tough debate, Chase's and Madison's parents both convinced them to go on their honeymoon. They assured the couple that they would exhaust every effort to make sure Hope didn't walk and also make sure no bail was granted. Hope's family was just as wealthy as Chase's, and since she was a flight risk, the judge she went before was tough and denied bail for her. There was nothing the Gardeners could do to get their darling daughter out of jail. She would have to stay until the trial date, and the Storms and Atkins would pay any amount to any firm to assure Hope Gardener paid for what she did.

After one year of waiting for a trial, Hope went before a jury of her peers and was found guilty of attempted murder. She was sentenced to life with the possibility of parole in ten years, the maximum in the state of Texas, and both families made a vow that they'd be at every parole hearing to make sure Hope never walked free again.

Not even three months after they were married, Chase and his wife conceived and gave birth to a little girl they named Nakia as Madison promised, and a year later, they had another little girl and named her Deena. There was always a healthy competition between her two best friends, but they all got along. Chase never once missed his single days and loved being a husband and father, and Madison was so happy in love. She agreed to give Chase another baby, and he finally got a son who they named Chase Junior. Chase Senior vowed that he'd make sure that his son never mimicked his old ways.

Madison and Chase lived the rest of their days in marital bliss.

The End